A Place To

A Place To Bury Strangers

By

Grant Nicol

Fahrenheit Thirteen

The Lord will fight for you; you have only to be still.

- Exodus 14:14

CHAPTER ONE

Friday 6th February

Freezing cold water dripped from somewhere high overhead as Óli Þór crept through the deserted building site. It was silent at this time of night but during the day it was a hive of feverish and noisy activity. He knew this because most of the men who worked on the site were customers of his. All of them worked long hours but they liked to play as hard as they worked. The guy he'd talked to on the phone wasn't one he knew personally but the size of the deal he'd proposed was too good to turn down. The boss was always on his back about keeping his sales up as high as he could and if he pulled this one off it would be his best month ever. That would keep him quiet for a while.

Óli Þór wiped another giant drip off his forehead and checked his phone one more time. The hour was right and the place was right. All he needed now was for the buyer to show and he could get off to the pub where he belonged. A noise from the far side of the site distracted him from thoughts of Brennivín and cold beer for the moment. He was as sure as he could be that he was at the right place for the meet but it was possible he'd got it wrong. As usual he'd been a little stoned when he'd taken the call so anything was possible. He checked the time on his phone again and cursed his stupidity for not writing anything down. He thrust his hands into his pockets and set off across the thin layer of ice that covered the newly-laid concrete floor, lighting his way with his flickering flashlight with the dodgy old batteries in it as he went. He tripped on a brick and stubbed his toe through his cheap trainers. It was lucky that this deal was going to eclipse the business he'd done for the last two months in one fell swoop otherwise he would have already given up on this idiot and left. If he didn't show soon Óli Þór would cut his losses and leave.

'Where the hell are you?' he mumbled to himself as he picked his path through the dark.

He turned his head to find where the noise had come from. Then he heard it again. Only this time from another direction altogether. 'At last', he whispered. But as he turned towards the sound he realised he had made a terrible error of judgement. Not the first by any stretch of the imagination but this time was definitely to be his last.

The blow split his scalp open from the crown of his head all the way down to the base of his right ear. The crowbar tore the skin away from his skull, broke the bone and exposed a horrid pale landscape of soft fleshy hills accentuated on either side by growing rivers of blood. Óli Þór's knees gave way beneath him and he collapsed in a heap on the frozen concrete floor. Strong hands lifted him into the air and dragged his limp body through the gloomy half-completed building. Óli Þór's final resting place was to be as demeaning and disgusting as the rest of his life had been. He was deposited feet-first into an empty and rusting forty-gallon drum and a thin noose was then tied tightly around his neck. The cord was pulled back behind him and looped around a piece of exposed steel three times. Once it had been tied firmly in place it held him against the back of the drum so he stood upright albeit as lifelessly as a broken toy. His head hung forward like a dying flower as the very essence of his existence ran down his cheek and dripped off his chin into the drum below. Nearby the sound of a metal lid being unscrewed from a can grated against the silence of the empty site. As drops of a bright shiny liquid bounced off Óli Þór's head the smell of petrol filled the air. The can was tossed aside and a match sizzled to life before being tossed onto the back of his head. The flames burst into life and engulfed him as the figure they silhouetted against the plaster wall took a few steps back to get away from the flames. The tall muscled figure rubbed his hands together to warm them as he made the most of the spectacle before pulling an aerosol can from the inside pocket of his jacket. He walked up to the plaster wall and gave the can a good shake as the flames crackled and spat next to him.

Somewhere across the building site a bottle rattled along the concrete floor casting an empty lifeless chime to the wind. With the spray can in one hand and the crowbar still gripped tightly in the other he sucked the cold air in through his teeth and quickly left his message scrawled in black paint. He was going to teach those stupid Icelanders a lesson they wouldn't forget in a hurry. If ever.

CHAPTER TWO

Friday 6th February

Even as Grímur Karlsson slammed the car door closed behind him he knew what he was about to do already had an ominous feel to it. It had been snowing relentlessly since just before Christmas and the city had now frozen solid beneath his feet. Ignoring the uneasy feeling in his gut and his throbbing head he set off up the hill as fast as his feet would carry him. The man and girl he'd followed from the club on Lækjargata had disappeared along a path between two rows of pine trees almost as if they'd headed into a tunnel. From somewhere in the darkness the girl made a noise that was almost a scream but not quite. The sound was muffled and apologetic as if she wanted to let her captor know she was already moving as fast as she could. They had left the bottom of Öskjuhlíð now and were headed up the hill towards Perlan and its giant shiny water tanks. They would soon be able to turn onto paths that led either right or left and then there would be no way Grímur could catch them up.

'Stop. Police!' Grímur yelled at the top of his voice but he wasn't sure if they could even hear him through the biting wind.

He pulled his phone from his pocket and fumbled with the touchscreen as he continued to run. He managed to find Ævar's number and was just about to dial it when he lost his footing on a patch of ice. Because he'd been concentrating on the phone and not where he was putting his feet he fell heavily and didn't have time to break his fall properly. The impact took him by surprise and knocked the wind right out of him. He let go of the phone as he spread his arms in front of himself in a comedic attempt to soften his landing. As he hit the rock-hard ice he made a sound not unlike a dog being kicked in the guts. His phone didn't slide as far as he'd feared it might but he was still fast losing track of his quarry.

He pulled himself to his feet and rubbed the elbow he had hurt in the fall. It was as sore as hell and would be badly swollen in the morning. Once he was upright he fumbled about on the ice for his phone. He needed to keep up with them or they would get away and that would be the end of his pursuit. And if that happened the girl was as good as dead. Another face that would stare back at him as he tried to fall asleep at night. She had tried to warn him this would happen but because she was just another junkie he hadn't listened to her. He didn't listen to anyone any more. He always knew best even though he knew nothing.

With one eye on the ground and the other on where he had last seen them he set off again only this time much more carefully. Another fall like that and he could kiss the two of them goodbye. They would just disappear. The path he was on, such as it was, led straight between the two rows of pines and then into something of a clearing beyond that. That was where they had gone and that was where he had to get to now. Up above them he could see the exterior of the famous Perlan building. Its giant water tanks illuminated by powerful up-lights which made it look like a UFO. An image that was only exaggerated by the huge searchlight which sat atop its glass dome sweeping across the Reykjavík sky.

As he emerged from the cover of the pine trees he looked to his right where he felt they had probably gone. There was no way to see the path that ran north across the top of the hill because there was no light to see it with. The lights from the water tanks were obscured by a stand of short tough-looking trees. The ground underfoot was uneven and covered in small streams of ice that danced and weaved their way in between the large rocks that were scattered about the place. It would have been tough going in broad daylight let alone in the grip of winter darkness. He hadn't been thinking straight when he'd decided to follow them on his own. He could see that now. He was going to need help if he was to get out of this without making a fool out of himself. That was the last thing he needed right now simply because it was exactly what everyone expected of him these days.

As he unlocked the screen on his phone he heard the girl again. This time her scream was much higher pitched than before and full of fear. Turning his attention away from the phone he ran towards where the terrible noise had come from. As he neared an isolated stand of trees he slowed and looked down at his phone. Indecision had set in. He had become the dithering old man he'd always feared becoming. A noise to one side distracted him and he turned to see what it was. Silence. Then his phone shattered the cold night air with its electronic warble. The screen told him the incoming call was from Ævar. He was saved from having to decide what to do. He would tell Ævar where he was and that he needed help. Then all he would have to do was keep track of the noises around him and wait for the other officers to arrive. Exactly what he should have done in the first place. He answered the call.

'Grímur. We've found her,' Ævar said.

The silence all around him was terrifying. He felt that if he spoke he would be identifying himself to the entire hillside and giving away his position. His elbow throbbed, he was cold and tired and the booze in his stomach no longer felt welcome and warming. It felt like an enemy within him which is exactly what it was. Another noise. This time much closer.

'Grímur, did you hear me? We've found Svandís.'

Out of the black night a gunshot tore open the air around him. Grímur looked up and realised his phone was illuminating his face like a candle. If the bullet had been meant for him how it had missed was anybody's guess. He ended the call, turned the phone off and took several steps away from where the deafening noise had come from. He fumbled about for a tree trunk to hold onto. Anything that he could use to steady himself. As soon as he felt something in the darkness he wrapped his fingers around it and tried to balance himself but it snapped as soon as he put any weight on it and another shot rang out even louder than before. This time he wasn't hanging around.

He turned back towards where he had come from and ran for his life but only managed to take three steps before he fell again. This time his arms were still flailing as he hit the ice with his full weight. He heard something in his left wrist snap and his phone went skidding across the ice and into the inky night. The pain scythed up his arm and across his chest. For a moment he thought he was having a heart attack or a stroke. He held his damaged wrist wishing that the pain would go away but knowing there was no chance of that happening. As he lay on his side trying to decide what to do his mind was made up for him again as he heard heavy footsteps coming through the trees straight towards him. Grímur looked around him but his phone was gone. Swallowed whole by the night's black tide and along with it any opportunity he might have had of getting the help he so badly needed. Theoretically Ævar would be trying to figure out where he was but that wasn't going to do him much good right now. Ævar would have heard the gunshots and would have guessed that he was in trouble but it would take time for him to figure out where to send back-up.

With his one good hand Grímur pushed himself upright and moved through the impenetrable dark back towards where he had come from although it was tough to tell if he was moving in the right direction. He took three maybe four steps and tripped again over another rock. As he fell and rolled onto a wrist that was no longer of any use he had no choice but to scream out in agony. The last thing in the world he wanted to do was make any noise but the pain was more than he could bear. Somewhere behind him the gun fired again. This time the bullet found its mark and the pain in his wrist became inconsequential as his left side felt as if it were tearing itself apart from the top of his ribcage to his hip. He rolled onto his back and tried to concentrate on breathing. Such a simple task normally and yet now so very, very hard. With each inhalation his lungs felt as if they were being pulled in and out of the brand new hole in his chest. He reached out for his phone even though he knew it was gone. He wanted to cry out for someone to help him but the only person there wanted him dead.

He wished he had stayed in his car now and waited for other officers to come but then the girl would probably be dead. She was probably going to die anyway but at least he had tried. His eyelids ignored all orders to remain open and fell like lead. His left arm wouldn't move any more and everything hurt like hell. He could feel blood gurgling in his throat as he tried to breathe and then he heard two more shots. The girl screamed again and Grímur passed out on the ice.

Somewhere beyond where Grímur lay unconscious and bleeding the girl fleeing through the dark stopped in her tracks. She wanted nothing more than to keep running but there were a couple of notions in her head that wouldn't allow her to do that. First of all she had no idea where she was going and knew that heading in the wrong direction could well be more dangerous than standing still. The ground all around her was treacherous to say the least. She had reached the top of Öskjuhlíð and passed the iconic Perlan building and was about to head down the other side of the hill but even in the moonlight she could see what a bad idea that would be. Instead of the gravel paths that normally ran down the slope there were now streams of solid ice that snaked like miniature luge tracks all the way to the bottom. One foot out of place and she would wind up doing almost as much damage to herself as a bullet would. If she fell and hurt herself she could feasibly lie there in the dark until she froze to death in her skimpy clothes. With the temperature at around seven below it wouldn't take long before she would go into shock and then without any assistance she would die. The other thing worrying her was she could tell the policeman was in a really bad way. She couldn't live with herself if he died just because she was just too afraid to go back to help so she crept back through the dark towards the spot where she had originally broken free. With each step she took the determination in her drained and the courage slowly but surely left her legs. In spite of that something deep inside her pulled her across the rough ground to a stand of small trees she thought she recognised.

If only they didn't all look exactly the same in the dark. Short, stunted and leafless birch trees that were still fifty years away from being a proper and decent size. She reached out and held onto one of them to catch her breath. As she waited for her breathing to reach a more regular rhythm she thought she heard something just beyond her very limited range of vision. After the cop had been shot she had heard two more shots and panicked thinking they were meant for her. She had looked down at herself at one point expecting to find blood all over her but she had been alright. When the shock had worn off she had turned and run not caring where it was she was headed as long as it was away from the sound of the barking gun.

The wind whistled through the bare branches above her head but otherwise there were no other sounds. Another branch snapped somewhere off in the distance. This time further away than before but still close enough to put the fear of God into her. She squinted and strained her eyes to try to make out any movement in the gloom but she appeared to be on her own. Only she knew that definitely wasn't the case. Somewhere out there was a killer. Then a barely distinguishable shadow moved across her field of vision as the light tripped over a moving figure before allowing it to disappear into the night once again. She was well aware that if her curiosity got the better of her it was likely to get her killed but still she inched forward in the direction of the movement she'd seen. If only she could check on the policeman to see if he was still alive or not then she could leave with a clear conscience. If he was already dead she wouldn't feel too bad about what had happened. She hadn't asked him to come after them and she couldn't comprehend what he'd been doing there in the first place following them in the dark. His brave actions had given her the opportunity to escape though and it was that thought which forced her forward now as she tried to make out any sort of detail whatsoever across the ice. A shadow moved in front of her again dancing wraith-like in the dark. A figure bent over in the moonlight and picked something up off the ground. At first she couldn't see what it was and then when she could she simply couldn't believe her eyes.

She knew straight away that she didn't need to worry about the cop any more. It was time to do something she should have done already. Get the hell out of there and save herself. She kicked something across the ice with her foot then bent down and picked it up. She stuck it her pocket and then turned and ran. And this time she didn't even think about turning back.

CHAPTER THREE

Friday 6th February

The stench was unmistakeable. He hadn't been kidding at all. When the stinking-drunk tramp had waved down their patrol car Eygló and Ari had both taken his wild claims with a pinch of salt but now they'd actually seen what he'd been talking about for themselves Ari was bent over a nearby wall throwing up over a pile of bricks. The smell of the charcoaled corpse had just been too much for him. Eygló, his more world-weary partner, was examining the crime scene from a safe distance making sure she didn't tread on anything that might be useful later on. The forensics guy, Björn would be unimpressed enough with Ari's shenanigans as it was without her adding to his list of gripes. The building site was going to be a nightmare for him to examine when he arrived. It was wet and dark and covered hundreds of square metres. There would be dozens of men who worked on the site every day making it almost impossible to determine if anything he found had been left by the murderer or just jettisoned in the course of a day's work by an employee. On top of that they would all be showing up for work at eight o'clock wanting to get on with the job. She didn't envy him in the slightest. The entire site would have to be sealed off and there were two van loads of officers on their way to do just that. Labourers, sightseers and the press would all have to be kept a safe distance from the scene until such time as Björn and his colleagues could state that there was no more useful evidence to be found. She pointed her flashlight at Ari as he wiped the detritus from the side of his mouth and wondered if she should make an attempt to cover up the small yet disgusting pile he'd left on the floor. She felt sorry for him but at the same time he was going to have to adapt to life on the force sooner or later and explaining himself to Ævar in the morning might just provide him with the intestinal fortitude to become a better police officer.

From where she was standing Eygló could only see the very top of the deceased. His or her head, it was impossible to tell which, was somehow still protruding from the oil drum despite the enormous damage that had been done to it by the fire. The face was burned beyond recognition and it would take a thorough forensic examination to identify the victim of what had been a ruthless and brutal crime. As she stood and stared at the gruesome sight she could hear Ari spitting up again on the ground nearby. He obviously wasn't done quite yet. The longer she stared at the corpse the more details she could make out even from the distance she was keeping. She was running her flashlight back and forth across the scene in slow methodical arcs. The reason the head was still visible above the top of the drum was because a ligature of some sort had been tied around the neck which was holding the victim in place. It had been severely damaged in the fire but not completely destroyed. It must have had a solid core that had kept it from burning all the way through. Some sort of metal perhaps. The deceased had either been strangled from behind or tied in place and left to burn, possibly even while still alive. The thought made her skin crawl.

Behind her she could hear her partner slowly reassembling his dignity and trying to put a brave face on things. She turned around and smiled at him. It was in all honesty all she could do to stop herself from laughing at the poor lad. He hadn't been on the force all that long and obviously didn't have the stomach for such things. Chances were this would be the one and only time in his career that he would ever see anything like this but he wasn't handling it terribly well at all. With any luck he would be fine from here on in so she chose to leave him alone. This time. She doubted if she would be so lenient on him in the future.

'Maybe you should go and wait in the car,' she said.

Ari nodded and walked back to their vehicle. Life was presently a great deal grimmer than he'd anticipated. Eygló on the other hand was old enough to know what to expect.

The years she had under her belt had given her plenty of scars both physical and emotional and some of those scars had scars on top of them too. She knew that everything in life was temporary and that to think otherwise was just stupid. Too many people spent so much time striving for things that were never going to make them happy that they forgot to enjoy anything else that they passed along the way. She hoped that hadn't been the case with the poor soul in the oil drum. Their good times were over now, once and for all.

Even though the walls around the drum were charred in varying degrees from slightly singed all the way through to completely black where the flames had licked their way up to the ceiling it was clear that a message had been left for someone to find. It looked as if black spray paint had been used but it was difficult to tell for sure with so much fire damage.

'Jeg har funnet stedet hvor du begraver fremmede!' she said to herself.

The warning was a simple one even if it was in a foreign language.

'I have found the place where you bury strangers!' it said in Norwegian.

Eygló knew a little of the language and had been around long enough to know that if it had anything to do with the Norwegians then it had to do with drugs. Whoever it was in the oil drum they had done something to get on the wrong side of one of the Norwegian biker gangs, either the Hells Angels or the Bandidos, and had paid the price. As she watched Ari amble back to the car with his tail between his legs she did start to feel sorry for him. It wasn't easy seeing this sort of thing at his age. He had probably envisioned his first few months somewhat differently. Handing out speeding tickets, collaring late-night drunks in 101 and the occasional domestic dispute. Nothing like this. The skin on the corpse's head had blistered right back to the bone in many places leaving porcelain-like discs that made the victim look like something off the television. An unrealistic horror movie from the eighties. Not real life. Not in little old Iceland.

She felt a heavy tap on her shoulder which made her jump despite her best efforts not to. It was the tramp trying to get her attention. She was surprised she hadn't smelt him coming first. She turned to ask him what he wanted and had to take a step back to avoid the nauseating vapours emanating from his mouth. How he was still standing in the state he was in was beyond her but he seemed to be in full control of his senses despite smelling like he'd consumed several Icelandic breweries.

'Do you have some coins you could give me?' he asked.

'Coins? No, but I have some questions for you,' she said as she shone the light in his face.

He shook his head and covered his eyes with his hands and looked at the concrete floor.

'And then maybe you can give me some coins?'

Eygló ignored his question. This was probably where he slept every night once the workmen had gone home for the day. It couldn't be easy living like that but it was still no excuse for not looking after yourself. There were public swimming pools all over the city where you could shower for less than the price of a cup of coffee and yet he stank to high heaven. Where he got the money to get so drunk was another mystery. One she didn't care to investigate.

'I'm not giving you a thing until you've shared everything you know about what happened, and I mean everything. I'm guessing this isn't your first time here so you must have a good idea of who comes and goes every day.'

She didn't intend giving him a single thing other than a trip to the station where he could get a roof over his head for the night but she wasn't about to tell him that just yet. Not while he still thought that talking to her might get him somewhere. He scratched his hair as though there was something alive in it and continued to stare at the floor.

'Let's start from the beginning. When did you notice the body?' she asked.

'I smelt it before I saw it. You could smell it all the way out on the street so when I came in here I already knew what I was looking for. Something bad.'

'You've smelt that kind of thing before somewhere else?'

He nodded without looking up.

'Years ago, before this happened to me I used to work out east in an abattoir. There were plenty of unforgettable smells in there but there was one that stood out. One day a bunch of us got our hands on a pig. We cooked it up that very same night round the back of one of the houses. We had a spot of bother getting the fire under it started and one of them came up with the idea that we could use a little kerosene to get it going. Well, a little kerosene turned into quite a lot of kerosene after we'd had a few schnapps and we managed to set the pig on fire. It smelt a lot like that guy over there does right now.'

Eygló raised one of her eyebrows.

'How do you know that's a guy? I can't tell one way or the other.'

The tramp looked up at her for the first time and squinted at the flashlight's beam. His face was covered in deep creases as though the outgoing tide of his life had taken pieces of him with it. His eyes were full of shame and fear. Eygló didn't like the way they made her feel. She felt as if she had done something wrong but this poor man's life wasn't her responsibility. It was times like this that she was grateful for her boring dependable life full of trivial gripes and moans. There was nothing fancy about it but there were no great tragedies imposing themselves on her either. Sometimes the line between keeping yourself safe and winding up on the streets looking for somewhere to sleep at the end of every day was a fine one. This poor guy had crossed over it and had never been able to pull himself back. Everyone followed their choices in life both big and small and this is where his had led him.

'It's just a guess,' he said. 'Someone made an example of him.'

'How long have you been doing this?' Eygló asked.

'Doing what?'

'Doing what you do out here every night. Sleeping rough, begging for coins.'

'It's been years. Are you sure you don't have any coins? I could really use them. Just whatever you've got. I did the right thing by waving you two down, didn't I? I could have just as easily have kept on walking and forgotten all about it but I didn't.'

'You did what any self-respecting person would have done. I'm not going to reward you for that. I want you to answer my question so I'll repeat it for you. How do you know that's a guy in that drum?'

'I don't. I don't know who's in that drum or why they're in there. I'm tired and I'm cold and I'm hungry and all I want is somewhere to lie down tonight before I fall down. Is that asking too much?'

'No, that's not asking too much but you're going to have to come with me if you want me to help you. What's your name?'

'Ragnar.'

'Okay, Ragnar. Come with me and we'll look after you.'

She put her hand on his shoulder despite his odour and led him back to the car. They found Ari sitting in the driver's seat looking at his phone with a concerned expression on his face.

'Can you take Ragnar back to the station and look after him with some food and somewhere to lie down for the night. I'm going to wait here for the others to show,' Eygló said.

Ari shook his head.

'No.'

'What do you mean?'

Ari looked up at her with a pale harrowed face.

'There's been an officer shot at the bottom of Öskjuhlíð. Leave this guy here, we've got to go.'

CHAPTER FOUR

Monday 26th January

Grímur peeled the Post-it note off his phone and held it up so he could get a better look at what was written on it. The handwriting was abysmal, it was written by the new guy who'd been filling in for Valdís while she was on holiday in Portugal. Even though the two of them had been introduced in the lunch room he couldn't for the life of him remember what the guy's name was. Whatever he was called he had been reassigned temporarily from Akranes and had been very excited about his move. He had been looking forward to getting in on some of the 'big city action' as he'd put it but that had been before he'd realised that all he would be doing in the 'big city' was answering phones.

The note had a name and contact phone number on it so Grímur decided it would be best to just ring it and ask whoever answered what is was that they had wanted. The number wasn't Icelandic it was from somewhere in Norway. It was answered after the second ring and Grímur introduced himself and asked in his no-frills English if someone there had called him recently. The guy on the other end laughed and said something in Norwegian about something being important or possibly not that important and then he also switched to English.

'All I asked your colleague to do was to leave you a note,' he said.

'He did that. It's just that I can't read what he's written here and rather than go hunting about the building for him I thought I'd ring you and see what was up,' Grímur said.

'Nothing is up, I just wanted to let you know about a visitor you can expect to be having at the end of the week. Knut Vigeland is his name. You probably recognise it.'

The wheels turned over in Grímur's head as he tried to recall the name. He had heard it somewhere before and then it dawned on him. He knew exactly who Knut Vigeland was. A Norwegian biker who caused all manner of grief whenever he came to Iceland. It was never a major disaster but you always knew something was going to happen when he visited. The guy didn't come for the Northern Lights or the Blue Lagoon that was for sure. He'd never been arrested and had actually never done anything that had bothered the police too much. All he seemed to do was come over, beat up a few local drug dealers and then leave town again. No complaints had ever been made even though the police had seen the results of his handiwork and it was never very pretty. Everyone involved seemed keen to keep it in-house and let things sort themselves out without any unnecessary interference from the authorities and so as a rule the police left them to their own devices. As long as it was only each other that they were hurting no one really gave too much of a shit. The guys on the wrong end of the beatings were all known to the police and they were all bad news. Knut might not be a particularly nice person but when it came to breaking the law he seemed to have a knack for doing the cops a favour. He would need to do something out of the ordinary before he caused them too much concern.

'Now that you mention it I do know his name,' Grímur said.

'I thought you might.'

'To be honest he's never really given us too much cause for alarm but we'll keep an eye out anyway. He seems to fly under our radar most of the time. He goes about his business in a very quiet fashion but I guess you just never know. As soon as I say that something will happen.'

'That's right.'

'I'll let you go,' Grímur said. 'Thanks for the call.'

He hung up and made a mental note to tell Ævar when he next saw him. No matter how many times he looked at the note he'd pulled off his phone he couldn't make out the words Knut, Vigeland or trouble. That was all that Valdís's substitute with no name had needed to write.

Grímur toyed briefly with the idea of leaving a note of his own on Ævar's desk but figured they'd bump into each other sooner or later and he wasn't entirely sure it was even worth mentioning it since he knew Ævar already had more than enough on his plate. On the other hand if he didn't say anything and then Ævar found out he'd known Knut was arriving and hadn't told him he would think he was keeping something from him. There was nothing for it but to find Ævar and tell him the news personally. At least that way he would have covered his rear end in the event Knut did anything out of the ordinary on this visit. The chances of that happening were slight but it would be just his luck that this one time Knut decided to go and do something that would make them all look foolish, and that was the last thing any of them needed. Grímur had no pressing desire to draw any further attention to himself in the twilight years of his career.

It took him almost twenty minutes but Grímur finally tracked his boss down in the men's toilet on the third floor. It worked out well because by that point he needed to go himself. As the two men relieved themselves side by side Grímur brought up the phone call he'd had with their Norwegian counterparts. Ævar listened in silence and still seemed to be thinking hard long after Grímur had finished his brief tale. Eventually he broke his silence as he zipped himself up and walked to the sinks to wash his hands.

'Maybe we should keep more of an eye on him this time,' Ævar said.

'If you want to but I don't think it's necessary. It's always the same with this guy. He jets in and then jets out again a few days later leaving a selection of black eyes and broken noses behind. There's never been so much as a phone call from any of his victims.'

Ævar dried his hands and ran his fingers through his hair.

'I know. Having him here makes me nervous though.'

Grímur smiled and joined Ævar at the sinks.

'You're not the only one. Every time he's here there's virtually no drug related problems for about a week. They're all too scared to stick their heads out from underneath their rocks. The guy's only a problem if he doesn't like you.'

'And he likes us is that what you're saying?'

Grímur washed his hands and straightened his hair in the mirror.

'I've met guys like him before. Live and let live. We don't get in his way and he won't get in ours. If we put him under surveillance or bring him in for questioning it'll only get his dander up and that's not a good idea. The last thing you want is this guy taking a personal interest in you. Let him go about his business and then fuck off back to Norway,' Grímur said.

Ævar took a long hard look at Grímur and shook his head.

'I don't know. There's some truth in what you say but I don't want anything coming back to haunt us. Part of me thinks it's high time we put an end to his shenanigans here and chased him out of town like in those old Westerns. If we're ever seen to condone these sorts of activities it could go very wrong for us. If we know about this sort of thing we're supposed to do something about it. That's our job. No matter who he's hurting and regardless of whether or not we care.'

Ævar continued to stare at Grímur and waited for him to at least nod in agreement. He couldn't help wondering how many miles the ageing detective had left on his clock. When the time was right he was going to bring up the topic of early retirement with him again. Not now though. For now he had better things to be getting on with.

CHAPTER FIVE

Thursday 29th January

Halldór Valdimarsson took another sip of his coffee but it was still a bit hot to really throw it back as he would have liked. He'd just pulled another all-nighter trying to get his speech ready but it probably still needed some work if he was to be honest. He wanted another coffee because he was going to have to be as alert as possible for the impending visit of Auður Jökulsdóttir. She was his contact on the inside of one of the country's biggest newspapers and he liked to be at his best whenever she paid him a visit. He had invited her today to have a chat and drop a few hints that he would have something big for her soon. She would have plenty of questions as per usual. It was in her nature to be nosy. It was what made her such a good journalist but he would have to watch his answers and measure them in such a way that he didn't give the game away. Not yet anyway. There would be time for that soon enough. For now she was to be baited and teased but nothing more.

An attractive blonde head stuck itself around the corner of the door to his office and smiled. Right on time as always. He liked that about her. Auður's face hung in the doorway for a few more seconds before she swung herself into the room and closed the door behind her. He had never figured out how she managed to be so chirpy no matter what the hour was be it last thing in the evening or first thing in the morning.

'Good morning,' she spouted and pulled up a seat opposite him with the casual air of someone who was quite at home in the office of the Minister for Finance and

Economic Affairs. 'It's good to see you. I must admit that I'm a little curious as to why we're here so early. I could have really done with another hour in bed. You look like you could do with catching up on some sleep yourself.'

Auður and Halldór had attended high school together at Menntaskólinn við Hamrahlíð where they had embarked on an enjoyable but short relationship which had ended when Auður had disappeared to Copenhagen where she stayed with relatives and worked in a café while deciding what to do with her life. Halldór had followed his dream to work in politics by signing on as an intern with Iceland's foremost right-wing political party which he saw as the way forward for himself and the country. Auður had returned eventually and embarked upon her own career with a large national newspaper.

They had both succeeded in chasing their goals. Auður was now the political editor for the newspaper and Halldór had worked his way in to the position of Minister for Finance and Economic Affairs as well as that of Deputy Prime Minister. They had done exceptionally well for themselves but one suspected that they both still held ambitions to climb that one step higher at some point. Neither of them would be satisfied until they had reached the very top of their respective trees.

'Coffee?' Halldór asked.

Auður nodded and poured herself a cup.

'So what is it that has me called to your office at this early hour? I'm thinking it's so no one would see me coming or going. That wouldn't be the case would it?' she asked as she added some milk and a spoonful of sugar to her coffee.

Halldór couldn't help but smile. That was exactly why he had insisted on such an early meeting although he would never admit it out loud.

'Of course not. I just thought this would be a good opportunity for the two of us to touch base. You always see ulterior motives whether there's one present or not. Your profession has made you unnaturally suspicious of even your oldest and dearest friends,' he grinned broadly as he said the last part and almost got a chuckle out of the steely-eyed journalist.

'That's because there's always one there if you're willing to look hard enough. With politicians it's always the subtext you have to concern yourself with never what is actually being said. If I've become overly suspicious in the last few years it's only because you and your parliamentary companions have become overly devious. If this had been something innocent you would have invited me down here for lunch or met me in a bar later this evening. Where people could see us together,' she grinned.

It was the same insightful logic he had been so attracted to all those years ago. There hadn't been any fooling her then and nothing had changed in the interim. She was as sharp as a tack and never missed a thing no matter how hard you tried to hide it from her.

'Okay, you've got me. I arranged this clandestine get together because I wanted an element of secrecy to be involved. In the next couple of weeks I'm going to have something for you that will be an unprecedented scoop for you and the newspaper. There are going to be some big changes around here and you're going to be first in line when they happen.'

Auður drank some of her coffee and leant back in her chair. She was appraising Halldór with what could only be described as a suspicious eye.

'How can you be so sure I'm going to be first in line for the story? If you're not going to give it to me today, and it doesn't look like you are, what's to stop someone else beating me to it?'

Halldór beamed across the desk at her and held his arms out wide as if he were about to embrace her.

'Because my dear, you aren't just going to break the story, you're going to be the story. When the time is right I'm not just going to feed you a lead. What I'm going to do is give you the tools to uncover the biggest by-line of your career to date.'

'Sounds exciting,' she said with a world-weary and sceptical tone.

'It will be, you'll see.'

'Why the prior warning then? Were you just keen to get me out of bed early this morning or is there another reason I'm here right now?'

'I just wanted to give you a little advance warning that something big is brewing. When this is all over things are going to be very different for both of us. I just want to make sure that you know that. This is going to make you a star.'

'I can hardly wait,' she said.

CHAPTER SIX

Friday 30th January

As Knut's plane touched down at Keflavík he turned his phone on and stared at the picture of Lise that he had on it. She was the reason he was in Iceland. The only reason. He hated the place with a passion and wouldn't have even entertained the idea of a visit if it wasn't an emergency. Even though most of the country's visitors adored the place he simply didn't share their sense of awe. Despite its natural wonders, incredible scenery and gorgeous women he had always loathed the isolated little pile of rocks. And yet again here he was and, as it always seemed to be, he was here on business. And Knut's business was killing.

Two weeks ago Lise had sent a distressed and confusing message. She had got herself into a spot of bother and had asked for his help. Again. During their brief time together in Oslo Lise had developed a heroin habit that had tested the limits of her physical endurance as well as the absolute boundaries of Knut's patience. It was an ugly stupid drug that stripped people of their charm and left them graceless and spiritually barren. Despite her assertions that she had everything under control it quickly became obvious that she didn't have anything under control and the addictive white powder soon had her under its thumb. It was a position she had been powerless to get herself out of.

The idea behind her move to Reykjavík had been to start over and get away from the circle of friends that did nothing but drive her addiction forward and supply her with drugs. In hindsight it had been an idealistic and rather naïve plan and no one should have been surprised when it had failed miserably. As soon as she'd arrived in the Icelandic capital she had sought out and found a dealer and a group of like-minded users to shoot up with. One thing led to another and she soon had the same old set of problems all over again.

Before long she had moved in with them and was in debt to the tune of several hundred thousand krónur. With no way to earn the money legitimately due to her continuously wasted state she had turned to other foreign girls for help. The ones who had found themselves in a similar predicament but had worked out ways to pay their debts off. Most of their debts anyway. Enough to keep their dealers off their backs and heroin in their veins. And if they were lucky a roof over their heads. That was what mattered. Somewhere warm and dry to inject when the night's work was done. A mattress with a kettle next to it. A needle, a spoon and her phone charged and with a little credit on it. That was what made a house a home.

She had sent a selfie along with her plea for help and Knut still wasn't sure if it had been meant to make him want her back or pity her. She had asked him for money. Of course. She was looking pale and tired. Long haul tired like she hadn't slept in weeks and had been up 'dancing' to earn her keep every single one of those nights. He knew all too well what 'dancing' meant. She'd left one city for another but the problems people have they take with them wherever they go. Baggage. Weighing her down like a load of bricks.

He'd decided not to send her the cash she'd asked for but to visit her instead to see what could be done to get her back on the straight and narrow. Dragging her back to Oslo to check her into a rehab centre sounded like the best option but before he'd even arrived something had gone wrong. She'd stopped replying to his texts and wouldn't answer his calls. After four days of calling her phone it was finally answered. Someone in the house had got sick and tired of listening to it ring probably and had pulled it out from underneath her mattress. Whoever the girl who'd answered was she hadn't seen or heard from Lise either. That was when he'd booked his tickets and headed for his least favourite island destination. He had better things to be doing with his time and a host of responsibilities that he would be walking away from in Oslo but he felt he owed it to her to at least try. She had done all this to herself but he still felt sorry for her and he'd seen it happen to much stronger people than her.

Walking through the airport he briefly thought about smiling at the passport checkpoint but they rarely even looked at you let alone smiled back so he didn't bother. Either they were going to let him through or they weren't. There weren't too many other options. A few of his associates had been denied access to the country over the last year because of some petty crackdown on Norwegian gang members. This time Knut had swapped his leather jacket for a suit which he'd disliked at first but was beginning to grow on him. He thought it made him look more dangerous than ever. Like someone who should be respected as well as feared. He liked the idea of the façade of respectability. The solemn-faced police officer slid his passport back through the glass divider to him and waved him on. As expected he didn't get a smile. It was time to forget about smiles and get down to business.

Two hours later he was staring at an inexplicably self-confident idiot smoking a cigarette while trying to look tough at the same time. And failing. The young man leaning against the door frame flicked his cigarette butt to the ground and coughed.

'Didn't you hear me? She's not here,' he rasped.

'I didn't ask you whether she was here or not. I asked you when you last saw her,' Knut said.

He was losing what little patience he had with this stoned moron. The guy was doing his utmost to be unhelpful while trying to come across as aloof. Knut was puzzled as to what sort of message this was supposed to be sending but he had reached the end of his tether with the guy. Whatever the message was, he was about to have it shoved back down his scrawny little neck. This was one time when the suit had conveyed the wrong tone altogether. He had probably been mistaken for a social worker or a lawyer. And now was the time to dispel any such illusions. As the little nincompoop reached for another cigarette Knut swung hard and low at the guy's solar plexus. It was a target he could hit with his eyes closed. The blow doubled the smoker up and he dropped to the ground holding his midriff and gasping for air.

Knut stepped over him as if someone had just puked on the doorstep. As he walked into the fetid air of the squat he screwed up his nose and turned back to where the guy still lay curled up in a ball.

'If I find her in here you're going to want to make yourself pretty scarce. And if I don't find her in here I'm going to have some more questions for you to try to answer and this time you're going to try much harder.'

Inside the house the walls were soft with damp as if someone had spent hours pouring water down them. He touched one of the radiators in the hallway. It was ice cold. If he hadn't already double-checked the address she'd given him he would have sworn he had the wrong place. Then again he should have known better than to expect anything else. When things started to go wrong they usually went wrong all the way. With temperatures in Reykjavík at this time of year consistently around freezing it would be a very unpleasant place to live. He pushed open the first door he came to but the room was empty apart from a mattress on the floor and a pile of dirty clothes next to it. He bent down and looked through them but he didn't recognise anything he could remember Lise having ever worn. He wiped his hands on his suit pants when he put the clothes back down again.

The next room contained another two mattresses and yet more clothes. These were in a more orderly state than the first lot but in much the same condition. No one had been to the laundry in a while. There were plastic bags full of stale kleinur in one corner of the room and half-finished bottles of cola all over the floor. They hadn't exactly been living high on the hog. It was the diet of the destitute and sugar-needy. It was cheap and would keep you going but nothing else. Knut had an image of Lise asking strangers for money outside the Hlemmur bus station and then buying herself these treats in the convenience store where all the late night trade was either from tourists or alcoholics. He was angry at so many people but mainly at himself. When she'd suggested a move away from Oslo and the scene she'd got herself caught up in it had seemed like a good idea. Anything had to be better than what she was doing to herself there or at least that was what he'd thought. It now appeared he had been wrong. Very wrong. As he walked through what was supposed to be the kitchen and into the living room he shook his head at the smell of the place and swore. Someone had definitely been to the toilet in one of those two rooms although he couldn't tell which one. There were bags of rubbish lying all about the place that had been torn open by desperate animals or even more desperate humans. He resisted the urge to cover his nose with his hand but only just. His tour of the decrepit hovel was soon over and he headed back to the front door which was still lying wide open. There was a packet of cigarettes and a lighter on the ground outside but his obstinate little friend had gone. Knut cursed again as he regretted not keeping hold of the guy so he could follow up on his threat to question the idiot some more.

Knut looked up and down the street but there was no sign of the escapee anywhere. In his rush to get as far away from Knut as possible he'd dropped the cigarettes and his lighter. Even if he'd noticed them fall it was doubtful he would have hung around long enough to pick them up again. The punch had been designed to lay him low for a few minutes but he'd recuperated quickly and made good his escape. Knut kicked the cigarettes into the gutter and bent down to pick up the lighter. It was a cheap plastic disposable one with a tacky logo printed on it. The kind of thing someone had spent at least twenty minutes designing or picking out of a Google Images search. It was a girl sitting in a champagne glass kicking her heels up in a sea of bubbles. He would have laughed at it if he wasn't so sure that it had to have come from the club Lise had ended up in. Next to it was an address on Lækjargata but apparently the establishment was so fancy that it didn't have a name. The image told you everything about the place you needed to know. The street was definitely the one where she'd said she worked. It was too much of a coincidence to not be the same place.

Ten hours later Knut leaned against the bar in the club on Lækjargata and signalled to the pretty Polish barmaid for another beer. His second of the night. She poured him another Einstök White Ale but this time didn't bother with the slice of orange. After the fuss he'd made about having fruit in his beer the first time she wasn't about to make that mistake again. He thanked her and cast his eyes around the place. The decor was as tacky as the lighter had led him to expect. Anywhere that was going to put a champagne glass with a girl sitting in it on its cigarette lighters was unlikely to be a high-class establishment but this place didn't even try. He guessed that the array of reasonable-looking women there, who all seemed to be foreign, were on the clock. He couldn't think of any other reason they would have assembled there. Apart from them the place was quiet and it seemed unlikely that the clients would outnumber the staff at any point as the night dragged on. In short it was just the sort of place he would have expected Lise to end up once she had run out of money. Part of him hated himself for not sending her the cash but he knew that it would have only gone up her arm and she would have wound up here sooner or later anyway. He had learned the hard way that giving hard-earned cash to a junkie was one of the more stupid pastimes a human being could find. Time and time again he'd been burned by a girl he thought loved him and while that may have been the case it was also true that she loved drugs. He liked to learn things the hard way.

After removing your clothes in order to make money had been made illegal in 2009 someone had come up with the 'champagne club' idea instead of the old-fashioned strip clubs and they were proving harder to close down than the police had anticipated. For a set price, somewhere in the region of between 20,000 and 60,000 krónur, you got fifteen minutes to an hour with the girl of your choice. Behind a velveteen curtain. The idea was that all you did was talk with her as you shared some champagne together but it was widely accepted that you got to do pretty much anything you wanted to with her for the top-end price.

For the equivalent of around £300, a glass or two of champagne and some discreet cash tips you would get yourself a conversation you wouldn't forget in a big hurry. The girls were foreign, desperate and poorly-advised about what was legal or even a good idea in their new country. He had thought about asking if Lise was working tonight but that plan was fraught with all sorts of pitfalls. They would want to know how a face they had never seen before knew her name and chances were good that she worked under an alias anyway. Too many questions in a place like this made everyone nervous and that wasn't what he wanted. Not yet anyway.

If he couldn't find Lise through this place then his attention would turn to the odd-looking building in one of the other photos she'd sent him. It looked like a black tin can that had been cut in half and turned on its side. The windows had been boarded up and there was a chain and padlock on the door. It seemed to be an old army barracks hut that had been used by the either the American or British forces during the Second World War. Chances were that it was near one of the airports. Either near Keflavík where the international airport was or Reykjavík Airport, the much smaller facility beside the city centre that serviced Iceland's domestic routes as well as Greenland. What she should have sent him a picture of, or rather who, was the guy that had driven her down there to have sex with her. The guy who had threatened to kill her if she didn't behave herself. That was who he really wanted to talk to right now.

Either way it wouldn't take Knut long to find this character, it was what he did for a living. If anyone was going to know the whereabouts of Lise Sponheim it was this Janko guy she had spoken of in less than glowing terms. With a name like that he was bound to be from the former Yugoslav Republic. With any luck he would be wandering around his club at some point but there were only so many beers Knut could drink to kill time before his eyes would start wandering over the flesh that was on parade in front of him. That was the last thing he needed. To be caught with his pants down on the hunt for an ex-girlfriend.

He would struggle to explain that one to the wife back home that was for sure. No, he would finish this beer and then call it a night. In theory he could always come back another time. He downed the rest of his pint, thought about it for a moment and then ordered another. One more couldn't hurt and it was good beer. All the way from Akureyri in the north of the country so his new Polish friend had informed him.

'I was told that Janko might be in tonight at some point. Do you know if that's right?' he asked the smiling beauty behind the bar.

'He might be. Do you have a name handsome stranger?' she answered.

She was chuckling to herself as she poured another two glasses of champagne for one of the waitresses. When she was done she looked up at him and waited. Without taking her eyes off his she grabbed a wine glass and started polishing it.

'I've got all night you know,' she said.

The smile lingered but there was a steely air about her now. Maybe people coming looking for her boss made her nervous. Maybe she'd had a few bad experiences in the past with strangers asking for him. Knut certainly wasn't going to tell this girl what his name was but at the same time he wanted Janko to know that someone was looking for him. Someone who meant business and wanted answers.

He met her gaze and stared her down. He wasn't just another customer and now she knew it.

'I'm what you might call a friend of a friend. I know someone who was working here recently and she still owes me money. Janko probably knows where she is and it would really help me out if he could share that information with me.'

The Polish girl squinted ever so slightly as she put the polished wine glass back down on the bar.

'Why don't you leave your name and your number with me and I'll see that he gets it next time he's in,' she said.

'I can't do that. In my line of work it's just not a good idea,' Knut said.

'Well, how's he going to get hold of you then?'

Knut finished his beer in one go and put the glass down on the bar.

'He's not. I'm going to get hold of him.'

CHAPTER SEVEN

Friday 6th February

Ævar set his feet as firmly as he could on the icy surface and surveyed the hillside above and below him. The wind had picked up as soon as he'd arrived and was now as bitterly cold as he could ever remember. Friday the sixth of February was quickly becoming the worst day of his career with the Reykjavík Police Force. No sooner had the discovery of a badly burned corpse on one of the city's many building sites been made than he'd received the one call he'd dreaded receiving more than any other. One of his officers had been shot and was being rushed to the Landspítali Hospital for surgery. When he'd been told who it was and where it had happened he'd thought there must have been some sort of mistake. There was no way Grímur could have been anywhere near Öskjuhlíð at that time of night. He had sent him to Lækjargata to visit a champagne club about six hours earlier and he'd been told to have a quick look around and nothing more. How the hell he'd managed to wind up shot and bleeding all over the footpath next to Bústaðavegur was completely beyond Ævar. Someone had called the emergency services and told them exactly where to find him but when the ambulance had arrived only minutes later whoever had made the call was long gone.

With a flashlight in his hand he joined the search for clues along the trails that led both north and south along the sides of the hill. A couple of officers were inspecting the paths that led down the western side of the Perlan building but it had already been deemed that they were far too dangerous to attempt to walk down in the dark. If anyone had escaped that way they were crazier than any person he'd ever met before. The pathways had frozen solid and had become rivers of ice that descended towards Nauthólsvík so steeply that to walk on them in the dark would be lunacy of the highest order.

The search on the eastern side of the hill had originally concentrated on the area where Grímur had been found unconscious on the footpath alongside Bústaðavegur and had then worked its way slowly upwards in ever increasing circles. The pathway on which Ævar now stood had been disturbed at some point by someone walking or running along it. There were deep footprints and skid marks in the dark volcanic gravel where someone had slid or fallen. Some of the footprints seemed to suggest that the person who had left them must have weighed a fair bit. The impressions were deeper than one might have expected but there were a lot of them and they seemed to head in all directions. It was hard to tell exactly where anyone would have been going but they had made a real mess of the path as though there had been a scuffle of some sort. Perhaps even a fight to seize control of the gun that had been used to shoot Grímur. It would take some time to figure out exactly what had occurred and until then Ævar had to accept that almost anything was possible.

Ævar rubbed his hands together to try to get some warmth back into them as he tried to piece together the final moments before the shooting that had almost cost Grímur his life. The ageing detective was in a medically-assisted coma at the moment and the doctors weren't giving any information about his prognosis. From what Ævar could tell Grímur had answered his phone call but as soon as he'd said something he had heard the shot ring out. Then the phone went dead and none of his attempts to get through to it since had been successful. There had been no phone on him when they'd found him lying on the footpath and there was no sign of it anywhere on Öskjuhlíð yet either. At some point there must have been a struggle or a chase on or around the path he was now standing on and then Grímur had been shot somewhere near the base of the hill. That seemed the most likely scenario but there were still plenty of things that needed explaining before he could believe any one version of events. What he wouldn't give right now for his detective to regain consciousness and tell him exactly what had happened and why he'd been there in the first place.

Exactly one week ago a troublesome Norwegian had entered the country at Keflavík airport. Knut Vigeland was his name. He and Ævar's paths had crossed before and now all hell had broken loose in the space of less than eight hours. There was no way in the world it could be a coincidence. Trouble followed this guy everywhere he went the way bad days followed good ones. As soon as they could ascertain where he was staying he would be arrested and they would put an end to this ridiculous crime spree of his. If Ævar could have his way he would have never been allowed to enter the country. They could ban every single Norwegian biker ever born and he still wouldn't be happy. People like that were nothing but trouble and this had only served to reinforce his opinion of them.

Ævar shook his head and wondered what had led Grímur all the way from Lækjargata to where he was standing now. His instructions could not have been any clearer. Go down to the club and have a look around. That was all he had to do. Just a little visit to let them know they were keeping an eye on them and nothing else. They just needed to be able to say that an inspection of the premises had been made and they would be in the clear. Case closed. All he'd had to do was get in and get out again without getting himself in any sort of bother but now they had another set of headaches altogether and they had a distinctly Norwegian flavour to them. One was a murder victim with burns to ninety-eight per cent of his body. Somehow the soles of his feet had survived the ordeal but the rest of him resembled a barbecued chicken wing and now a police officer was in critical condition in hospital with a near-fatal gunshot wound. It was days like this that defined careers and Ævar felt as if his was on the edge of a cliff and about to topple off should the slightest breeze come along at his back. On top of that he had a sore neck and his hands were frozen stiff. The phone he so badly needed was nowhere to be found and was not about to show up of its own accord so it was time to call it quits and get on with the task of finding Knut Vigeland. Ævar was hoping that once that arrest had been made then everything else would fall into place and life could slowly return to normal.

With so many hotels and serviced apartments in the city not to mention the vast number of privately-rented properties that tourists had to choose from these days it could take them the rest of the day to find him if not longer. And speed was of the essence. Another murder or attempted murder in the next twenty-four hours and Ævar's resignation would be waiting for him on his desk ready to be signed. They had to find Knut Vigeland before someone else was shot or burned alive. With an armed threat like him on the loose the Viking Squad had already been put on standby.

Ævar pulled his phone from his pocket and dialled Grímur's number yet again. He was hoping he would hear it ring somewhere in the bushes nearby but deep down he knew he was kidding himself. Whoever had shot him probably had the stupid thing now. There was no phone ring to be heard anywhere on the frozen hillside and no one answered the detective's phone it just rang and rang as it had every other time. He would soon have the phone company tell him which mobile phone mast in the city it was connected to and that would at least narrow their search area a little. For now it was time to get in out of the cold and make some other calls about tracking Knut down. As he trudged back down the hill something caught his eye near the base of one of the trees. A glint of something shiny in his flashlight's beam. It was probably nothing more than a shard of broken glass but as he got closer to the tree he could see that it wasn't a piece of glass at all. It was metallic and about the size of his hand. He bent down to get a better look.

When he saw what it was he let out an involuntary groan. It was a small stainless steel hipflask. The very one he had given Grímur at a staff Christmas party several years ago long before he'd realised that Grímur had spent a significant part of his career hiding a drinking problem from them all. He picked it up, unscrewed the lid and inhaled the faint but unmistakeable scent of vodka. Making sure no one had seen him he slid the hipflask into his jacket pocket and said a quiet prayer that his decision to send Grímur to a bar in the line of duty wasn't going to cost him his life.

CHAPTER EIGHT

Saturday 7th February

Knut Vigeland signed his bill at reception and paid the outstanding balance for the drinks bill he'd run up at the bar. He thanked the receptionist for her help during his stay and received a pleasant smile in return before walking out to the minivan that was waiting to take him to the BSÍ Bus Station. From there he would transfer onto a large coach and head out to the airport at Keflavík. Two and a half hours later he would be back in Oslo with his wife. He nodded to the driver and showed him the return part of his ticket before walking to the rear of the minivan and swinging his bag on top of the other luggage. His was the smallest in the pile by a long way. He had to smile at that. He prided himself on travelling light. It was an art form he had worked on over the years. It was only necessary to carry the bare minimum with you when you travelled. Any more than that was just stupid. People never used half the stuff they lugged around with them. Just as he let go of the straps he heard vehicles pulling up behind him and doors opening followed by loud urgent demands in English that he turn around and put his hands on his head. They used his full name when they addressed him that was the first bad sign. Knut turned slowly to face the voices and raised his hands above his head as he did so. He had to smile at what he saw in front of him. There were seven Heckler & Koch MP5 submachine guns pointed at him. That was the second bad sign. All around him hotel guests were screaming and dropping to the ground with their hands covering their faces. The Viking Squad officers kept their weapons trained on him as he was instructed to drop to his knees. Once he had complied two officers approached him with Glock 17s aimed at his head while another officer handcuffed his wrists behind his back. It was going to be a long day. He would not be getting to see Oslo this afternoon or any time soon for that matter.

Knut was pulled to his feet and dragged towards a black Dodge van with blacked-out windows. The back doors flew open as they approached and he was pushed into the back of the van and told to sit on a small bench seat that ran along the side of the vehicle. It was really tiny for a guy of his size but it wasn't as if he had much choice in the matter.

Not all the Glocks had been put away. One was still pointed at him at eye-level as if he were about to make a break for it despite being handcuffed and locked in the back of a van. They had clearly been told not to take any chances with him and they were following those instructions to the letter. He had no idea how much they knew about what he'd been up to but until two minutes ago he hadn't been aware that the cops in Reykjavík even knew he was in town. And now, instead of getting ready to catch his 12:40 p.m. Scandinavian Airlines flight back to Norway he was going to have the hospitality of the Icelandic police thrust upon him for the foreseeable future. His arrest would be on the evening news both in Reykjavík and Oslo. He would not be overly popular in either capital tonight. His wife would curse his name. Under her breath if their two daughters were within earshot or out loud if they weren't. Her plans for their evening meal ruined by the zealous members of Iceland's elite 'Viking Squad' as they liked to refer to themselves. He wondered if it would be appropriate to remind them just where the Vikings had come from in the first place at this point in time.

The drive to Hverfisgata took less than five minutes. His calves were soon sore from trying to keep himself upright against the wall of the van as the two guys in full battle gear stared at him from no more than a few feet away. He felt that if he'd lurched forward at them without warning it might just be the motivation they required to make him only the second ever man shot by the Icelandic police. It wasn't something he was desperate to add to his resume. That really would give the wife something to get upset about. Within minutes of pulling into the car park at the rear of the police station he was unloaded and then ushered through the back doors of the building and into one of the holding cells.

Before he was left alone an officer removed his handcuffs and Knut was left staring at the walls wondering where it had all gone so wrong. They would leave him alone in the cell for a few hours now. The idea being that it would make him more talkative when they finally felt like questioning him. There wasn't a hope in hell he was going to tell them anything but they had to try. It was nothing new to him. They would learn that soon enough. He had spent weeks and months staring at cell walls before. Three months once in Department B of Oslo Prison for nothing more than a misunderstanding over an idiot dealer who had refused to pay his bills on time. He should have never let the little twerp live but then it would have been much longer than three months that he would have spent waiting to get back in the game. He didn't like being out of action for any extended period of time. It didn't do you any good putting your feet up like that. You got out of practice and slow in the head if you weren't careful. He couldn't afford to spend too much time in Iceland. He had too many other things to attend to but they would have to be put on hold for now while he let this thing take care of itself. He belonged to them until such time as they could put him in Litla Hraun for a stretch or were forced to let him go. Considering his circumstances he wasn't too worried about how things would play out. Things had a way of working themselves out. They always had before.

After what felt like about three or four hours his cell door opened and he was handcuffed once again. Knut was led through the cold silent corridors by two sombre officers and deposited in an interview room. Much to his relief he found

Nína Andrésdóttir sitting at the table waiting for him. They had never met before but he recognised her face and knew her by reputation. Someone back home had already agreed to give her a substantial amount of money to look after him otherwise she wouldn't have been there. She had heard of his troubles somehow. The ins and outs of exactly how that had happened didn't concern him too much. She was the best criminal lawyer in Iceland, everyone knew it. A hard-ass among hard-asses. The cream of the crop.

He would keep his mouth shut and listen to what she had to say and then perhaps later on at some point he would ask her what he had done to deserve such an honour. Or maybe not. He had learnt a long time ago to never question the good things in life. Sometimes you just had to accept that certain things were simply meant to be. This included the bad stuff too but especially the good stuff. If you started worrying about where that was coming from you would take all the fun out of life. Nína motioned for him to take a seat next to her just as the door behind them opened again and Ævar Rafnsson walked into the room. The expression on his face was difficult to pick. He didn't look particularly happy about anything but there was an air of smugness about him too. He gave Nína a withering look which she completely ignored and then sat down opposite them. While he waited patiently for Nína to finish whatever it was she was doing on her laptop Ævar pretended to make a few handwritten notes himself and then cleared his throat.

'Knut Vigeland, you are under arrest for the attempted murder of an Icelandic police officer on Öskjuhlíð last night and the murder of an unidentified individual on a building site on Einholt several hours earlier. You do not have to make a statement just yet but is there anything you would like to say at this point?'

Nína stopped what she was doing on the laptop and looked up at Ævar before turning to face Knut. She could tell by the smile on the big Norwegian's face that he did not have anything he wanted to say at this particular moment in time.

CHAPTER NINE

Monday 2nd February

Jón Páll lent back in his chair, looked across his desk at Svandís and rested his hands on his chest. He laced his fingers together and tried to put on his best non-judgemental face even though he couldn't help but wonder what the hell was wrong with her. He had seen her in a bad way many times before but today she looked as pathetic and frightened as he could ever remember. She was holding her side as though it was really sore but kept insisting she was fine and refused to let him examine her. When he'd asked her what was wrong she'd lied and told him that she'd pulled a muscle. From the way she was grimacing she had done considerably more than just pull a muscle but if she wasn't going to let him touch her then there was next to nothing he could do to help. She no longer trusted him but she still came to see him each and every time she hit rock bottom. She had been fighting a heroin addiction for close to five years now and in that time he had seen her try to give it up thirty maybe forty times. Her problem was that no matter how much she insisted she wanted to stop using the drug she really didn't. She loved it. She loved the chase around town to find a supply even if it was below freezing and it took her all night. She loved the feeling when she finally got that little plastic bag in her hand and she loved the pressure and the pin-prick penetration of the needle as it slid through her skin's nerve endings and into her vein. More than anything she was a needle addict. As addicted to the sensation and the pain of the cold metal as she was to the drug itself. She was never going to be able to quit. And now here she was again looking up at him with those sad watery blue eyes of hers.

'Why do you continue to come here, Svandís, when you won't let me help you?'

'You can help me if you'd just listen to what I'm saying.'

Jón Páll let out an exasperated sigh and sat upright again.

'You know as well as I do that I can't prescribe you drugs just because you happen to think it's a good idea. If there's something wrong and you genuinely need painkillers then you're going to have to let me examine you.'

He waited for a reply of some kind but all she did was grit her teeth and stare at him. Jón Páll smiled and held his hands out to signal that they were done as far as he was concerned.

'That's it?' she asked.

'Without the proper procedures being followed I cannot simply prescribe medicines to anyone who wants them. I'm a doctor not a dealer. As you know I have a reputation built on helping young people in your position and it's something I've been very successful at. This has not been achieved by handing out drugs like lollies. You may not see it at the moment but I'm doing you a favour. You will only succeed in getting yourself addicted to something else. The problem lies in your need to fill the void in your life with yet another void. The void of self-loathing with the void of addiction. There are, surprisingly enough, people who still love you. Let them in before it's too late.'

The tears that had been threatening to come for some time now spilled over and down her cheeks. She rubbed them away with the back of her sleeve and spat across the desk at him.

'You sick old fuck. If people knew what you really did with the girls who come in here looking for help you wouldn't be so popular any more. I do what I do because I don't have a choice not because I want to. Do you think I enjoy coming here and begging for help? Snivelling in here like a bitch with its tail between its legs asking you for a favour and being told to go fuck myself.'

Jón Páll couldn't help but smile a little but soon regained his composure.

'That's right, you can wipe that fucking smile off your face too. Those days are over, trust me. I'm never going to be that desperate again. Not ever.'

Jón Páll's face dropped as his façade cracked and finally gave way.

'Don't get all high and mighty with me. It doesn't suit you. Even less than spitting across the room like a common whore. And let's not forget that that's exactly what you are these days. If it's not me you're fucking for a fix it'll be someone else. Either way you'll be paying your way to that land of twisted dreams of yours on your back. That cheap and nasty little habit of yours has made you cheap and nasty. Very, very cheap and extremely fucking nasty.'

Svandís sat in silence and looked down at her hands. There were scratch marks on her forearms where she had taken the frustrations of daily life out on her skin. Her wrists itched constantly for no good reason she could think of other than she was getting sick without the drugs that her body demanded. They didn't even make her feel happy any more. Those days were long gone. The best they could do now was to stop her from going mad and they weren't going to do that for much longer either. Her fingernails dug into her skin. It was as if she was trying to tear the flesh from her bones every time she reached under the table and scratched. If she didn't get something to calm her down soon she would rip open the skin and find herself with an infection which would mean going to hospital and having to do some very awkward explaining to the staff. They would try to keep her in bed and off drugs and she would lose her mind if they did that to her again. She hated withdrawal more than anything else she had ever experienced. Even more than sleeping with men she loathed and who disgusted her. She looked across the table at her once benevolent doctor. If she was going to sleep with someone she hated then it would be for heroin and not some half-arsed drugstore imitation. She needed that feeling of the floor opening up beneath her and swallowing her whole. There wasn't a pill in the world that could replicate the real thing.

'You're a fucking prick,' she said barely loudly enough for him to hear. 'Do you know what I have to go through to get this stuff? Do you have the faintest idea?'

'Yes I do, but this is the life you have chosen.'

Svandís stood up and tried to straighten the kinks out of her clothes and her posture at the same time. Both attempts were unsuccessful. She hadn't bothered doing laundry in something like a month and her back was permanently stooped from the load that her lousy life-decisions had given her to carry around. She tried hard to give herself as much dignity as she could muster but it was a losing battle and the smile that started to creep back across Jón Páll's face said it all. Her stubbornness would prevent her from caving to his sordid demands but it would not prevent her from taking the first job that came her way as soon as she'd left his clinic. She had run out of options. Without heroin in the next twenty-four hours she would start tearing her hair out by the roots. The dependency on the drug she had developed had blossomed from a small-time habit into the poisonous core that her life now revolved around. Her orbit was shrinking daily and it was becoming obvious that at some point in the very near future she would crash and burn. It was only a matter of when and where.

'Next time you see me I'll be the one laughing not you. No matter how bad things get I won't be stooping to your level again,' she spouted.

'Stooping to my level? The next time our paths cross again, Svandís,' Jón Páll said with just a hint of a sigh, 'it will be the way it always is when we see each other these days. You'll be begging me for some unreasonable favour that only a fool would agree to and I'll be telling you no over and over again. If you could only see yourself as others do you might just understand how incredibly tedious you've become.'

'I'll never ask you for anything again as long as I live,' she said and walked out of his office for the last time.

CHAPTER TEN

Friday 6th February

Janko could not believe his ears. One of his dealers had been found dead on a construction site in the city centre not twenty minutes ago. Óli Þór wasn't exactly the shiniest penny in the jam jar but it was still difficult to imagine what he could have done to piss someone off this much. One of Janko's police friends had just sent him a text message to let him know the fate that had befallen his dim-witted friend so he would hear about it before he saw it on RÚV's late night news. His contact had attached a photo of the crime scene as an added bonus and it wasn't pretty to say the least. What Janko found really upsetting though was what had been painted on the wall just behind Óli Þór's charred corpse. He hadn't spent too much time in Norway but he knew enough of the language to understand the black letters spray-painted across the fire-damaged wall – 'Jeg har funnet stedet hvor du begraver fremmede.'

'I have found the place where you bury strangers.'

Someone was taunting him. Someone who knew his secret. He had no idea how anyone could have worked this out all on their own and he needed to know for sure that it wasn't some kind of elaborate joke. One that could get him in a great deal of trouble. And one that could easily get whoever had left the message for him killed.

Twenty minutes later he was parked next to the fence that ran along the back of Reykjavík's domestic airport. He lit a cigarette and waited. If it was some kind of trap they would be watching him so he was going to wait until he was sure there was no one around. He could have easily been followed or they could just be lying in wait for him. Regardless of what the risks were he had to see inside the hut. When his cigarette was finished he lit another and waited some more. It was a process he repeated eleven times before he made his move.

After just under two hours he decided that enough was enough. He had other things to be getting on with and more importantly he had run out of cigarettes. Janko got out of the car and looked around. If anyone was still watching him they were more patient than he was and he was a very patient man. His time spent fighting in the former Yugoslavia had taught him that the ability to outwait your enemy was as valuable as any weapon you might be carrying in your hands. Once he'd decided there was no one anywhere near the abandoned hut he walked over to the door that sat halfway down one of its sides and pulled a set of keys out of his pocket. He selected one of the keys and tried to insert it in the lock. It was far too big for the padlock and wouldn't fit. Someone had been in his hut and they'd changed the lock on the door too. Chances were they'd also found what was hidden beneath the old floorboards but there was no way he could know for sure without making a real racket. Until he was able to make a return trip with the right tools he would have to assume that they had and change his future plans accordingly. Who could it possibly be and why had they chosen to let him know in such a strange way? Had they intended to murder Óli Þór anyway or was his death just part of the message? Have a good look at this and see what I've done. You're next. Whoever it was certainly seemed to have a point to prove but Janko had offended so many people over the years that the list of potential candidates was virtually endless.

As he got back in his car and started the engine he failed to notice the trailbike nestled in amongst the trees at the base of Öskjuhlíð. As he turned the car around and headed back to his club to get a stiff drink and figure out what to do next the trailbike started its high-pitched engine too. Its rider waited until Janko was almost out of sight before letting the bike roll out from beneath the trees. It accelerated away to catch him up but once it was in sight of the rear of Janko's car it slowed down so the preoccupied Serb wouldn't notice he was being followed.

CHAPTER ELEVEN

Monday 2nd February

The girl was waving at him and shouting something at the top of her lungs from outside the café on the other side of Austurstræti. He didn't know how she knew he was a police officer but it was obvious that she did. He took a deep breath and jogged across the street to see what she wanted.

'Oh, thank you. This crazy girl is trying to steal our tip money.'

Grímur opened the front door and stepped into the café to find a truly chaotic scene unfolding in front of him. A young woman, who did indeed appear to be crazed, was wrestling a large glass tip jar away from a frightened-looking waitress. Or at least she was trying to. The contest looked to be a fairly even one but the waitress seemed to waning in her determination to see off her small but determined assailant. Even from behind he recognised the girl trying to steal the jar. Her name was Svandís Finnbogadóttir and it was not the first time their paths had crossed. Far from it in fact. Svandís managed to free herself and the tip jar from the clutches of the angry waitress and made a break for the door at the rear of the café. The one that opened onto Austurvöllur Square. The waitress gave Grímur a look of abject despair as he ran past her to the back door and launched himself through it after Svandís. When he called out after her she only turned her head slightly but it was enough to distract her from the task at hand. In the split second that it took her to recognise him she tripped over her own feet and instinctively let go of the jar as she braced herself for the fall. She managed to get her hands out in front of her but the jar dropped like a stone and a particularly heavy stone at that. It exploded as it hit the concrete sending a wave of coins across the ground. Hundreds of virtually-worthless silver króna coins spilled in every direction along with a few gold ones.

Passers-by gasped at the noise the jar made as it shattered and one old lady clutched her chest as if she were about to drop dead from the shock of it all. Grímur grabbed Svandís by the arm but he hadn't bargained on the reaction he would get. Even though she was short and badly undernourished she was wiry and much stronger than she appeared. When she felt his hand on her arm she rolled over and lashed out with her fingernails. Grímur was caught off-guard as he leant down towards her and didn't even see her hand coming at him. He did however feel the pain as her fingernails dug into the flesh of his cheek. She clawed him as hard as she could and managed to lift a considerable amount of skin as she raked her talons from top to bottom. Grímur recoiled from the pain and put his hand up to his face in a belated attempt to protect himself.

Svandís saw her chance and rolled away from Grímur. He wasn't about to let her escape though and grabbed her leg with his free hand and pulled her back towards him. She struck out with her other leg and knocked him backwards rather unceremoniously onto his rump. This time she was up and away and as soon as Grímur had regained his footing and a little of his dignity he was off after her. All thoughts he had of taking it easy on her had disappeared in a flash as soon as she'd lashed out at him. He could feel blood dripping from the scratches on his face and a fire burning from within the painful wounds. He caught up to her just as she was about to round the corner onto Pósthússtræti. He wasn't sure where she thought she was going to lose him in the middle of downtown but she seemed determined to give it a go. He was equally determined that she wouldn't get as far as the corner so he dove and grabbed at one of her ankles sending her sprawling to the ground once again. His acrobatic manoeuvre drew more gasps from the people assembling in small groups on the footpaths but he didn't care. He wasn't about to be attacked in public like that and let her get away with it. As she struggled to get up again he got on top of her with his full weight and pinned her to the ground.

Once that had been achieved he was able to handcuff her and take several badly needed deep breaths. He was too old and far too out of shape for this sort of crap and he knew it. She had come pretty close to getting away from him. One more twist and she would have been gone. Pinned beneath his considerable weight Svandís's level of protest went from noisy to ear-shattering within a matter of seconds. As soon as she felt the cold handcuffs snap around her wrists she started shrieking as if she were being killed. Grímur ignored her tantrum, loud as it was, hauled her to her feet and then marched her through the crowd of bewildered shoppers back to his car on Hafnarstræti. Her tirade continued the whole way there as well as throughout the short drive back to the police station. Grímur chose to drive around to the side entrance on Snorrabraut rather than to the front door on Hverfisgata and stopped just at the entrance to the car park. His face was stinging like he'd been sliced with a razor and his ears were ringing from the relentless mix of senseless chatter, hollow threats and expletives a sailor would have been proud of coming from the back seat. He didn't need any of this in his life and had already made the decision to cut his losses and set her loose. He applied the handbrake and left the engine running as he got out of the car into the freshening breeze that was coming up Snorrabraut from the bay. In the background Esja was covered in a fresh coat of shiny white snow.

Flinging the back door open Grímur pulled Svandís towards him and out of the car eliciting yet another series of high-pitched curses and unlikely promises from her relentlessly busy mouth. Her overly colourful language only reinforced the idea that he was making the right decision even when he knew full well he wasn't. He was just trying to justify it to himself. As he unlocked her handcuffs she took a brief moment to draw breath as she tried to decipher what was going on and actually stopped talking for a few seconds.

'Come on,' he said. 'I haven't got all day. I need to deal with you right now like I need a hole in my head.'

Svandís stared at him dumbfounded and unsure of what was coming next.

'You just want me to run off so you can crash tackle me again,' she said.

She held her palms up so he could inspect them. They were skinned and raw-looking.

'See what you did? And now you want another crack at it. You must think I'm stupid.'

'Just get lost,' Grímur replied.

Svandís studied him in silence and waited as he backed away from the car with his hands in the air.

'You're serious?' she asked.

Grímur nodded.

'I'm not going through all that shit with you again over a smashed tip jar. What the hell's wrong with you anyway?'

Svandís laughed a dark and bitter laugh.

'You know what's wrong with me,' she said.

She pulled one of her shirt sleeves up and showed him her arms. There was a collection of new and not so new track marks all over the inside of both of her elbows.

'I'm a fucking mess is what's wrong with me, Mr High and Bloody Mighty. I'd like to see how you'd look with a habit like this and how smooth and charming you'd be then. Not that you're any Cary Grant to begin with.'

She laughed again, derisively and daring him to retort.

'You come from a nice home, Svandís. It's up to you what you do with your life but don't make your problems everybody else's.'

Svandís's smile turned to a sneer as she looked up and down the street trying to decide what to do next.

'So you're just going to let me walk away then?'

Grímur nodded. He held one arm out to indicate that all she had to do was just that.

'And the sooner the better,' he said.

Svandís realised that she was going to get away with her little stunt and avoid a potentially horrendous night in a cell.

'Your face looks like shit. How are you going to explain that?' she teased.

Grímur went to raise one of his hands to his cheek but stopped halfway through the motion. Svandís smiled her evil smile again and then took on a more serious look. She ran her fingers down her side and grimaced slightly. The fall outside the café had aggravated her sore ribs.

'You're just too embarrassed to face the other officers in there and admit that a girl did that to you. I bet it's been a while since a woman ran her fingernails over you for any reason at all. Even at that club. You should take a good hard look at yourself before you go judging me or anyone else you sad old prick. See you later.'

Svandís turned and stormed off up the street towards Laugavegur. Grímur stood and watched her go. He hated the fact that she had been right about him not wanting to face his fellow officers. His reasons for letting her go were all wrong and he knew it. And because they were wrong they would come back to haunt him. It was just a matter of time. He was getting old and ineffective. He was letting laziness and personal fears cloud his judgements and he would regret it. If not today then very shortly and possibly for a very long time and he wasn't doing her any favours either. This sort of treatment would only reinforce the idea that her behaviour was not only acceptable but would be rewarded. She was right. He was a sad old fool.

As she walked up the hill Svandís pulled her phone from her pocket and made a call. The conversation was short and very one-sided.

'Come and pick me up, now. I'll be on the corner of Laugavegur and Snorrabraut underneath that hotel.'

She listened briefly to the reply from the other end of the line.

'I don't care what you're doing. Drop whatever it is and come and get me,' she continued.

She ended the call and shoved her phone back in her pocket and trudged through the semi-frozen slush towards the café. The wind bit through her jacket making her hunch her shoulders up even more than normal. Despite Gylfi's half-hearted protests she doubted she would have to wait very long and she was right. He pulled around the corner in his car a couple of minutes later, came to an abrupt halt on Snorrabraut, and then threw the passenger door wide open. Svandís smiled to herself. Yet another uptight male getting impatient with her. There were plenty more where that came from too. She slid into the car and closed the door with an exaggerated slowness that she knew would irritate her boyfriend no end. She loved belittling him any way she could and had never understood why he let her get away with it. But he did. They all did. She couldn't understand what was wrong with men.

'Well, aren't you happy to see me?' she asked.

Gylfi pretended he hadn't heard her and concentrated on executing a U-turn.

'Don't you have anything to say to me? I almost got arrested today you know.'

Gylfi continued to concentrate on the road as he turned the car around.

'You've got a job tonight. If you want it that is. I didn't give him an answer straight away. I said I've have to check with you and get back to him. We had some trouble with him last time but I told him I'd ask anyway.'

Svandís's eyes lit up at the news. She was broke beyond belief and as desperate as it got but she would never tell Gylfi that. Not now she had a chance to earn something. Money that she could use to spend tomorrow blissed out in the house rather than running around town making a fool out of herself like she had today.

'Who's the guy?' she asked but waved her hand as if to tell him not to bother answering. 'It doesn't really matter. I'm doing the job anyway but you can tell me if you want,' she said.

Gylfi scratched his head as he manoeuvred his way through the traffic on Snorrabraut wondering if that meant that she wanted to know who he was or didn't want to know. He turned to look at her but she was just staring at him with that gormless expression she got when she was tired and had run out of smack.

'It's Guðmundur Bodvarsson.'

Svandís shrugged her shoulders and smiled.

'Do I know him?' she asked.

'You know him alright. Last time you went out there I had to come in and rescue you after he started slapping you around. That's what you said anyway.'

He continued looking at her but she just turned away and stared out the window. When she snapped back she noticed him staring at her and realised that he was still waiting for an answer. She just nodded and pointed through the windscreen.

'Watch where you're going. I remember him now, okay,' she said.

When he finally turned his eyes back to the road she let out a long sigh.

'You remember him now?'

'Yes, I remember him now.'

'And you still want to do the job?'

'I need the money, Gylfi. Now will you please watch where you're going? If you're not careful you'll get us killed.'

CHAPTER TWELVE

Saturday 7th February

Ævar cracked his knuckles and looked across the table. He'd been looking forward to this ever since he got the call about Grímur being found with a bullet in him. This was one Norwegian who would wish he'd never set foot in Iceland.

'You were so smart and yet you managed to be so stupid too. You were smart enough to destroy any forensic evidence linking you to that building site with the fire you started but you were stupid enough to leave that message. A bit of a warning for the locals, was it? In Norwegian. You must think we're really thick?'

Knut smiled and shrugged his shoulders in a display of mock confusion. The door to the interview room opened and a female officer entered and handed Ævar a piece of paper before she turned around and left again without a word. Ævar scanned the page carefully before looking back across the table at Knut.

'Óli Þór Sigurdsson. Does that name ring any bells?'

'No. Should it?' Knut replied.

'You burned him alive in an oil drum last night. I would think it should. Or do you not bother finding out who they are before setting them on fire?'

Knut stared across the table at his interrogator. He remained emotionless and cold on the outside but he desperately wanted to leap across the table and punch this snotty Icelandic cop right in the face.

'I've no idea what you're talking about.'

'Okay. I'll give you a few clues then. Óli Þór worked for the local chapter of the Hell's Angels. He was a small-time member who ran errands for them and yesterday your paths crossed for one reason or another. Maybe you knew him before then, maybe you two had never met before. Maybe he was sent to give you a message. Is that what it was? You didn't particularly like what he had to say and so you decided to send them one back.'

'I have no idea what you're talking about,' Knut repeated himself without a trace of emotion on his face.

'You've been saying that a lot since we brought you in but I think you do.'

'Is that so?'

'I have found the place where you bury strangers,' Ævar said and then studied Knut's face for any flicker of recognition but there wasn't one.

'If you'd written it in Icelandic or even English we wouldn't have had the foggiest idea who it was and you'd be back in Oslo now with your wife and daughters. But you needed to write it in Norwegian so the "Angels" would know exactly who it was who had incinerated their little friend. Óli Þór drew the short straw when it came to having to meet you face to face and what he had to say pissed you off. So you strangled him, dumped him in that drum and then set him alight leaving a message in your mother tongue for us to find. That was just your way of telling us all to go fuck ourselves. The fact that they picked one of their most inconsequential members to meet you probably didn't help. You probably found that a little insulting. Probably thought that they should have afforded you the respect you deserve and so Óli Þór had to be made an example of. How's that sound, Knut?'

'Like the load of horseshit it is.'

'Is that right?'

'That's right, hotshot.'

'I know you did this, Knut. And I'm going to prove it. Not only that but when Grímur Karlsson wakes up he's going to tell me it was you who shot him as well. That flight home's starting to look an awfully long way off now isn't it?

In fact your chances of getting off this little pile of rocks are looking pretty slim.'

There was no response from Knut. No emotion on his face, not a sound out of him. Nothing. He just sat and stared at Ævar as if his mind was somewhere else. Nína looked at the two men and waited for someone to say something. Anything at all. It was a stand-off that neither was about to break. Not any time soon anyway.

'Perhaps you would care to fill us in on what it is happening with this officer?' Nína asked. 'You said my client was being charged with attempted murder. Does that mean that you expect the victim to recover?'

'Last night on or near Öskjuhlíð an officer was shot by an unknown assailant around eleven o'clock. He was found lying on the ground next to Bústaðavegur in a pool of his own blood and is extremely lucky to be alive. As of right now he's in a medically-assisted coma and his doctors have little or no idea when or if he'll be coming around. They have said that they expect him to regain consciousness at some point but they're being especially vague about when this may or may not occur. We can safely assume however that when he does he'll be pointing the finger at the shooter and I fully expect that he will be pointing it at Knut.'

'Based on what evidence? Do you have anything that places my client on Öskjuhlíð at the time of the shooting?' demanded Nína.

Silence hung over the three of them until Knut started chuckling to himself. Softly at first and then much louder as he realised that Ævar didn't have an answer for Nína.

'You guys don't know shit do you? You've pulled me in here with the biggest show of armed force in the history of this hick town expecting that I'd roll over and tell you exactly whatever it is you want to hear. Well here's some news for you. I'm not rolling over, I didn't shoot your cop and you're never going to be able to prove I did something I didn't fucking do.'

Ævar leaned back in his chair and stared at Knut while Nína made some notes on a pad. Knut just sat and stared back at Ævar without blinking and not even trying to wipe the smile off his face. When Nína was done scribbling she looked up at the two of them and sighed.

'If you don't mind Ævar I wouldn't mind some time alone with my client. There's a few things I need to go over with him in private.'

'Be my guest,' Ævar said. 'There's a few things I need to get done too.'

Nína made a face that said she wasn't very impressed with either of them.

'It's only a matter of time before we tie you to Óli Þór's murder, Knut. No one, no matter how good they are, can hide all their tracks. Then we'll see how funny you are. And when I prove you were the one who shot Grímur Karlsson last night too you won't be leaving this hick town for a very long time so you might want to get comfortable,' Ævar said.

This made Knut smile even more. Ævar got up and left the room. He'd had enough of this smug Norwegian prick for the time being. There was plenty of time yet for him to get the better of him but for now he wanted some coffee. It was going to be a very long day. As soon as Ævar had left the room Nína turned to Knut. The smile on his face slowly fell away as he sensed just how irritated his lawyer was. He wasn't about to let her spoil his mood though.

'You don't need to go out of your way to antagonise the police here. It won't do you any good at all. These are some very serious charges you are facing.'

Knut put his feet up on the desk and leaned back in his chair.

'They're only serious if they can make them stick,' he said.

'Not yet they can't. Give them time. These hick cops know what they're doing. You shouldn't be so sure of yourself.'

'Unless I've got nothing to hide,' he said.

Nína laughed a little before regaining her professional composure.

'Come on. Who are you kidding? We've all got something to hide,' she said.

CHAPTER THIRTEEN

Saturday 7th February

Ævar stood next to Grímur's bed looking down at him not really knowing what to think. The doctor had left him alone with his colleague so he could have a few moments to collect his thoughts and let the seriousness of the situation sink in. From what he had just been told it was obvious that Grímur was in a very bad way. The bullet had hit him in between two of his ribs and entered his lung. It had missed his heart by about two centimetres. After removing the bullet in surgery the doctors had induced a coma so that he would have the best chance possible of recovering. He was in the 'very lucky to be alive' category there was no doubt about that and there were still no assurances from the medical staff that he would pull through. Ævar's threat to Knut that their star witness would be ready to testify against him at some point had been nothing more than a bluff and of course the Norwegian had seen right through it.

Ævar had needed to get out of the station for a while to clear his head and he'd wanted to see first-hand how his colleague was doing. The doctors had been very non-committal over the phone and he'd decided that the best idea would be for him to take a look himself. Now that he was at Grímur's bedside he had a much better idea of what they were dealing with. Grímur's face was pale. As white as the sheets on his bed. Whiter even, as if the life-force in him was trying to leave but hadn't quite been successful yet. Ævar was hoping that the cantankerous old bastard was a fighter and would pull through. Without him they were lost. Knut might fit the bill for both crimes but without a motive for either the fatal assault on Óli Þór or Grímur's shooting they weren't going to be able to prove a thing. Maybe Grímur had just got in his way. The wrong place at the wrong time. Men had died for less. A doctor appeared at his side and put his hand on Ævar's shoulder. Ævar felt himself jump a little.

'You shouldn't expect too much at the moment. It will take quite some time for your friend to show any signs of recovery.'

Ævar nodded.

'I was hoping that he'd be able to talk to us soon so he could tell us who did this to him. It's important to a lot of people that the person responsible is punished.'

'Of course, but you must understand that Grímur came very, very close to dying last night. How he survived is still a mystery to all of us who operated on him. Had he not been found when he was then he most definitely would have passed away on the side of the road.'

'The funny thing is that's not even where he was shot,' Ævar said.

'What do you mean?'

'This morning we found blood much further up the hill towards Perlan. His blood. He was shot over two hundred metres away from where we found him. Somehow he managed to make it all the way down to Bústaðavegur before he passed out.'

The doctor smiled and took his hand off Ævar's shoulder.

'I don't think so,' he said.

'What do you mean?' Ævar asked.

'What I mean is quite simple. With the injury your friend sustained there is no way that he could have possibly walked, crawled or even fallen down that hill. He simply wouldn't have been physically capable.'

'But he must have been. There's no other way he could have made it down to the road. There was no one else up there except for the shooter.'

The doctor looked from Ævar to Grímur and then back again.

'Then the man who shot him must have carried him down off the hill,' the doctor said.

'No I don't think so,' said Ævar.

'There is no other explanation. Unless he has a guardian angel who follows him around.'

'There is always another explanation. We have the guy who shot him in custody and I'm telling you he did not carry Grímur down to the road after he shot him. The guy doesn't have it in him. He would need to have a heart in order to do something like that.'

The doctor shrugged and started walking out of the ward. As he departed he called back over his shoulder.

'I don't care what you say, your friend did not make that journey on his own.'

The doctor stopped at the door and turned to face Ævar once again.

'Either your cold-hearted killer helped him down to the street and saved his life or an angel carried him under its wings. With a wound like that Grímur would have been unconscious seconds after he was hit. Before he hit the ground even. Have a good day.'

Ævar turned back to Grímur and put his hand on the unconscious man's arm.

'If you can hear me in there I need you back. I want to nail this bastard and you're the only one who can help me do it. Come back and help me make everything alright again. We owe it to each other to get this done. Let's forget about everything else and just get this guy.'

There was no response from Grímur's pale face. Ævar moved his hand onto Grímur's forehead and held it there willing some form of communication to take place between the two of them but there was only silence and within that silence lay the key to all understanding.

CHAPTER FOURTEEN

Tuesday 3rd February

Svandís pulled the rear-view mirror towards her so she could get a better look at herself to put her lipstick on. Gylfi rolled his eyes but didn't say a word, he knew better than that by now. She had just caught his slightly comical gesture though.

'You don't need it to see where you're going. Stop being such a drama queen,' she said as she looked at the colour of the first lipstick she picked before putting it back in her handbag and fishing another one out. Once she was convinced she had the right colour she started applying it while trying not to grin at Gylfi's half-hearted attempt at indifference.

'I don't know why you even bother. It's not like he's going to care if you're wearing lipstick or not,' Gylfi said.

'You're just jealous because I don't wear it for you.'

'Why waste money on something he's not even going to notice?'

'It's not like I paid for it. I pinched them from Hagkaup when you were getting those sweets yesterday so I may as well wear it. And anyway, it's not for him it's to make me feel better. I had a shitty day yesterday and I want to feel good about myself for a change.'

Gylfi chuckled to himself. He changed lanes to get past a motorist who was taking it easy even though they were the only two vehicles on the road at 3:00 a.m. He had long ago stopped wasting his time trying to talk her out of her peculiar ways. She was as stubborn as she was self-destructive. Enormously so. The more you tried to get her to take it easy the more of everything she drank, smoked, snorted and shot up just to prove that she could do whatever she wanted and that there wasn't a thing you could do about it.

They had just passed through the suburb of Mosfellsbær and were heading north out of the city. They would soon be at the Hvalfjörður tunnel and Gylfi started fishing around for the 1,000 krónur they would need to pay when they reached the toll gate on the other side.

'You can just shut up and drive anyway. If I wanted your advice I'd ask for it,' Svandís said.

She put the lipstick away and moved the mirror back roughly to where it had been before but made sure it was still out of position just enough so that he couldn't see out the back window. That wiped the smile off his face while he adjusted it again so it was just the way he liked it. When he was done he looked across at Svandís and groaned out loud which made her start giggling like a little girl.

'Do you have to do that in the car?' Gylfi asked.

Svandís was busy dividing a small pile of cocaine into two thin lines on top of a plastic takeaway food container that had held her dinner of leftover pasta only a few minutes earlier. Her diet consisted primarily of carbohydrate-rich foods that could be easily reheated whenever the urge to eat took her. And amphetamines. She also drank as much coffee as she could get down her throat and only slept a few hours at a time normally just after she'd finished her night's work. As a result she looked at least ten years older than she really was and was tired almost all the time. Except when she was high on drugs. She ignored Gylfi and snorted the lines through a shortened drinking straw that she kept in her handbag especially for the job. When she was done she moved the rear-view mirror again to check her nose for detritus and laughed the contented laugh of the freshly high as a kite. She reached under the seat and found a half-empty bottle of white wine. She unscrewed the top and drank the remaining South American Chardonnay in one go. She wound down her window and threw the bottle out onto the road. Gylfi cringed as it disintegrated somewhere behind them in the dark.

'Jesus Christ, what is wrong with you? Do you want us to get pulled over or what?'

'So what if they do? There's nothing left for the idiots to find now anyway,' she yelled triumphantly. 'Are we there yet?'

She giggled uncontrollably while Gylfi adjusted his mirror back to its rightful place yet again.

'We'll be another thirty minutes or so,' Gylfi said. 'I don't know what your hurry is. Where did you get that stuff from anyway? I thought you were broke.'

'I've been saving that for a rainy day.'

Gylfi shook his head as they descended into the Hvalfjörður tunnel. By the time they were halfway through he'd located the 1,000-krónur note he'd been hunting for and had it in his hand ready for the automatic toll booth.

'I'm all revved up and good to go now is what my hurry is,' she spouted.

'Great,' Gylfi said as sarcastically as he could.

Svandís ignored him and bounced about in her seat humming along to some tune that only she could hear. Once they had passed through the toll gate the rest of the trip to Borgarnes passed in silence. Gylfi was wary of starting any new conversations that might lead to an argument and the cocaine seemed to have something of a calming effect on Svandís and her drug-addled physiology.

Before too long they'd crossed the Borgarfjarðarbrú Bridge and were entering the small town of Borgarnes. They followed the main street for a short distance and then headed down a hill that wound its way back towards the sea. They were roughly sixty kilometres outside of Reykjavik now and Gylfi was starting to feel tired. He was ready for a break from her and was secretly hoping to get some sleep while she entertained Guðmundur. Hopefully there would be no repeat of the antics of their last visit.

That night he'd sworn he would never return to the guy's house but apparently those decisions weren't his to make any more. He still suspected that Svandís had made up a large proportion of her story about him attacking her. Guðmundur was a mildly creepy guy as were most of her customers but he hadn't really seemed the type and she had been a real handful that particular night, even more so than usual. Even on her good days she could be a real pain in the arse. He had become accustomed to her fits and tantrums but they still irritated him. In the time they'd been seeing each other Gylfi had discovered that more often than not when some sort of crisis exploded around Svandís it was a really good idea to get all the facts from an impartial source before believing a single word that came out of her mouth.

He spotted the house he was looking for in its lonely position at the end of the winding road and as they pulled up outside it he breathed a sigh of relief unaware that he was even doing so out loud.

'You'll be pleased to be getting rid of me I expect,' Svandís said without any hint that she'd taken it personally. 'You should get some sleep while you can, this could take a while.'

'I think I'll do just that,' he said and stretched his arms out realising that he was a lot more tired than he'd realised.

She reached over and grabbed his chin between her fingers and gave it a not so gentle shake.

'Don't sulk, you wouldn't know what to do with yourself if you didn't have me around to look after. I'll be back out in a few hours but keep your phone on just in case.'

And with that she bounced out of the car and wiggled off up the driveway pulling her skirt down over her backside as she went. Gylfi waited until she had disappeared through the front door before turning the car around and driving off to an even more remote spot where he knew he wouldn't be disturbed. It was entirely possible they wouldn't be getting home until six or seven o'clock so it was a good idea to get some rest while he could.

Even though Svandís would be tired when she'd finished her night's work she would only sleep for two or three hours before bouncing out of bed again and once she was up there would be no chance of him getting any more rest. It was like living with a five-year-old in many ways but it was just the way it worked with her. If she was up so were you. When Gylfi had found his parking spot he killed the engine and reached into the glove compartment. He lit the joint he'd stashed there for just such an occasion and reclined the driver's seat as far as it would go. It wasn't long before he was stoned and sound asleep in his little metal cocoon.

A while later he was woken from his marijuana-induced slumber by his phone ringing. He rubbed his eyes and fumbled around in the dark for it before conceding defeat and switching on the interior light. He shielded his eyes against the glare and picked the phone up off the floor. On the other end Svandís was talking so quietly that he could barely make out what she was saying.

'They're going to kill me,' she whispered.

Even though her voice was quiet there was no mistaking the fear it contained.

'What?' he asked.

Gylfi tried turning the volume on the handset up but it was already as high as it would go.

'What's that again?' he repeated.

'I'm behind the sofa.'

'Behind the sofa? What the hell for?'

'He just called here. You've got to save me.'

'What? Who called? What are you talking about?'

'They're in it together. I can see that now.'

'Who's in what together? Can you speak up? I can hardly hear you.'

'If I'm still here when he gets here I'm dead. Do you understand what I'm saying?'

'No, Svandís, I don't understand what you're saying.?'

'Just get here as fast as you can and get me out of here. I'm serious. If you don't you'll never see me again. Gylfi?'

Gylfi cleared his throat and sneezed.

'Okay, I'm coming.'

'Hurry.'

The line went dead and he knew he now had no choice but to go and see what was wrong for himself. This is what he'd been expecting all along from a return visit to Guðmundur's place. He started the engine and spun the wheels as he sped back to the house.

By the time he came to a stop at the end of the driveway Guðmundur was standing at his front door staring out into the night as if he'd lost something. Gylfi leapt out of the car and ran up to him.

'Where is she?' he demanded.

'I couldn't tell you.'

'Why on earth not?'

'Because,' he said with a smug smile on his face. 'I don't know.'

'Is she inside?'

'No, she's not inside. What do you think I'm doing out here. She's run off.'

'What do you mean she's run off?'

'Exactly what I just said. She's run off like a fucking lunatic without so much as a word of explanation. I got my money back though. She didn't even take that with her. Can you believe that?'

He looked at Gylfi as if he were responsible for the girl's erratic behaviour.

'She wouldn't just run off for no reason. What the fuck did you do to her?' Gylfi demanded.

'I didn't do anything to her and you can drop that tone of voice with me. I remember you from last time, don't worry about that.'

Gylfi took a couple of very deliberate steps towards Guðmundur and grabbed him by his shirt collar.

'Listen to me smart-arse. She called me a couple of minutes ago and said that someone was trying to kill her. Now I get here and you're telling me that she's just decided to run off in the freezing cold. You seriously expect me to believe that? Why don't you drop the fucking attitude yourself and tell me what really happened?'

Guðmundur peeled Gylfi's hand off his collar and pushed him back a couple of feet closer to where he'd been standing before.

'Just calm down. I am telling you the truth. No one here is trying to kill her. I'm the only one in the house and I haven't so much as touched her. We were having a bit of a drink and I went into the bathroom to take a piss. When I came out she wasn't upstairs any more and when I came down here the front door's wide open and she's gone. That chick of yours has a few screws loose, pal. I'm sure she's a lovely girl and everything but she's a bit unstable if you know what I mean. One minute she's all smiles and laughs and the next she's ranting like a crazy bitch.'

Gylfi told himself that he needed to calm down and that it just might be possible that Guðmundur was telling the truth and that Svandís was acting like an idiot all over again. It was quite a coincidence though that these things always seemed to happen with the same customers. He ran his fingers through his hair and tried to decide what to do.

'Okay. Let's just say that you're telling the truth.'

'I am telling the truth,' Guðmundur protested.

'Let's just say that you are then. Where would she have gone?'

'I haven't a clue,' Guðmundur said. 'Take a look around. You won't see another place anywhere around here.'

Gylfi had to agree with him. There was nothing nearby where she could have gone to find shelter from the cold. If she had run away as he'd said, and wasn't still hiding behind the sofa, the only place she could have gone was another house that stood about half a mile away along the coast. There were lights on outside it and even from where the two of them were standing he could see it clearly perched up above the ocean.

'Who owns that place over there?' Gylfi asked.

Guðmundur pretended to look in the direction Gylfi was pointing.

'I don't know. They're too far away for me to care.'

'I'm going to check it out then,' Gylfi said.

'Good luck. I'm going to bed. If you don't find her don't bother coming back here. I won't be answering the door.'

Guðmundur went back inside and closed the door behind him. Gylfi looked towards the lights in the distance and cursed his girlfriend's name.

CHAPTER FIFTEEN

Tuesday 3rd February

By the time Gylfi had found out how to get to the house with the eerie outdoor lights on it and parked the car he was starting to feel more nervous than angry. What if she wasn't there? What then? How would he explain himself to the occupants without coming across as some kind of psychopath? But, if he sat around and thought about it long enough he would lose the courage needed to ring the doorbell so he was better off not thinking but just doing. Realistically the worst thing that could happen would be that they called the police but the way things were going he was going to need to do that sooner or later himself. This night was beginning to feel a lot like one that wasn't going to go away in a big hurry.

As he walked up to the front door he noticed something. From a distance the house appeared to be asleep as any self-respecting house would be at this hour despite the security lights but when he got a little closer he could see that there were lights on behind the curtains as well. It was certainly an odd hour to be up watching television or reading. In fact it was an odd hour to be up doing much of anything for that matter. Surely they must have seen her then or maybe she was waiting inside for him. He took a deep breath, rubbed his hands together and rang the doorbell. Faint sounds of feet shuffling along the floor got louder and louder as they got nearer until a gentle-looking elderly man opened the door.

'Thank God you've decided...'

He didn't finish what he was saying but instead looked Gylfi up and down as if he was possibly a criminal or at the very least a nuisance of some sort.

'I'm sorry, do I know you?' he asked looking genuinely puzzled.

'No, I'm looking for my friend. Maybe you've seen her?'

The man looked at him intently as if examining him for clues but didn't say another word so Gylfi continued.

'I'm sorry for disturbing you at this hour but it's really important I find her. It seems she's decided to run off from a house nearby and I thought she might have come past here as there don't seem to be many other places around.'

The demeanour of the elderly man changed and he didn't seem quite so pleasant any more.

'Now, you listen to me young man. I haven't the faintest idea what you're talking about but if you don't get off my doorstep right now I'm going to call the police.'

Gylfi could suddenly see the night stretching out into the next day and possibly beyond if he couldn't find Svandís and get her home. His patience came to an abrupt end. He knew the old man was lying to him and he'd had enough.

'Look, I know you've seen her. You're the only house within miles and your lights just happen to be on so either you've talked to Svandís in the last ten minutes or so or you've been up playing cards until five in the morning. Whichever it is I'd like to come in and take a look around. If that's a problem then you will need to call the police because I'll kick your fucking door in if you don't let me look for her.'

The elderly man tightened his dressing gown around his waist and smiled warmly. His blue eyes lit up as he realised that Gylfi wasn't going to be intimidated. He took a step back into the house and let Gylfi in.

'Come in young man. It's far too cold a night to be arguing out in the open like this. If we're going to do this then we may as well do it indoors. It's freezing out and I can see you're upset.'

Gylfi followed him into the tastefully decorated hallway and through to the kitchen where he found a woman in the process of making coffee.

'I'm Jón Páll and this is my wife, Lára. Please take a seat.'

Gylfi sat himself down at the table and watched Lára pour them a cup of coffee each before silently leaving the room. Jón Páll took a seat at the other end of the table and took a sip of his coffee. Gylfi couldn't help but wonder what was going on. Jón Páll's demeanour had changed dramatically since they'd come indoors. The antagonism had left him and he seemed quite happy to talk now.

'I know what you're thinking and you'd be quite right. I wasn't being entirely honest with you,' Jón Páll said.

'I thought as much. Are you going to tell me what the hell's going on?'

'Your friend was here just before you arrived but I'm afraid she's run off.'

That was a phrase Gylfi had definitely had enough of. Who the hell just runs off in the middle of the night if there's nothing wrong?

'What do you mean she just ran off? Where exactly is she going to run to all the way out here?'

'The young lady in question is rather headstrong as you are probably aware and I'm not sure she listened to a single thing I said to her. I'm sure that if you were to set off after her now you'd find her in no time whatsoever. She couldn't have got very far. She didn't even have any shoes on and like you say, there's not really anywhere for her to go.'

Gylfi shook his head. He'd had enough. Hooking up with Svandís had been a mistake. His friends had warned him that she'd be nothing but trouble and they'd been right. It had taken him a ridiculous amount of time to see the light but now he was being blinded by it.

'I don't believe you,' Gylfi said. 'What is it you're not telling me?'

Jón Páll's words had made perfect sense but there was something not quite right about the story both he and

Guðmundur had told him. Neither of them seemed surprised enough by what was by anybody's reckoning some pretty strange behaviour. He was used to Svandís's antics but neither of these guys knew her well enough to take it all in their stride the way they were.

'A girl comes knocking on your door in the middle of the night and you just let her run off without any shoes knowing she has nowhere to go. Not only that but you don't seem particularly surprised by any of this and that's what really concerns me. You're just a bit too cool, calm and collected for my liking. I'm going to go look for her now but if I don't find her I'm coming back here to find out exactly what it is you're trying to hide.'

Without touching his coffee Gylfi stood up and made his way back to the front door. He didn't have a clue where to start looking but he had to make an effort. When he stepped outside into the cold air again he could tell that the weather was changing for the worse. It had started to rain and the wind was picking up. They were right on the shoreline and the gusts were not just freezing cold but getting stronger as well. He wished now that he'd brought a jacket with him but he hadn't planned on charging around Borgarnes in the middle of the night when they'd set out from home. As he pulled the door closed behind him and stepped out into the dark void just beyond Jón Páll's security lights he heard the unmistakeable sound of a phone ringing from inside the house. He looked at his own phone to see what the time was. It was quarter to six in the morning. It seemed like a very odd time for someone to be getting a phone call.

CHAPTER SIXTEEN

Saturday 7th February

Ævar made his way back to the station and found Knut in his cell trying to get some rest. He was roused from his attempt to relax and taken back to the same interview room as earlier. Nína was long gone having fulfilled her duties for the day. She had other pressing matters to attend to now that she had got to grips with what was required to represent her latest client. The big Norwegian was starting to look a little frazzled around the edges for the first time since his arrest. The endless hours of sitting around answering questions and staring at the ceiling of his cell had to take its toll eventually. The exterior of the guy was as cool, calm and casual as anyone Ævar had ever seen in an interview but they all had their weaknesses. As Grímur sat down and got himself organised Knut tried his best to lean back in his chair and relax but he looked tired. He folded his arms and tried a smile but it didn't quite work out so he gave up on the idea.

'How's your friend?' Knut asked as he yawned.

'He's still unconscious. There's no real news just as yet. Your bullet did a lot of damage.'

'He's lucky to be alive then,' Knut said.

'He is lucky to be alive and let's hope for all our sakes that he stays that way and that he's back with us sooner rather than later.'

'My sentiments exactly,' Knut said. 'I bet the guy's going to have a really good story to tell us when he wakes up.'

This time his smile was real and he'd regained his air of self-confidence. The look in his eyes was defiant but not in the slightest bit angry.

'You're one cool customer aren't you, Knut?' Ævar asked. 'Nothing phases you. Things just don't get to you the way they do to normal people.'

'Here's how I see it,' Knut said. 'You've got one body in the morgue looking like a piece of burnt French toast and one of your officers in the hospital fighting for his life. The guy in the morgue is some bum-fuck nobody that no one, and I mean no one, is ever going to miss and your officer can't tell you anything because he's in a coma for the foreseeable future. When he comes to, depending on what his story is, he'll either be a national hero or you'll want to throw him out on his arse. But until that day comes you have no idea what happened to him. None. Not a clue. Meanwhile the list of people who might have enjoyed killing the pissy little drug dealer is so long you'd need until next year to tick all the names off it but nonetheless you'd like to pin his murder on me because that way you'll look like you're doing your job. Just thinking out loud here.'

He took a moment to flash his teeth across the table and stretch some of the tiredness out of his arms while Ævar scratched his chin and collected his thoughts.

'You do know that as soon as Grímur's conscious again the two of us are going to wipe that ridiculous smile off your face.'

'Yeah but thing is that even if he does wake up again he could quite easily wind up being the biggest vegetable in the Reykjavík police force even though from what I've seen so far he's going to have some fairly stiff competition. There are no guarantees in this life. If you're depending on him to convict me I think you're making a mistake.'

Ævar breathed in deeply through his nose and exhaled as calmly as he could.

'Jeg har funnet stedet hvor du begraver fremmede.' Ævar said in the best Norwegian accent he could muster. 'The message was obviously for someone in particular. Maybe you'd like to tell me exactly who it was for.'

Ævar's pronunciation got a big smile from Knut. He wouldn't admit it but his eagerness to leave a calling card at the scene of Óli Þór's murder had been his only real slip-up. His ego had got the better of him. Sometimes he just couldn't help himself. Other than that he had remained sufficiently under the radar to be able to go about his business unnoticed and he had so very, very nearly made his flight back to Oslo. He shrugged his shoulders at Ævar.

'I have no idea what you're talking about.'

'Yeah, you keep saying that but when I tell the prosecutors that you were the one who left that message they're going to want to keep you here until Grímur wakes up. Whether that's one week or one year it's not going to matter to them because it's a murder charge and it's a police officer. And seeing as you're the only Norwegian lunatic we have in town at the moment I don't think it's going to take too much to convince them that you're our guy on this one.'

He took a moment to let what he had said sink in and then continued.

'You're right in one respect, that at the moment I don't have the necessary evidence to take you to trial but that is only at this moment in time. Give me a while and I will. No doubt about it. I have forensics guys all over that construction site and in your hotel room and your luggage. If you were there then they're going to find something. We have shell casings from the gun that was used to shoot Grímur. We don't have the gun yet but when we find it we will trace it to whoever fired it and if that was you then you're going to be stuck here until you're an old man.'

It was Ævar's turn to look smug. But not for long.

'I'm looking forward to that poor bastard coming out of his coma because he's going to tell you that the whole time he's been unconscious the guy who shot him has been running around loose out there and you'll be out of a job so fast it'll make your head spin.'

CHAPTER SEVENTEEN

Six years earlier

Halima Wangai cursed out loud and tossed the crumpled-up piece of paper across the dusty potholed street into the gutter on the other side. Just one more bill she was never going to be able to pay and one more step towards having nowhere to live and nothing to eat. If something didn't change soon she and her three daughters would be out on the street with the ever-growing pile of black trash bags that no one was ever going to collect. They would become four more faces staring out at the world for help with no one caring who they were or what would become of them. She was desperate and getting more desperate by the hour. She had tried hard for the last few months to put on a brave face and forget about their worries and that was probably part of the reason why they now found themselves in the situation they were in. It wouldn't be long before the kids got home and she would have to sit them down and be honest about just how far she had let things wander beyond her control.

She wanted to cry but there was no time for that luxury. She was going to have to be strong. There was no room in her life for needless emotion nor shedding of tears. There would be time for that when she had gone away. Then the girls would be on their own and she would have a real reason to cry. Nyo, Msia and Issa were going to have to grow up fast now. In less than an hour their little faces would be sitting around the kitchen table as she tried to explain to them what had become of the money their father had sent them. That had been four months ago now and she was amazed that what he'd sent had lasted that long. He hadn't been seen or heard from since and it was probably safe to assume now that they wouldn't be hearing from him again any time soon. His guilty conscience had been assuaged for the time being and that was probably good enough for him.

He had left to look for work in Nigeria just over six months ago lured by the scent of the big pay cheques on offer from the companies running the oil wells there. Halima had asked him not to go, begged him in fact, but she knew even as she was doing so that she was wasting her breath. What she was afraid of was that it wasn't the prospect of a job that had Muhammed all fired-up to head across the continent but rather that it was just an excuse to get away from her and the kids. So when first the phone calls and then the money had dried up she knew she wouldn't be seeing him again. It had been all too well planned. He had known what he was doing all along and never intended setting foot in Nairobi ever again. She had outlived her usefulness to him and now she and the kids were on their own. And this time it would be for good. Now she was the one who was going to have to look elsewhere for work and it was going to have to be a lot further afield than the other side of Africa.

When the girls got home they could sense straight away that something was wrong. Their mother wasn't her usual self all smiling and happy to see them. She looked sad and serious as if someone she knew had died. When they asked her what was wrong she told them to sit down and be quiet. She had something to tell them and she didn't want them interrupting her with their girlish chatter and foolish questions. The three girls looked at each other in turn and then dutifully took their seats around the table keeping their mouths shut just as they had been told. It was painfully obvious that their mother wasn't in any mood for their jokes and jibes. When Halima was satisfied that the girls were going to remain quiet and pay attention she started the speech she had been rehearsing in her head all day long.

'Girls, I've been trying to keep this from you for a while now but the time has come. We have a serious problem and we need to talk about it. I never wanted to have to admit this to you but I can't afford to look after us any more. The money your father sent us is gone and I'm going to have to go away to earn us some more so you're going to have to go live with your grandmother for a while.'

'Grandma,' the three girls said almost in unison.

Nyo, Msia and Issa realised they had opened their mouths and all raised their hands to their lips. Halima smiled at them proud that she had raised such obedient children and now even more sad that she was going to have to leave them in order to look after them. It seemed such a terrible solution yet she knew it was the only way.

'What about Dad?' Nyo asked.

Halima sighed deeply and scratched the side of her head.

'Your father is not coming back, girls. I hate to tell you this but I haven't heard from him for a lot longer than I've been letting on and I don't even know how to get hold of him any more. He's gone and left us and it's high time we got used to the idea.'

The three girls looked at each other in dismay. This really was news to them. Their mother had been so busy putting on a brave face that she had convinced them that he was still in touch on a regular basis, still sending money home and still fully intending to return to Kenya when none of those things could have been further from the truth. She had lied to them in order to protect them but the plan had backfired horribly. The expressions on their faces told her in no uncertain terms that she had made a serious miscalculation. Instead of keeping them safe from harm as she'd hoped she'd let them think everything was normal and that they would be seeing their father again just as soon as he'd finished his contract in Nigeria.

'I've got more bad news too I'm afraid,' she continued, ignoring their pleading looks and concerned expressions.

Issa started crying and was reprimanded by her elder sisters for interrupting their mother.

'I'm going to have to move away to find a job too. There's nothing for me here and your grandmother will need money to look after you too.'

She looked at their sad little faces one by one and tried to put on a brave face herself but it was killing her to have to say these things. Even though it had been her who had been let down and lied to she still felt like the one who had failed them and the only way she could think of to put things right again was to go away and leave her children.

'I'm not going to be away for long,' she lied and it was as she spoke this untruth that she could finally feel the tears welling up in her eyes for the first time as the enormity of the journey she was about to undertake hit home.

'How long's not long?' Msia asked timidly as if she didn't really want to hear the answer.

Halima closed her eyes and hung her head slightly unable to decide whether to lie to them further or tell her children the cold hard truth that she had absolutely no idea how long exactly not long was going to be. All she really knew was that it was going to be a lot longer than they thought it would be. To them a weekend away would feel like forever.

'Your grandmother is really looking forward to seeing you all again,' she began but when she looked up she could see the fear in her daughters' eyes.

They knew what a non-answer meant just as clearly as if she had told them she would never be seeing them again. She couldn't possibly know what the future holds. She couldn't know where she was going to end up and there was no way whatsoever she could anticipate a return date or even know if one existed.

'How did this happen?' Nyo asked and then started crying.

Msia and Issa looked at their mother waiting for an answer but she didn't have one for them. She had asked herself the same question over and over again and was still no closer to knowing how or why she had simply sat back and hoped that this wouldn't come to pass.

'I held on to hope too long girls. Sometimes it can be a dangerous thing. I should have realised a lot sooner what kind of a man your father really was but I didn't want to admit that I had made a big mistake by trusting him. My pride got in the way. Now I can't look after my own children and I'm more ashamed than I've ever been in my life and worried that if I don't do something now things will get even worse.'

Halima took her daughters in her arms one by one and whispered apologies in their ears just loud enough that they could hear and no louder. She felt as if someone was watching her from above and that she had failed whoever that was too. She had failed them all and she was going to have to carry that around with her for the rest of her life.

CHAPTER EIGHTEEN

Tuesday 3rd February

Although Gylfi had spent the last forty-five minutes going over the story of Svandís's disappearance with the detective again and again he wasn't at all convinced he was being taken seriously yet. The guy seemed grumpy and unhelpful and even though he claimed to know Svandís personally he didn't really seem to care one way or the other that she was missing. He had in fact suggested several times that she would probably show up of her own accord at some point like she was a family pet that had run away from home and would be back when she got hungry or cold. Grímur had filled out the missing person's report but didn't seem at all enthusiastic about doing anything else to actually help find her. He had nasty-looking scratch marks down one side of his face that he didn't want to talk about and he wouldn't answer any of Gylfi's other questions with anything more than a cursory shrug of the shoulders and some form of monosyllabic response. In short, he wasn't being as helpful as Gylfi had hoped. It was no secret that he had as much trouble dealing with Svandís as anybody else but he couldn't imagine his sad little life without her in it.

'Her phone just keeps ringing and ringing when I call it. She always answers the damn thing. Can't you just send some people out along the coast to search for her? You say you know her, then you should know what she's like. She's one of the most difficult girls you're ever going to meet in your life but it's just not her style to disappear like this. If she was trying to make a point or teach me a lesson she'd do it to my face. She doesn't shy away from confrontation, she actively seeks it out. She has never once in the time I've known her gone for more than one hour without getting in touch with me. Something's happened to her and I need someone to help me look for her.'

Grímur folded his hands and tried to remain as calm as possible. It wasn't that he didn't like Gylfi, quite the opposite in fact. He had great respect for anyone who could put up with Svandís for as long as he had without killing her. But he had serious reservations about allocating manpower to search for a girl who had almost definitely been out of her head on drugs at the time she had vanished. She would do almost anything for attention and he was sure that this was just another case of her throwing the toys out of the pram. He felt sorry for Gylfi and wanted to tell him that if Svandís had decided to take off and leave him it would probably be the best thing that could ever happen to him. It definitely wasn't what the young lad wanted to hear at the moment but it was the truth.

'I'm sending officers out now to have a look along the coastline but as you know yourself it's very exposed. There's not too many places she could be where she wouldn't have been seen already. My feeling is that she's headed back to town under her own steam.'

Gylfi looked exhausted and for a moment Grímur thought that he was about to start crying. He wondered what it was that Svandís had seen in this guy but the fact that he was getting so upset probably meant he was prepared to do absolutely anything for her and that was undoubtedly a trait she valued above all others in men.

'Listen, I'm heading out there now to interview these two gentlemen that you say she was with and I'll let you know how I get on. In the meantime I suggest you get some rest.'

Gylfi hung his head and nodded more in acceptance than agreement.

'Go home. Get some sleep and when I have something to tell you I'll let you know. In the meantime if you hear from her please let me know.'

Grímur got up and left Gylfi where he was. He just wanted to interview Guðmundur and Jón Páll and check them off his list. It would take something spectacular to convince him that anything untoward had befallen Svandís. Anything that wasn't her own fault anyway.

While Grímur was driving all the way out to Guðmundur's house in Borgarnes he had plenty of time to reflect on his own relationship with Svandís. He'd met her parents several years ago back when they'd still held on to some sort of hope that she would turn her life around. At that point she had only just started down the road she now resided on permanently and they thought they might be able to get their little girl back. But, as the troubled ones so often do, she had spurned all offers of assistance and had become even more determined to do whatever she pleased. Her parents were good people. They had never done anything to deserve a human time bomb like their eldest daughter. She came from a nice home and yet chose to live a hand-to-mouth existence that embraced heroin as a friend rather than recognising it for what it really was. An enemy to be feared and avoided at all costs. She had actively sought out a road to ruin and she had found one. One she would now seemingly never stray from until she had destroyed herself.

Grímur checked his appearance in the rear-view mirror. His cheek still looked red and sore and didn't feel much better than it looked. She had done some real damage to it and it wouldn't start to heal properly until it had stopped weeping and dried out a little. Even then it was going to take some time to right itself.

When Grímur had reached his destination Guðmundur opened the front door and smiled at him as half-heartedly as he could. Grímur had called ahead and was expected but even still it was obvious that the news of his visit had done little to brighten Guðmundur's day. He was invited in and they took a seat in the living room. The last known place that Svandís had been seen. According to Gylfi she had been hiding behind the very sofa he was now sitting on when she'd called to tell him that someone was going to kill her. She hadn't elaborated on who it was that was going to kill her or why but Gylfi seemed to think that the terror in her voice was real. She had genuinely feared for her life and now it was Grímur's job to find out whether she had been telling the truth or not.

'Thank you,' Grímur said as Guðmundur placed a cup of coffee on the table in front of him.

'As you know I am here because Svandís Finnbogadóttir has been reported missing and one of the last places she was seen that we know of was in this house. By you. In the early hours of this morning. We both know why she was here but I'm not interested in that even though we both know that what the two of you were up to is illegal.'

He leaned forward a little and tried his coffee. He was hoping that Guðmundur would relax a little once he thought that he wasn't going to be prosecuted for purchasing sex.

'Good coffee. I've known Svandís for some time now and frankly she's nothing but trouble. Whatever it was that you two were up to here will not become an issue for the police unless we fail to locate her so it is very much in your interest to help us out.'

He stared across the coffee table to see if what he'd said had sunk in or not. It was hard to tell. Guðmundur looked a little nervous but no more so than nearly everyone did around police officers. Even people with nothing to hide tensed up when confronted by questions from the police. And this guy definitely had something to hide. He started talking but just a little too fast.

'The last time I saw her was in my bedroom just before I went to use the toilet. She was sitting on the edge of the bed having a drink. By the time I came out again she'd disappeared. I heard her moving about down here so I came down to see what she was playing at but when I got down here the front door was wide open and she'd gone.'

'And you have no idea where she went?'

Guðmundur shook his head and tried his coffee.

'None whatsoever. She left in such a hurry she didn't even take her shoes.'

'Could I have a look at those and anything else she might have left behind?'

Guðmundur got up to head up the stairs. Grímur stood as well.

'Mind if I just have a quick look around? Just to get a feel for where she was and where you were. Just so I can picture it all in my head.'

'Be my guest. There's not much to see.'

Grímur waited for Guðmundur to turn and head towards the stairs before having a look over the back of the sofa. The carpet all through the living room looked as though it had recently been vacuumed. Nothing else seemed out of the ordinary so he turned and headed up the stairs just a few steps behind Guðmundur. At the top of the stairs the master bedroom was a relatively simple affair. Grímur took a seat on the queen size bed and asked Guðmundur if he would walk into the bathroom and close the door behind him. The request elicited a puzzled look but he complied. Once Guðmundur was in the bathroom Grímur stood up again and took a good look around the room. There were wardrobes with mirrored sliding doors, heavy curtains over the windows and two bedside tables, both with reading lamps and one with a telephone. Grímur opened the door to the bathroom and a puzzled Guðmundur peered back at him.

'So you were in here while she was sitting on the bed?'

Guðmundur nodded.

'Did she say anything to you while you were in here?'

'No.'

'And then when you came out she was gone?'

'That's right.'

'But her shoes were still here? Just sitting on the floor somewhere I guess?'

'That's right. She kicked them off next to the bed.'

'Where are they now?'

'In the wardrobe. The left-hand one.'

Grímur walked over to mirrored wardrobe and slid the left door open. He bent down and picked up a small pair of black heels. They were fairly battered and had definitely seen better days, a little like their owner. He held them up and showed them to Guðmundur who just nodded.

'She didn't take them off downstairs?' Grímur asked.

'No. I always ask people to take off their shoes at the door but she pretended not to hear me.'

'And then what?'

'I went looking for her downstairs but like I said when I got down there the door was open and she'd gone.'

'Just like that? Didn't you think it was a bit strange? Did she say anything about leaving or where she might possibly head to in the middle of the night when it's absolutely freezing outside?'

Grímur was starting to think that Gylfi's suspicions might not be as crazy as he'd first thought. There was something that didn't add up with this guy. And it was very possible that his own personal dislike of Svandís had been clouding his judgement up until this point.

'She never said anything about leaving,' Guðmundur insisted.

'What possible reason would she have had for calling her boyfriend and telling him someone was going to kill her? And why would she then run out of the house without her shoes? Was she high on drugs? Something freaked her out. Help me out here.'

'I don't know,' was all Guðmundur had to say.

'You don't know? That's not much help and like I said before you need to be helping me if you don't want me to take an interest in why she was here in the first place. And trust me on this one, you don't want me to do that. Something you said or did caused her to get up off that bed and run out of this house as if her life depended on it and I intend to find out what that was.'

Guðmundur just stood where he was staring at Grímur.

'She wasn't wasted? You didn't threaten her? Nothing you did made her fear for her safety? She just decided to get up off your bed, run downstairs, call her boyfriend and tell him that she was about to be killed and then take off before he could get here? Are you sure that's how you want to play this? I would have come up with a better story than that if I was you.'

Still no answer from Guðmundur. Grímur turned around and pointed at the phone next to Guðmundur's bed.

'When I get hold of the records for your phone am I going to find that you made or received any calls in the early hours?'

'No,' Guðmundur said.

'None at all?'

'None at all.'

Grímur knew he was being lied to. What he didn't know yet was why. He told Guðmundur that he would be in touch and let himself out. As soon as Guðmundur was sure that the detective was gone he picked up the phone and made a call.

CHAPTER NINETEEN

Tuesday 3rd February

The next address on his rather short list was that of Jón Páll Sigmundsson. His was at least a name that Grímur knew. The doctor was a well-known man. He had been in the news around a year ago for setting up a clinic near the city centre to help young addicts to get over their problems and get on with their lives. Better themselves rather than succumb to pointless temptations. He still made the occasional appearance there when he could but he had much less of a hands-on role these days while he spent most of his time working as a consulting specialist at the Landspítali hospital. Today however he hadn't had any work commitments and he'd been more than happy to meet with Grímur whose conversation with Guðmundur had left him feeling more than just a little suspicious. The guy was hiding something and he planned to get his hands on his phone records as soon as he could.

Jón Páll answered the door in a suit and tie looking every bit the professional. He was in his late sixties now but still in great shape and his handshake was every bit as firm as Grímur's if not firmer. He took a fleeting look at the side of Grímur's face but didn't pass judgement out loud and then invited him in. The coffee table in the living room was covered in plates of rye bread, cheese and even some cured salmon. A pot of coffee sat in the middle of it all.

'Take a seat and we'll get comfortable,' Jón Páll said and pointed to one of the chairs.

The atmosphere was the complete opposite of his last host's. Where everything about Guðmundur's manner had been overly cautious and defensive Grímur could tell at once that Jón Páll was relaxed and happy to see him.

'Thank you,' Grímur said and sat down.

Jón Páll poured them each some coffee and then took a seat himself.

'I'm guessing you want to know whatever I can tell you about my unexpected visitor in the early hours,' Jón Páll said.

Grímur tried his coffee and nodded. He looked at the array of food in front of them and wondered what they did when they had serious guests over. Jón Páll obviously came from the old school who thought your ability to make people feel welcome in your own home was a sign of your social standing. A dying art in Grímur's opinion.

'Help yourself to the salmon,' Jón Páll said and passed Grímur a plate.

Grímur helped himself to some rye bread as well as some of the salmon. He was genuinely hungry and it would be rude to refuse such gracious hospitality. When he'd constructed himself an open sandwich he nodded his thanks to Jón Páll and settled back into his chair.

'Start at the beginning. What happened when Svandís came knocking at your door?'

'As you can imagine we were rather taken aback to have a visitor at such an hour but I went to see who it was regardless. The young lady was very upset and not dressed at all well for the weather so I invited her in and tried to get her to calm down.'

'What was she upset about?' Grímur asked.

'It's hard to say. The poor thing was in quite a flap over something but trying to get her to tell me what was next to impossible.'

'Did she say anything about someone trying to kill her or coming to kill her?'

'No. Nothing like that. I tried to get her to come in and sit down. I thought if she did then she might tell me what was going on but she insisted on standing out in the cold in her bare feet and screeching at me about this and that.'

This and that. Guðmundur has said the exact same thing. It seemed to be a popular phrase at the moment. Was there something about Jón Páll that was just a little too good to be true or was he imagining it?

'So she wouldn't come in? Then what?'

'She got a fearful look in her eye like she'd just remembered something important and then turned and ran off without so much as a word of explanation.'

'Just like that? She didn't say where she might be going?'

'I'm afraid not. Whatever it was that was bothering her she had obviously decided to keep to herself.'

'So why did she come here in the first place?'

'I haven't a clue.'

Svandís had run away from two different houses in quick succession and apparently neither occupant had a clue as to why. Svandís was admittedly a highly-strung bundle of nerves at the best of times but nothing about either story made any sense. Something had spooked her badly while she'd been at Guðmundur's house and it was Grímur's feeling that both Guðmundur and Jón Páll knew exactly what is was but for one reason or another they weren't letting on. He was getting nowhere fast with his questions and the only reasonable thing to do now was to admit that Gylfi had been right all along and call the search and rescue teams out for a full search of the coast.

'Haven't a clue?' Grímur asked.

Jón Páll shook his head and started building himself an open sandwich with the bread and the salmon along with some lettuce and slices of boiled egg. Grímur finished his sandwich and his coffee and thanked Jón Páll for his time.

'One other thing before I go,' Grímur said.

Jón Páll looked up from his sandwich-building.

'The young guy who came here looking for Svandís just after she'd disappeared. He said that he heard the phone ring just as he was leaving. Would you mind telling me what that phone call was about?'

Jón Páll smiled as he finished spreading some graflaxsósa on top of his salmon.

'I'm quite often on call at the hospital in Reykjavík and phone calls at that hour aren't terribly unusual I'm afraid.'

Grímur nodded and turned to go.

'You know, you should really keep those scratches covered for a few days and then let them get some air after that. They'll heal faster that way,' Jón Páll added as a farewell.

Grímur let himself out and walked back to his car running his fingers over his sore face which was starting to itch badly as it began to heal. Something didn't add up at this house either but this time he knew what it was. If Jón Páll had been on call last night and someone had decided to call him at that time of the morning then what would they have been calling about? If he was actually on call as he said he had been then the only possible reason could have been to get him to come into work. If that had been the case then why had Jón Páll told him that he hadn't had any work commitments today and why was he still at home? No one would ring at that time of day to tell him he wasn't going to be needed. They would only ring if there had been an emergency and they needed his help. Somewhere in the middle of trying to appear helpful Jón Páll had made a mistake. Now it looked as though he had a second set of phone records to request.

CHAPTER TWENTY

Thursday 5th February

What had already been a rather irritating day was made worse by the unexpected arrival of Svandís's parents Finnbogi and Guðrún along with her sister Inga Lind. Grímur had been meaning to speak to them at some point but had kept putting it off because he couldn't face the prospect of their pained expressions as they looked at him waiting for news of their troubled daughter. He was dreading trying to convince them that nothing had happened to Svandís. That would take a special kind of disingenuousness. The kind that would let him look three perfectly lovely people in the eye and not only lie to them but also pretend that he still cared one way or the other. The truth was that he knew something had happened to her but he had no idea what it was just yet. The list of possibilities was as long as his arm. She had been on a collision course with disaster for years and the timeframe had been speeding up of late. Gaining a momentum and a purpose that gave it a will all of its own. The fiasco at the café in the city centre had all the signs of her having hit rock bottom. She had entered a tailspin she wouldn't be able to pull out of this time. Not only was he sure that this was what had happened but part of him also knew that his life would be easier without her around. It was an unpleasant thing to admit, even to himself, and wasn't something he felt terribly proud of but it was the truth. His conversation with Gylfi had been symptomatic of the way he really felt about her. He had been able to tell from the expression on the young man's face that his own lack of interest in her disappearance had been all too apparent. And now he was faced with the same dilemma all over again. Only this time it was family. With three of them sitting facing him there would be nowhere to hide. Part of him wanted to tell them to prepare for never seeing her again but there was only so much truth most people could handle.

The three of them were ushered into Grímur's office by a junior officer who then spent several minutes fumbling around with an extra chair he had brought in from another room. Grímur only had two chairs for visitors in his office and there was barely enough room for them let alone three. Eventually the officer asked Finnbogi and Guðrún to take a seat and then once they were sitting he placed the extra chair in the remaining space for Inga Lind. Once he'd left them in peace Grímur cleared his throat and tried to put on his bravest face.

'It's good that you've come to see me. I was planning to call today but now we can do it face to face instead,' Grímur said attempting to smile as he did so.

An uncomfortable silence hung over the room as Grímur wondered where he should start. It was Svandís's younger sister Inga Lind who broke the awkward silence.

'We were just wondering what was happening with the search. Have you found anything yet or do you know where she might be?' she said as she looked at her parents and then at Grímur. 'We know she's only been missing a little over two days but it's really unlike her to just go off like this.'

'We know something's happened to her and we want to know what's being done about it,' Guðrún said suddenly finding her voice.

'I've talked to the occupants of the last two houses she was seen at and so far all I've been able to ascertain is that she left one for the other and then ran off without telling anyone where she was going or why.'

Guðrún looked at Finnbogi as if Grímur had just told them their daughter had recently grown a second head. Grímur wasn't sure if he should continue or not. He thought the statement was fairly self-explanatory but both of Svandís's parents looked terribly confused.

'Well don't you think that's a little strange?' Guðrún asked.

'Listen,' Finnbogi said. 'We've spoken to that idiot of a boyfriend of hers and he tells us she rang him just before she disappeared. He said she was convinced someone was going to kill her. That would explain why she ran off in such a hurry wouldn't it? Surely you must have some idea who this person threatening her is. That's your job isn't it?'

Grímur wiped his hand across his forehead and through his hair. He was starting to sweat despite the fact that the room was barely warm at all.

'As far as I'm aware there wasn't anyone trying to kill her. I've interviewed the last two people to have seen her and there's no sign of foul play or anything else untoward. There is a search and rescue team looking up and down the coast around Borgarnes for her now but so far there's been no sign of her.'

He paused to take a couple of breaths and to gauge what their reactions were to this news or lack thereof but none of them said a word. Both of Svandís's parents looked shell-shocked and Inga Lind's expression was impossible to read.

'I'm sorry there's nothing more I can tell you but it's very early days yet and I'm still hoping she will turn up of her own accord very soon.'

He reached into his wallet and pulled out one of his business cards. He slid it across the table and left it in front of Guðrún who made a big deal of ignoring it before getting up and signalling to Finnbogi to do the same.

'I don't want your card. If there's any news you can call us thank you very much,' she said. And with that she turned awkwardly in the confined space and made her way back out through the door with her sullen husband following close behind. Inga Lind looked across the table at Grímur and shrugged. She focused on her hands for a bit as if thinking of what to say next. While Guðrún and Finnbogi both looked more angry than upset Inga Lind looked genuinely sad as if a certain resignation had settled in her shoulders and neck.

'We didn't really expect anything much in the way of news but they're both really upset. They're convinced something's happened to her. It's just too weird for her to just disappear. She's a complete idiot as I'm sure you know but she always keeps in touch. Something's wrong, I can feel it too,' Inga Lind said.

She reached across the desk and pocketed Grímur's card before navigating her way through the chairs to the door and then turning to face him with a smile on her face.

'You know how she makes a living just as well as I do. That's where you need to start looking for her,' she said and closed the door behind her.

Grímur started tapping his pen on the desk. Before they'd arrived he'd been waiting for the phone call that was going to change everything. That was how it felt anyway. Once he had the phone records for both Guðmundur's and Jón Páll's houses he would have a much better idea of what had happened. He knew he'd been lied to while interviewing Guðmundur as well as Jón Páll but he had no idea what it was they were trying to hide. As far as he knew there was no connection between the two men but he could easily be wrong. If there was something or someone that they had in common, then the case would take on a different feel altogether. He took the opportunity to stretch out his legs and close his eyes for a few minutes while he tried to clear his mind and ponder what might come next. When his phone rang he had almost drifted off to sleep in his chair. He reached out and grabbed it hoping it would be the breakthrough he'd been waiting for.

'Hello?'

'Grímur, I'd like to see you in my office. Straight away,' Ævar said.

'I'm waiting on a very important call. Can't this wait?'

'Straight away please,' Ævar said and hung up without further explanation.

Grímur muttered something impolite under his breath and walked the short distance to his boss's office. As he entered the room Ævar signalled that he should take a seat.

'I've something to tell you that you're not going to like very much but which can't be helped,' Ævar began. 'I've just received a phone call from the Office of the National Commissioner and you are to be taken off the Svandís Finnbogadóttir case immediately.'

Grímur sat in silence for a few seconds as he tried to figure out if Ævar was joking or not. When he'd decided he was serious he took another couple of moments to let the information sink in.

'Did you hear what I said?' Ævar asked.

'Why?'

Ævar fidgeted in his seat and stared at his hands which were spread out on the desk in front of him briefly before answering.

'They wouldn't explain any further than to say that it wasn't really any of my business and that the decision had been made at a ministerial level.'

'I thought that was your job. And since when are we told what to do by the Alþingi? What on earth can it possibly matter to them who investigates what around here?'

Grímur's face was reddening as his control over his temper began to slip away. Ævar held his hands out in front of him in an attempt to get his detective to calm down.

'I'm waiting on a call right now that I'm sure is going to explain what happened to her. It could all be explained in the next hour or so,' Grímur said

'Everything from here on in is to be handled by Haukur Hauksson. He's been appointed as the new investigator. And before you say anything, that wasn't my decision either.'

Grímur went to reply but decided to bite his tongue instead. Arguing with Ævar wasn't going to achieve anything. Their working relationship was strained enough as it was.

'Okay,' he said. 'So I've just got to let it go then?'

'Yes. That's exactly what you should do. The decision has been made and we both need to move on.'

Grímur strummed his fingers on his thigh and nodded.

'I've got some other things to be getting on with,' he said and stood up.

'Please don't do anything stupid, Grímur,' Ævar said. 'And do something about those scratches. People are starting to talk. I'm not going to ask you how you got them because you won't tell me anyway but you've got to start looking after yourself a little better.'

Grímur turned away from Ævar as quickly as he could and left the room. He only went back into his office long enough to grab his coat and then took the stairs down to the ground floor. He waved to the girl on the front desk and headed for the front door. He had no intention of doing anything for the rest of the day nor did he anticipate returning to the building in a big hurry. He pushed the door open and stopped dead in his tracks. Walking up the steps towards the front door was Halldór Valdimarsson, the Minister of Finance and Economic Affairs. The chances of this visit simply being a coincidence were infinitesimal. Grímur let the door close behind him and held his arm across it so Halldór couldn't enter the building. He stood where he was and waited for the politician to react. At first he stared blankly at Grímur as if no more than slightly puzzled by his behaviour.

'Do you mind?' Halldór said.

Grímur stared at him for a few seconds without replying. Halldór started to look a little irritated. He stared back at Grímur but didn't repeat the question.

'Do you know who I am?' Grímur asked.

Halldór continued to stare at him and still didn't answer. When it became clear that Grímur wasn't going to let him through the door he cleared his throat.

'I don't believe we've met,' he said.

While the statement was in itself true enough Grímur could tell that he knew all too well who he was.

'I was just wondering when it became the government's policy to decide which detectives get to investigate which cases. Is this something you've come up with recently or has this been standard practice for some time now?'

A look of resignation crossed Halldór's face as he looked the pesky detective over.

'Am I to assume that you aren't pleased with the way things are being run at this station? If that is the case I'm sure we could arrange for you to work at another,' Halldór said.

His look of resignation was quickly replaced by one of steadfast determination. He wasn't about to be badgered by a mere police officer. He reached over Grímur's arm and grabbed the door handle. Grímur stood his ground and didn't move.

'I would get the hell out of my way if you don't want to be handing out speeding tickets in Siglufjörður this time next week,' Halldór said as his own level of irritation rose. He mumbled something under his breath and pulled Grímur out of the way.

'The day has not yet come when I have to explain that or anything else to the likes of you. You would do well to mind your own business and concentrate on matters that are better suited to your somewhat limited capabilities. Has anyone mentioned those scratches to you? They don't look at all good. I would think an officer of your advanced years would know how to look after himself a little better.'

Halldór gave Grímur a condescending smile. It was common knowledge that Grímur had failed to secure an arrest let alone a conviction in either of his last two major cases. Two strikes and one left was the general consensus. His stock was low around police headquarters. Many people, friends and enemies alike, thought it was high-time he took the easy way out and opted for an early retirement. They didn't even bother whispering it behind his back any more. He'd overheard it by mistake in the corridors and the lunch room more times than he cared to remember.

'Have a pleasant day won't you,' Halldór said as he disappeared into the building.

CHAPTER TWENTY-ONE

Thursday 5th February

Gylfi threw himself down on the sofa and looked for the remote control. He couldn't see it anywhere and couldn't be bothered hunting under the cushions or on the floor. Wherever it was it could just stay there for the time being. What he really needed more than television was a drink. The day had been an unmitigated disaster. He had been losing patience with the progress and lack of effort from the police and had decided to take matters into his own hands and do a little digging himself. First he had tried the various dealers around town that he knew Svandís bought drugs from. There were quite a few since she liked to spread her business around as much as possible. That way when she owed someone money she could just move on to another one until her goodwill ran out there too. None of them had seen her lately and none of them seemed to have missed her very much either. She had burnt a few bridges over the last few months by the sound of things. One of them even laughed and told him he was better off without the 'stupid cow'. Gylfi had bitten his tongue and walked away. She was far from perfect but she was all he had. She drove him crazy just like she did everyone else but he didn't know what he'd do without her. She was his girl.

He pulled himself up from the sofa and walked over to the bookcase where he knew there was a half-bottle of Brennivín stashed behind some books away from any prying eyes. He pulled it out and took a swig wishing that he had some cold beer to wash it down with. After three hours chasing drug dealers around town he'd decided to call it quits as it was becoming increasingly apparent that even if any of these lowlifes knew where she was it was seriously unlikely that they would have told him. She appeared to be universally disliked. After that he had stopped off at the club she had worked at on and off on Lækjargata.

It was one place he knew she wouldn't be but he hoped that someone there might have an idea of where she might be holed up or why she might have disappeared. He was clutching at straws and knew it. The club had been fairly empty when he'd got there and his questions had soon drawn the attention of the owner. As soon as he'd seen Janko making his way across the room straight at him he knew he'd made a huge mistake. He was the last guy you would ever want angry at you and he'd looked plenty angry as he strode in Gylfi's direction. He'd heard about his nosing around and had told him to get the hell out of the club and never come back. Gylfi had made the awful mistake of trying to reason with the most unreasonable man in Reykjavik rather than just keeping his mouth shut and leaving like he'd been told.

He got the distinct impression that the only reason he'd been able to leave the club on his own two feet was because there were too many people around for Janko to do what he really wanted to do to him and that was to cause him some serious injury. He hadn't understood why Janko had got so upset and still couldn't. He wasn't trying to cause him any trouble he just wanted to find his girlfriend. Why that was such a big deal to her ex-boss was a mystery but the Serb had certainly taken exception to his questions. Once he'd realised what an idiot he was making of himself Gylfi had admitted defeat and scurried back down the stairs. Everyone in the place had seen him getting screamed at and he had felt like a fool.

He sat down on the sofa again and drank some more of the vaguely aniseed-flavoured schnapps. It burnt his throat all the way down to his stomach. He looked around the living room at the mess Svandís had left on the floor and wished she was there to tease him about having to clean up after her. He threw the rest of the Brennivín down his throat and lay across the sofa wondering what more he could possibly do or if he should just give up. He'd managed to piss off everyone he had talked to so far and didn't know if there was anywhere left to turn. He closed his eyes and wished he had never told her about the job in Borgarnes. If he hadn't taken her out there she would be with him now and everything would be okay.

Sometime later a sharp rap on the front door woke him up. He lifted his head and asked whoever it was what it was they wanted. There was no answer. He pulled himself upright and checked the time on his phone. It was four o'clock in the morning. No one in their right mind would come looking for him at that time. Then again with the knocking. This time more agitated and insistent. Whoever it was didn't sound like they were going to go away in a hurry.

'Who is it?' he called out again.

Still no answer. He was loathe to open the door but it was very unlikely they would go away now they knew he was home. He had left himself no option but to open up and find out who it was and what they wanted. It proved to be something of a mistake. As soon as he'd undone the lock the door was shouldered open leaving him sprawled on the floor like an upturned turtle. Janko's hand clamped itself around his throat cutting off his air supply and lifting him to his feet at the same time. The look in Janko's eyes made Gylfi fear for his life before he'd even said a word. He was thrown across the room onto the dining table which knocked the breath out of him and left him doubled over and gasping for air. Janko closed the door behind him as best he could now it was hanging off its hinges and walked over to where Gylfi lay sprawled across the table trying to get some air back in his lungs. Janko looked like a man on a mission. He pulled Gylfi to his feet again and smacked him across the face with the back of his hand. Enough to bloody his nose and get his attention but nothing more.

'I don't know what the fuck you were playing at tonight but you don't walk into my place and start asking questions about anyone especially that stupid little tramp. Do you understand what I'm saying?'

Gylfi tried speaking but it was completely beyond him. He was having enough trouble breathing as it was so he just nodded. Bits of saliva dropped from his mouth.

'Take my advice and wait for her to come home. The only thing you'll find by sticking your nose in where it doesn't belong is trouble. If I catch you anywhere near my club again or any of my girls for that matter I'm going to kill you. If you had any brains you'd forget all about her and get on with your life. Do yourself a favour and find yourself another girl.'

Janko let go of Gylfi and walked out of the apartment leaving the door swinging from a single hinge. Gylfi looked down at his pants and the wet patch that had spread all the way down the front of them.

CHAPTER TWENTY-TWO

Thursday 5th February

Inga Lind sat herself down at her bedroom desk with yet another cup of hot coffee. Her sister's disappearance was giving her sleepless nights and her insomnia was in turn driving her to distraction. Too much time on her hands had her thinking too much and that was rarely a good thing. Her solution was to drink coffee like it was going out of fashion in the hope that she would be too tired to keep her eyes open when it came time to go to bed. But as usual her logic was flawed and verging on the ridiculous. She yawned as she stared at the computer screen. She was looking at the account she had just set up for herself on a social community website for kinksters. Fetish World. She had finally chosen a username for herself: DamselForDistress. She smiled to herself and wondered how it was that she could be so clever when she was so very, very tired.

She was probably the only person who had any idea how Svandís had gone about her online business. One night when the two of them had been very drunk on vodka-inspired cocktails the story of how Svandís was supporting herself came out in something of a late-night confessional. She had set up a profile on Fetish World and used it to contact horny businessmen in and around the capital area to offer them her outcall services for a price that was dependent on what they wanted to do to her. Or what they wanted her to do to them. It tended to work either one way or the other but for the right price she was willing to do pretty much anything such was the heroin habit she had acquired. They sent her private messages on the site and she then arranged a time that suited both of them for her to visit. At first she had struggled to find many takers but as word of mouth spread about her small operation she found herself getting busier and busier.

It was about the same time as her business operation really started to take off that she met the hapless Gylfi. She had done everything in her power to put him off building an attachment to her but despite her best efforts the guy had remained hopelessly infatuated with her. Eventually she had relented and allowed the relationship to happen even though it was against her better judgement and she found him to be a weak and ever so slightly pathetic individual. She just decided that he would have his uses.

What had changed her mind was the role she had come up with for him to play in her business venture. She realised early on that she was going to need someone to drive her around and keep an eye on her as she visited her customers. It was often very late at night and there were frequently alcohol and drugs involved. And that was her as well as them. A lot of her customers were highly-strung at the best of times and things could occasionally get out of hand if there was some sort of misunderstanding about what had been agreed upon and at what price. In those sorts of situations Gylfi wasn't that much use but he was better than nothing. His puppy-like dedication to her had come in handy on a couple of occasions.

Inga Lind had chosen a selfie that looked as much like Svandís as possible to use as her profile picture. She figured that if she was going to attract the same customers as her sister had then it would be a good idea to look as much like her as she could. Most men she knew definitely had a type they preferred and she figured that the ones who'd wanted to sleep with her sister would be no different. She had dollied herself up in much the same way as Svandís did and had taken a dozen different shots of herself until she finally had one she was happy with. Luckily the two of them looked quite a lot alike so finding a suitable facsimile wasn't too much of a problem. As she uploaded the photo and her profile went live she leant back and smiled to herself. She was convinced that it was only a matter of time before the man or men behind her sister's disappearance contacted her. Then it would just be a matter of finding out who the faces behind the online profiles were and taking it from there.

As it turned out she didn't have to wait too long at all. Within an hour she had received several friendship requests from curious men who wanted to know what she was looking for in a partner and whether she enjoyed being tied up or if she was happier being the dom. Some of their questions took her a little by surprise. People were a lot weirder than she'd ever imagined possible. The world of wrist restraints, paddles, blindfolds and prostate massagers was all new and somewhat alarming to her. She was however on a mission and that mission was to find the man responsible for her sister's disappearance. No matter how weird, disturbing or downright disgusting things got. So she took her time and replied to the requests one by one as best she could trying not to sound too keen nor too much of a novice.

The main thing she had no idea about was what to charge these guys if they did show an interest in spending an evening with her. It was one thing Svandís had refused to talk about and although she knew her sister was making a good living out of it she had no idea how much of a good thing she was on to. As she befriended these strangers one by one she went through their profiles in an attempt to get a feel for what each of them might be like. What it was exactly that made them tick as it were. None of them showed their faces online so she couldn't really tell much about them apart from the fact that they all seemed to enjoy varying amounts of nudity and leather. She began to wonder if she would be expected to dress that way when she went to work. Almost definitely. They would want their fantasies to come to life before their very eyes and what she was wearing no doubt played a big part in that.

Some of the messages were from men who enjoyed being in charge a great deal more than others. These were the ones she paid particular attention to. She indicated that she was both able and willing to do as they pleased and waited to see if their interest was genuine or if they were just using the site to amuse themselves. One of them responded almost immediately and suggested they meet. For a price. She asked him if he had done this sort of thing before and he said that he had used the site previously to meet partners and knew the routine.

After a brief back-and-forth he accepted her assurances that his need for absolute privacy would be met and gave her his address and promised her payment of 30,000 krónur when she arrived at his city centre apartment for an hour and a half of bondage and discipline, she would be expected to operate as a dom primarily but possibly also as a sub, followed by straight sex. Inga Lind had no idea what exactly would be expected of her but assumed it would involve her tying WhipLashBoy up and spanking him and him quite possibly doing much the same to her. She didn't really care as long as it gave her a chance to see if he was the one she was looking for or not. She was also starting to get an understanding of why Svandís had chosen this as a means of employment. For 30,000 krónur she would tie her own mother to a bed for an hour and a half and spank her backside until it was bright red. The upside of the arrangement, as far as she could tell, was that at some point she would have this guy at her mercy and as soon as she had him cuffed or bound or whatever the hell he liked she could begin her interrogation in earnest. He had obviously done this sort of thing before and therefore had to know Svandís. It was too small a town for their paths to have not crossed at some point. If he wasn't the one responsible for her disappearance then chances were he knew who was.

CHAPTER TWENTY-THREE

Thursday 5th February

Grímur poured himself another drink and put the half-empty bottle back on the floor next to his reclining armchair. If it sat down there at his feet he wouldn't be constantly reminded of how much of it he had already drunk. That was the theory anyway. He patted Bobbi on the head and slumped back into the chair. His life wasn't supposed to have turned out this way. He didn't know what he'd been expecting but he was sure this wasn't it. He'd put off making any kind of commitment to any of the women he'd dated when he was younger because he had been sure that he was still to meet the right one. He had always been fussy when it came to the company he chose to keep. He had convinced himself that he was entirely happy on his own and could quite easily survive that way if need be. But interest from the opposite sex had dried up and left him with little choice in the matter. He was simply too old to do anything about it any more. He couldn't imagine any woman wanting anything to do with him now and he had no one to blame for that but himself.

There had been too many times when he'd wished everyone would just leave him alone and now he'd got exactly what he'd wished for. It had just crept up on him the same way all the years had. He had closed his eyes to what had been going on in his life and now that they were open again he didn't care very much for what he saw. Having carefully kept everyone at arm's length there was now nothing and no one left to hold on to. He had hoped there would be more to life than sitting alone in his living room trying to drink as much vodka as he could swallow before he passed out but as it turned out, there wasn't. Grímur threw back the drink he'd just poured himself and reached for his packet of cigarettes accidentally kicking Bobbi in the head as he did so. Bobbi moaned quietly in his sleep but didn't even open his eyes.

He was used to getting bumped, shoved out of the way, cursed at and trodden on. Grímur lit his cigarette, inhaled deeply and closed his eyes. He wondered how many years of smoking and drinking he had left in him before that caught up with him too. It wasn't a particularly pleasant future he had if things continued the way they were going. Solitude, unemployment and the inevitable boredom that would come together with the gradual atrophy of his lungs and liver. It would all leave him a lonely and bitter old man. Many people who knew him would argue he was well along that road already. Exactly how much more lonely and bitter he could become was debatable.

Even though hindsight was a powerful tool he would struggle to pinpoint what he would change even if he did have the ability to go back in time and start all over again. The problem was that there wasn't any one event that had created the malaise which had slowly but inexorably engulfed him. It had taken decades of apathy to allow this quicksand to suck him down. He had committed the unforgivable sin of no longer caring about himself and because of that others had stopped as well. It was impossible to love anybody who held themselves in such low esteem and that was why he was now all alone and drinking to forget the fact that he had allowed his life to fade into such insignificance.

On the few occasions in recent years he had been in a position to do some good he had inevitably failed those he could have helped. First there had been the kidnapping of Elín Einarsdóttir and her sister Kristjana. When their younger sister Ylfa had come to him for help he had barely tried to hide his disbelief at her wild theory that her family was being targeted by a madman. Of course she had been right and both her sisters had been killed. Somehow she managed to escape a terrifying ordeal at the hands of the very disturbed individual but her journalist boyfriend had not been so lucky. Eventually the killer had been found dead in an inner-city squat but not before he had made the police and Grímur in particular look hopelessly ineffective in the face of such overwhelming horror.

Grímur's world-weary cynicism had cost people their lives and even though it was generally accepted that there was very little anyone could have done to prevent such a tragedy from occurring it had weighed heavy on his conscience and accusing eyes now followed him wherever he went as his self-loathing and paranoia grew.

He ground his cigarette into the ashtray next to the television remote control and poured himself another drink. This time he took care not to disturb his sleeping canine companion. It was entirely possible that Bobbi would be his only company from here on in so it was about time he started looking after the poor old thing. What he would do when Bobbi passed away or had to be put down was a real concern. That would mark a brand new chapter in his life. Isolation. Without a job to go to and without his faithful dog he would find it hard not to lose all hope. He had once read somewhere that happiness was nothing but an illusion.

'Show me the man whose happiness was anything more than illusion followed by disillusion.'

It was hard to argue with that. He was beginning to see why people killed themselves. It wasn't weakness or 'the easy way out' at all. It was a frank and clinical admission that life, as it had become, was no longer worth the effort it took to force yourself out of the house every day and face the increasingly ugly music all over again.

When he closed his eyes now what he saw was failure on a grand scale. And death. First it had been a teenage boy and a horse they had found murdered in Hafnarfjörður then it was the journalist and the two sisters just outside of Hella. Once they had discovered the body of the man responsible for these killings Grímur had hoped there would be some sort of relief but that hadn't been the case. The face of the killer had brought tears to his eyes and startling pictures to his dreams. Pictures that left him wanting to scream when he woke each morning and made him wish he never had to fall asleep again such was the fear they bore with them. As Daníel Lauguson sat propped up against that cold concrete wall in the abandoned house where they'd found him he looked spent. As if life had used him up and then let him go. Another vodka was poured and another cigarette lit as Bobbi twitched in his sleep chasing invisible prey or perhaps running away from something. Grímur patted his head and ran his fingers along his long black ears before standing up to stretch his tired legs.

The case that had really given him a name, for better or for worse, had been the one that came next. Gunnar Atli Davíðsson had been the only suspect in the case of a woman found grotesquely murdered outside his small inner-city apartment block. Grímur had been convinced they had the right guy, everything pointed to the slightly unhinged Gunnar Atli being the killer. The dead girl's father had come to Reykjavík to see that the police were doing their jobs properly but his enthusiasm for justice had got the better of him. When Gunnar Atli had escaped from the psychiatric hospital he had been placed in for evaluation two things had happened. First, a package had been delivered to the daughter of the head doctor of the facility containing a recording of the doctor talking to the murder victim not long before she was killed and then secondly, Gunnar Atli had disappeared into thin air. And he had never been found.

The next day Grímur had met with the dead woman's father as he was preparing to head back to Leirubakki and bury his daughter. He had seemed on edge and preoccupied but under the circumstances that was not altogether surprising. What had been surprising was that he had repeated a phrase Grímur had heard somewhere before. It had taken him a while to recall exactly where he had heard it and by then Kjartan was long gone. He had heard the phrase in the hospital that Gunnar Atli had escaped from. He had said it while under sedation and it was hard to imagine Kjartan hearing it from anybody else. He had repeated it word for word. Grímur strongly suspected that Kjartan had somehow intercepted Gunnar Atli after his escape or even engineered his disappearance and exacted his own personal revenge.

It was a difficult theory to prove given that Gunnar Atli was never found nor did his body ever turn up but there were ways of making bodies disappear in Iceland. It had gnawed away at Grímur as he wrestled with himself trying to weigh up the pros and cons of going after a man who had already lost so much. In the end he had decided to keep his suspicions to himself and let fate steer the course of events whichever way it wished.

If Gunnar Atli's body was ever found then they would have no choice but to open a murder investigation but until such time as that happened he was prepared to keep what he knew, or what he suspected, to himself. The end result though was that he knew he had let someone get away with murder. And it made him feel like a fraud. At the beginning of the investigation he had seen the poor girl's mutilated face every time he closed his eyes. And now all he could see was a different face. That of a troubled young man whom nobody, including himself, had liked very much. It wasn't too long before he was out of cigarettes and the bottle of vodka was empty. With any luck he would be too drunk to remember his dreams tonight.

CHAPTER TWENTY-FOUR

Four years ago

Oksana Ulanova made the short trip from her tiny bedroom along the basement corridor with the low ceiling to the laundry room. It was time to wash away the accumulated filth of the night and the sooner the better. If she'd had the energy to do it when she'd got home she would have but she simply hadn't. As usual she'd been so exhausted it was all she could do to get herself undressed and onto her bed. She had never been so happy for sleep to overwhelm her and take her away from her sad and wretched life. It was one thing to hate the people you despised in your life but it was quite another to save that emotion for yourself and she now hated herself with a violent passion.

As she walked into the laundry room she looked up at the hot water pipes that ran across the ceiling and wondered what it would feel like to hang at the end of a rope from one of them. If she could find one that would do the job she would kill herself today. Once she'd had a shower. She didn't want to die feeling as used and soiled as she did right now. Earlier in her life suicide had seemed such a dirty word and a terrible waste of life but not any longer. Thoughts of ending her own life bubbled to the surface on a regular basis now. She closed the door behind her even though she knew that was a waste of time too then undressed and stepped into the bathtub. She pulled the shower curtain across and stared out the basement window across the paved backyard as she did at about this time every day. It was a view she had grown to loathe. Outside were the bins for the tenant's rubbish and recycling. Beyond that were five washing lines tied between the building and the back fence. She could steal one of those lengths of cord to hang herself with but someone would see her and ask her what she thought she was doing and where they were supposed to hang their laundry now.

She turned the hot water on and mixed some cold water in with it so she didn't burn herself. The hot water in the building smelled of rotten eggs. They told her it was the sulphur in the water when she'd mentioned it. She could hear the pipes groaning as the water forced its way through the ancient plumbing. She knew what that noise meant and sighed at the thought. If she didn't feel so filthy there was no way she would have got into the tub during the day. If only she wasn't so exhausted when she got home she would shower then but she never had the energy. She counted the seconds off in her head until she made it all the way up to two minutes and just like clockwork she heard the door at the top of the stairs open and close and then she counted the fifteen steps he took to get down the concrete stairs and into the basement. The footsteps along the floor from the bottom of the stairs were silent across the fake parquet floor. Everybody in the building walked around in their socks. If she didn't take her shoes off as soon as she came in someone would always say something to her. Most of them loved giving the foreign girl advice on how to fit in but didn't realise that it just made her feel all the more like just another stupid foreigner.

She let the warm water run over her sore, tired eyes and wondered when she would stop feeling so tired every day. It was getting to the point where she was exhausted when she woke up and it only got worse as the day wore on. It was a tool they used to keep her in line. If she was that tired all the time she was less likely to cause them any sort of trouble. This way she wouldn't ever have the strength to run away. It was just beyond her. The thought brought tears to her eyes which she washed away with the warm spray from the shower head. This place was not where she wanted to die. All alone on a strange island miles away from anywhere that even remotely resembled home. She wanted to see Kiev again. She wanted to teach her people how to dance. Her own people. Ukrainian people. As well as that she wanted to spend one more day speaking her own language with her friends as they sat inside and drank coffee away from the prying ears of their Russian-speaking neighbours.

It was their inside language. The one they only spoke indoors and the one that would never get them a job or a loan or anything else of any use but the one they always spoke to each other as they were growing up and which she now feared she would never hear again. The sound of her own voice just wasn't the same.

Oksana fumbled around for some shampoo but she'd forgotten to replace the last bottle when it had run out and now she would have to do with washing her hair with soap again. The thought made her cringe but it was better than nothing, though only just. The top hinge on the laundry door creaked as it opened and she could smell the stale cigarette smoke on his clothes as he stepped into the room and closed the door behind him again. She rolled her eyes up at the low ceiling with the water pipes running along it and wondered when he was going to tire of his tedious little game. The day she had arrived there had been a key in the laundry door that she could use to lock the door from the inside but it had disappeared as soon as he had seen who had moved into the tiny basement room just below his. She had never heard him speak a single word even when she had very occasionally tried to engage him in conversation. It wasn't because he was shy because he didn't seem to have a problem with walking into the laundry while she was in the tub washing herself. Quite the opposite in fact. As soon as he heard the water running below his floorboards he suddenly had laundry to do or something to find in the clutter that was strewn throughout the room or stashed away in the cupboards. She could hear him opening and closing doors as he pretended to look for something then he would walk back down the corridor, leaving the laundry room door wide open, and walk out through the external door and up the short flight of stairs to the backyard. She could count the number of steps it would take him to get far enough across the paved area at the back of the apartment block so he could see in through the ground level window. That way he would be able to see her from above the waist as she washed herself and even if it was snowing outside as it did for much of the last winter he would go outside for a walk.

He would still find something to do in the garden shed where he could stand under cover and stare through the window at her. Then he would pick something out of the shed and make his way back into the laundry room and wait for her to finish. She had found that she could wait as long as she wanted and he still wouldn't go away. Eventually she would have to turn the water off and pull the curtain back so she could step out of the bathtub and dry herself off. Oksana looked up at the ceiling just above her head, closed her eyes and tried to empty her head of all the nonsense that had accumulated around her and become her life. If she just acted like he wasn't even there then she could try to ignore him and get back to her horrid little room without any more hassle. That was all she wanted now. As little hassle as possible but it didn't work so she opened her eyes again and let out the breath she had been holding in her chest without even noticing she was doing it.

The ceiling above her looked as though it was made of wooden planks that had been painted blue. When the floor had been constructed it had been held in place by wooden planks as the cement on top of them hardened. They had all been slightly different thicknesses and widths and when they had been removed the ceiling looked as if it had been constructed of big, thick, uneven concrete planks. When she'd first moved in she thought there was wood beneath the blue paint but didn't realise how little wood there was in houses in this part of Reykjavík. Only the very oldest houses right in the middle of town had wooden floorboards in them. The block of flats she lived in had been built in 1939 just as the Americans had arrived to occupy the country at the start of the war. It had become common knowledge that the Americans would be appropriating any unfinished housing to use as accommodation for their troops. As the news spread the builders working on her street told people that if they didn't move in straight away they would lose their homes. As soon as they heard this they moved into their half-finished apartments with doors, windows and even parts of walls and roofs missing. They weren't about to let a bunch of foreigners move into their homes.

As a result some of the buildings had been completed with the builders working around the inhabitants who were eating and sleeping in what were sometimes not much more than building sites. It was a matter of national pride that they stuck it out through the freezing nights and hung on to their property that they had worked so hard to get. Every line in the ceiling told a story. Every one of those people had stuck to their guns and not let the Americans screw them over. Sometimes you just had to do what you had to do to get through the tough times. That was what Oksana told herself that she had to do now even though she knew she was doomed. Another couple of months of this and she would let go of what hope she had left and get her hands on one of those washing lines. As she turned off the water and pulled the shower curtain back she wondered if any of the people watching their homes being built around them then had ever imagined what would become of them once their children had grown up and moved away.

CHAPTER TWENTY-FIVE

Friday 6th February

Grímur had called work earlier in the day to tell them he wouldn't be around for a few days. He was apparently still recovering from a mystery virus he had succumbed to as a result of wanting to kill his boss and suspected that it might be highly contagious. It wouldn't be right to infect everyone and spread it around the office so he'd decided to quarantine himself at home. The receptionist on duty had wished him a speedy recovery and he'd started to feel guilty as soon as he'd hung up even though he knew he was doing the right thing. He hadn't taken any time off work in over three years let alone lied about the reason why. In all probability he was just in desperate need of a holiday but he didn't have much of a life outside his job and hated travelling on his own. But even sitting around the house doing nothing would be preferable to clashing with Ævar again. Things had been tense between the two of them for a while now and this latest incident had pushed him to the point of wanting to walk out and never come back. The only thing stopping him from doing just that was the fact that it was exactly what they all wanted him to do. Ævar included. There had been a silent campaign to usher him out the back door underway for some time now. It all dated back to the murder of Ísabella Thorgeirsdóttir and the disappearance of Gunnar Atli Davíðsson. The whole experience had left him feeling as if he were at the very fringes of effectiveness and that maybe it was high time he did as everyone wanted and retired. This latest episode with Halldór only drilled the point home further that he was no longer the detective he had once been. He no longer had the respect of his peers, he very rarely had the stomach for making hard decisions and when he did he hardly ever got them right any more. But as soon as he'd ended the call he realised he had absolutely nothing to do to keep himself occupied.

He hadn't quite yet decided how many days he was going to be out of action for but he knew it wouldn't be long before boredom set in. As if he could tell what his master was thinking Bobbi appeared in the living room and gave him that look that could only mean one thing. He wanted to go for a walk. Grímur also wanted to stretch his legs so he grabbed Bobbi's lead and they headed out the door and up the hill to Klambratún. By the time they'd reached the park he wanted to let his lively companion off his lead but knew as well as anyone did that it wasn't allowed. He tried to slow the pace of the enthusiastic dog as they walked but Bobbi was having none of it and insisted that his out-of-shape owner keep up with him.

Grímur saw a young lady keeping an eye on them from underneath a stand of birch trees. She was hiding in the shadows but even in the darkness he could tell that she was staring his way. At first he thought she was merely amused by him being taken for a walk by Bobbi but she had an expression on her face that suggested otherwise. She looked vaguely familiar but with each passing year there seemed to be more and more faces that he recognised but couldn't place. This one was pale and very skinny as if she was either on drugs or just thoroughly undernourished. She had long black hair with a straight fringe that made her look like a sickly porcelain doll. She smiled at him as he and Bobbi approached but it was a sad pitiful smile and not a happy one at all. The kind he had seen dozens of times before on the faces of those living on the streets as if they were still trying to convince you they were okay when they had obviously given up on themselves. Bobbi lunged forward and tore the leash out of Grímur's hands and ran straight at her but instead of being frightened she reached out and embraced him as if he were a long lost friend. Maybe the two of them had met before and Grímur just didn't remember her. Bobbi certainly seemed to know who she was.

'Hi,' she said as he got closer to her. She was a pretty girl somewhere in her twenties who looked as if she'd seen about as much of the world and its inhabitants as she cared to. Jaded well beyond her years.

'Hello. I see you two have met then,' Grímur said pointing at his overjoyed Labrador.

The sickly-looking young lady smiled again as Bobbi licked her hand but this time she looked genuinely happy.

'I noticed you looking at me and wondered if you needed anything,' he said.

She looked a little embarrassed and brushed some stray hair out of the way of her eyes and nodded.

'I'm sorry. I thought you might remember me.'

Grímur nodded as he tried to recall where they might have met.

'I thought we might have met before,' he said. 'I'm afraid I don't remember your name.'

'I'm Sóllilja,' she said holding out her hand for him to shake. 'It's okay if you don't remember me. It was a long time ago and I don't think we were very nice to you.'

'We?'

'I'm a friend of Svandís's. You and I met maybe four or five years ago when I was living with her near Hlemmur. I can't remember what you were doing at the house but we were probably causing some kind of trouble and someone complained about us.'

She looked back at Bobbi and patted his greying muzzle.

'Anyway, we might have given you a pretty hard time,' she said.

'I vaguely remember those old houses giving us quite a lot of bother. We were glad when they were sold off to a developer. You haven't heard from Svandís have you?'

Sóllilja shook her head slowly as if she was thinking about something else.

'No. No one's seen or heard a thing.'

Sóllilja looked around the park nervously as if she half-expected someone to be watching them.

'Is there something you want to tell me, Sóllilja?'

'I don't know,' she said. 'That probably sounds pretty stupid but the truth is I'm not sure what I should tell you or if I should even say anything at all. I don't really know you.'

'I think you must want to tell me otherwise you wouldn't have been staring at me before.'

She grabbed Bobbi again and started running her fingers through his shaggy black coat but didn't say anything.

'If you know anything about what happened to Svandís you should tell me. Even if one or both of you might get in trouble it's more important that we find her. Her family and her boyfriend are very worried about her and they're scared something has happened. If you can help put their minds at rest, even if it's bad news, you should do what you can to help.'

He watched her pat his dog and hoped that his words had sunk in but it was impossible to tell. He felt a great loneliness coming off her as if something huge was missing from her life. Maybe he just recognised another lost soul when he saw one.

'Okay, but I don't want you asking any questions. I'll tell you what I know and you'll have to leave it at that. Okay?'

She looked at Grímur waiting for some sign of consent. Even though he wasn't thrilled with her he nodded for her to continue.

'Okay. Svandís and I were working together. I still work there and it's the only money I can get so I need it. We look after rich guys. Really rich guys. Guys with important jobs who don't want any one finding out about what it is they get up to with us if you know what I mean?'

Grímur nodded again.

'Well, a few nights ago Svandís kind of lost it at one of these guys. She was strung out and really needed a fix but hadn't been able to score for days. Instead of staying home and sweating it out she decided that once she got paid for her night's work she'd be able to get some smack and everything would be okay. The problem was that she didn't have any to get her through her shift so she was a bit of an accident waiting to happen.'

Grímur could imagine her in that sort of mood without any trouble at all.

'One of the guys took offence at what he thought was a bit of an attitude she had on her and he got a bit rough with her. More than bit rough actually. He tried to teach her a lesson which she didn't really enjoy very much and she completely lost it. She knew how important it was to get through the night without doing anything stupid. These guys aren't like normal customers, you've got to be really careful with them.'

'What do you mean?'

'We're talking lawyers, judges, politicians and quite a few cops too. Some of them even wear masks while they're fucking you because they think you won't be able to tell who they are.'

'But you still can?'

'Yeah, you can tell what a guy's going to look like naked when you first meet him. Not being able to see his face doesn't make the slightest bit of difference.'

'Okay,' Grímur said and smiled to himself. 'I'll take your word for it. So what happened?'

'There was some sort of commotion going on. This guy was going off his head at our boss. I think he wanted to kill her.'

'Do you know who this guy was?'

She looked into his eyes as if searching for something. She looked the way she had when he'd first seen her. Lost and a bit sick of herself.

'If this guy wound up doing something to her it would be a mistake not to tell me,' Grímur said.

The look in her eyes told him that she knew he was right but there was still something in the way.

'What's the worst thing that could happen if you tell me his name, Sóllilja?'

'I could lose everything. My job, my flat, even my life. She's not the first girl to go missing from where we work. She's probably just the first one you lot have noticed.'

'The first one we've noticed?'

'Yeah. Most of the girls aren't Icelandic and when they leave no one gives a shit about where they've gone or what's happened to them. The thing is, some of them just disappear. If they went back to living on the streets you'd see them around but you don't. You don't ever see them again and that's impossible in a place this size.'

She shrugged and looked around the park again.

'Unless they just disappear.'

'People don't just disappear,' Grímur said.

'Yeah, they do. Around here anyway. Svandís comes from a decent home and has parents that still care about her. Just. That's the only reason you're looking for her.'

'Let's just say for a moment that you're right. How many of these girls might have slipped off the radar?'

'In the last two years I'd say at least three or four girls. At least.'

Grímur smiled. She had to be having him on.

'You think I'm being funny?' she asked.

She didn't look at all happy and was about to get up and leave.

'Hang on a second. Look at it from my point of view. You're telling me three girls have disappeared in the last two years and we haven't heard anything about a single one of them. It's just not possible.'

Sóllilja turned back to him with a new look of determination on her face.

'These men are powerful. The guy Svandís pissed off, he's got a lot to lose if this gets out and from what I heard she made some pretty crazy threats. She knew what she was risking but she did it anyway. This guy isn't just some wannabe tough guy. He's the real deal. Anyone who gets in his way is dust. He couldn't care less about some random chick who's just there to do the stuff his wife won't do for him any more. We're expendable. We fuck up and we're gone. You don't have to believe me but I'm not making this up. Svandís crossed a line and now no one knows where she is. And if you think she's still going to turn up alive and well then you're out of your mind. She's gone for good.'

Sóllilja got up and walked off. Bobbi chased after her for a short way across the park but he gave up when Grímur called out to him.

CHAPTER TWENTY-SIX

Friday 6th February

Grímur was beginning to think that absolutely anything would be better than sitting around the house twiddling his thumbs. Since his talk with Sóllilja he had spent the rest of the day going through old news stories on his computer trying to reconcile what she had told him with what he could remember of missing persons reports from the last few years. He still couldn't believe that what she'd been talking about could have happened right under their noses but there had been something, a look in her eyes perhaps, that had told him she wasn't making it up. Just because it was difficult to believe didn't mean it hadn't happened. His phone rang. It was Ævar.

'Grímur. I know you're not feeling well and probably need your rest but we've got a bit of an emergency on our hands staff-wise and I was hoping you could help us out. We've had a complaint from a member of the public. An American tourist who just happens to be a cop back in Texas. He says he witnessed what he's calling a case of "false imprisonment" at the champagne club on Lækjargata last night. He says a girl who works there was physically restrained when she tried to leave the premises and that she was prevented from doing so several times despite the fact that it was clear she wanted to leave. I'm not sure what he thought was going on but he's insisting a crime was committed. Whether that is the case under Icelandic law or just where he comes from I don't really know but I need someone to go down there and give it a quick once-over just to make sure that everything's on the up and up. You don't need to spend too much time there if you know what I mean.'

'Good afternoon to you too. I'm not sure I understand what it is you need me for. I'm not feeling the best. What exactly do you mean I won't need to spend too much time there?'

'I mean have a look around and let them know that we're keeping an eye on them. All we need to do to get this American off our backs is to be able to say that we've had a look at the club and not seen anything that looks suspicious blah, blah, blah. He's already talked to the girl himself. Apparently he cornered her later on and tried to get her to file a complaint but she refused. If she's still unwilling to do so tomorrow morning, which I assume will be the case, then we can just let this one die a slow death.'

Grímur sighed for dramatic effect but when he looked around the living room he knew there was only ever going to be one answer. Sometimes there was nothing like feeling needed even if it was just to do someone else's job for them.

'Okay. I'll have a look around tonight and let you know what I see,' Grímur said.

Sitting around the house was driving him crazy and as angry as he was with Ævar he wanted to get back to the only thing he knew how to do. Even if he didn't do it particularly well.

'Do your best, Grímur. I'm sorry about what happened with you and the missing girl but you have to understand it was out of my hands. We all have to answer to someone. Even me.'

Grímur had a few choice words for him on that subject but decided that if he wanted to keep his job he would have to keep such observations to himself.

'Svandís. Her name is Svandís,' he said.

'That's right. Make sure you let me know how you get on at the club and don't waste too much time worrying about things we don't have any control over.'

Ævar wished him luck and hung up. Grímur looked down at Bobbi who was resting on the rug at his feet. The days when he had been a bright-eyed and bushy-tailed recruit seemed an awfully long time ago. He had slowly lost interest in changing the world one lost cause at a time and had first become comfortable and then complacent. That had been ten years ago.

He couldn't even call himself complacent any more. He was bitter and resentful and hadn't made one bit of difference in the last decade that he could remember. Not only had he started turning a blind eye to others breaking the law but he had been wilfully doing it himself. If there was to be any kind of road back to salvation for him it would need to be found soon and if the truth be told he hadn't even started looking for it.

By the time he'd found a parking space on Lækjargata within sight of the club's front door he was already regretting his decision to help Ævar out. If he was going to pretend to be sick then he should at least play the part properly and refuse to head out into the freezing cold to do someone else's job for them. He knew damn well that the rest of the detectives were sitting around doing nothing to find Svandís with their hands now firmly tied behind their backs by Haukur Hauksson. They would wait for the search and rescue crews to do their job and that would be it. As long as they were seen on the news to be looking for a body there was no pressing need for them to find out what had actually happened. From what Sóllilja had told him that might just be the last thing anyone wanted. It would certainly explain why he was visiting a champagne club to do nothing more than give the management a reminder that they knew what was going on in there but still weren't prepared to act. A uniformed officer could be doing this but by sending a detective they were emphasizing the fact that they took the complaint seriously. Just not seriously enough to do anything about it.

He had at least remembered to bring some coffee in a flask with him so he poured a cup and settled in for what could be a bit of a wait. It didn't take long to realise that he had come out far too early. In the first hour a grand total of two people entered the club and they only stayed a little over twenty minutes. Enough time for them to use the cards that were handed out on Laugavegur at the weekends for their free entry and one free drink. As soon as they saw the prices of everything else on the menu they would suddenly have a pressing engagement elsewhere. Champagne didn't come cheaply at this particular club.

He was going to have to wait for a group of foreigners on a stag night or a dirty weekend away from their wives to fill the place up. Once that happened then hopefully the staff would have better things to do than to pay too much attention to him as he slipped in through the door. The problem was that his face was known in there, perhaps a little too well. Over the last year since the death of Ísabella Thorgeirsdóttir he had spent considerably more time in this particular club than he should have. During his drunken attempts to forget about the disappearance of Gunnar Atli Davíðsson he had quite literally stumbled upon the place one night as he had tried to make his way home.

For some reason instead of throwing his drunken arse back out onto the street the owner had tolerated him. Not only had he tolerated him but he'd actually set him up with one of the girls who worked there. Somehow he had known he was a cop and had decided to take full advantage of the situation. What Grímur could remember of the incident, and it wasn't all that much, was just embarrassing. In his drunken stupor he had somehow managed to get undressed with considerable assistance from the poor young thing who had drawn the short straw to entertain him. He had then fallen asleep completely naked on a sofa. Fortunately enough this had all occurred in one of the private curtained-off areas but it had been a disastrous moment for him nonetheless.

When he'd woken with what was to be the beginning of a truly dreadful hangover it quickly became apparent that the manager had just decided to get a police officer in his back pocket. And he had succeeded without even having to try. Grímur had lurched in through the front door and given him exactly what he'd always wanted. Ever since that night Grímur had invented story after story about the club whenever it had been mentioned in the news or when, like now, a member of the public had seen something they hadn't liked going on in there. Ævar hadn't really believed most of the things he'd been told but he hadn't bothered to question them too much either.

And now here he was again. Back at the scene of his greatest failure. If he fucked up again and actually got caught doing something he shouldn't be doing it would be the perfect scenario for those who wanted him off the force. All their problems would be over in one fell swoop. He would confirm their worst fears about him and he would be hung out to dry. Halldór's face flashed in front of his eyes. He was just about the last person on earth he wanted to give a gift like that to.

He didn't have long to ponder the subject of his downfall though as a group of thirty-something tourists drinking bottles of beer reeled up to the club's front door looking like they were in the mood for a little action. The steroid case of a bouncer on the door stopped them and waited for them to finish their drinks before collecting all the bottles as they filed past him and up the stairs. Grímur saw his chance and sauntered across the street to tag on to the end of the party line. As he slipped inside he nodded to the bouncer who was far too busy trying to find somewhere to store all his empties to be concerned with one more arrival. Grímur put his head down and made his way up the stairs. He was going to need a drink soon too, maybe a couple. That had been another thing that had changed after Gunnar Atli Davíðsson had come into his dreams. He had never used to drink before but now it had become a way of life he just couldn't shake.

The group of men up ahead of him were British. They had obviously been drinking for quite a few hours and they provided a great distraction for the staff while Grímur made his way to the bar and got himself a double whiskey. He hadn't been in the club for quite some time now and had been hoping he could stay out of the place a little longer. The girl behind the bar looked at him as though she recognised him even though he couldn't quite place her face. The turnover of staff must be fairly high so he hoped she was a new arrival and just looked at everyone that way. He finished his drink quickly and ordered another straight away. The barmaid smiled at him when she handed him his second drink.

'This one's on the house,' she said.

Grímur nodded and self-consciously raised his glass to his mouth without actually taking a sip. The girl was in her early twenties and obviously not Icelandic but spoke the language very well albeit with a strong foreign accent.

'Thank you,' he said.

She smiled and walked off to serve another customer. Grímur took his drink and moved away from the bar. The place was dark in such a way that you could barely see the other side of the room. The lights were all pointed down at the floor so the place glowed up at you off the deep red carpet. While the British men made themselves at home Grímur wandered about aimlessly popping back to the bar every now and then for another drink some of which he had to pay for and some of which he didn't. He wasn't even supposed to be at work so he figured he would take a few liberties. As long as he got home in one piece Ævar wouldn't have anything to complain about.

Heavy full-length velveteen curtains hung along the back wall of the club. There were four curtains in all. They all looked exactly the same and were positioned at even intervals. It was behind one of these curtains that he had suffered his inebriated indignity. Behind each one a small space no bigger than an oversized cupboard containing a fake leather sofa and a wooden stool. One of them opened and a woman in her twenties with spiky jet black hair and far too much dark eye make-up looked out at him. She stood perfectly still and held Grímur's gaze while she tried to figure out what it was he wanted. When she'd decided that he was just curious she motioned with her eyes that he was to move along to the next cubicle. She stood aside and a man in an expensive-looking suit stepped passed her and brushed against Grímur as he straightened his tie and made for the exit. Grímur looked behind the next curtain. It was slightly open which he figured must be the sign that the booth wasn't presently occupied. Behind it was an identical set-up to the booth next to it with a sofa and a stool but this time the sofa was occupied by a tall skinny blonde girl in dark leggings and black boots. She looked bored but tried to smile when she saw Grímur.

'Are you busy?' he asked for no other reason than he could think of nothing else to say.

The girl smiled for real and looked around the tiny room as if to say that she was all alone.

'Don't be silly. Come on in and close the curtain behind you,' she said.

Grímur did as he was told. The girl motioned for him to take a seat on the stool. She waited until he was seated and then walked up to his ear until she was close enough to blow out his pilot light. He could feel her breath on his cheek and she smelled of coffee and something sweet. Not perfume but as if she'd spent her day sucking on candy in between cups of coffee and maybe an occasional cigarette.

'Tell me how long it is you want,' she said in accented English. 'And I'll see what I can do for you.'

She ran her hand down his thigh but when he moved his hand onto hers she took it off again and shook her head.

'No. At this point I can touch you but not the other way around. You tell me what you want me to do and I'll tell you how long that will take and what the price will be. I have a menu here if you want to see how much time your money will get you.'

'Sorry,' Grímur said trying to wipe the smile off his face.

'That's quite okay. It's only natural to want to touch a pretty girl.'

She cupped his chin in one of her hands and kissed him on the cheek. He wasn't sure who this girl was but he wanted her more than he'd wanted anything in his life.

'You're going to need plenty of money,' she said and slid her hand all the way up his thigh.

Maybe it was because she was new to the place or maybe it was just the way she had about her but the way she looked at him made him want to cry. If only she didn't make every guy who walked through the front door feel the way he felt right now. If only he wasn't such a sad lonely old excuse for a man. He lifted his drink to his lips and sucked the whiskey into his mouth. Without him noticing, the curtain behind him opened slightly. The girl smiled at Grímur and excused herself. From the other side of the curtain he could hear a hushed conversation. And then silence. He waited for the curtain to be pulled back and the girl to reappear. When neither of those things happened he stood up and pulled the curtain aside but she was nowhere to be seen. He looked down at the empty glass in his hand and wondered when exactly it was that he'd become such a hopeless drunk. It had crept up on him without him noticing like everything else in his life. He was being slowly swallowed by time's ragged tide and he didn't like it one bit. It just made him want another drink which wasn't going to help anything but it was all he could think of to keep his wavering spirits up since the girl obviously wasn't coming back any time soon.

Across the other side of the room he saw something move. A door almost hidden in the wall opposite the bar. One so well concealed he almost didn't notice it open. It led in the direction of a considerably more respectable bar in the next building along the street. One you didn't have to check the street before entering to see if anyone you knew was watching where you were going. Two men in suits stepped through it just as Janko Kova?evi? appeared out of the shadows as if by magic and shook their hands. He greeted them with some small talk as a waitress handed them a glass of champagne each. As they took the glasses and toasted each other Sóllilja and the blonde girl he'd just been talking to behind the curtain walked up to them and introduced themselves. Grímur didn't mean to stand and stare but he found himself fixating on the girl he had talked to only a few hours ago in the park.

Her eyes were glassy and she had a languid smile on her face that suggested she was high on something. She hadn't noticed him looking at her yet but Janko had. His hand landed on Grímur's shoulder like a falcon landing on a mouse. Grímur turned to see the Serb's grinning eyes staring straight back into his own. Those eyes had always made him feel as if something terrible was just about to happen. In something of an awkward moment he handed his empty glass to Janko and attempted a smile of his own not really sure of what he was supposed to do next or whether he should say anything at all.

'I don't know what's going on but I don't want you here tonight,' Janko said as he took the glass and rolled it around in his hand like a marble.

He stared at the glass for a moment and then looked back at Grímur who was still standing silently in front of him. Janko looked back at the glass in his hand and then into Grímur's eyes again with the look of a troubled parent who was losing patience with a needlessly annoying child.

'I don't know what you were playing at back there but you know better than that. If you want a girl you come and ask me. You don't walk into a man's house and help yourself to his larder. You wait to be invited to dinner. You know what kind of man I am. There will always be a seat at my table for you but you need to exhibit a little patience and a little humility. You've had some drinks on me so maybe it's just time to go home.'

Janko took a moment to pause but when Grímur didn't say anything he continued.

'I'm a little curious as to what brings you here tonight but I suspect I know the answer. I was told we were to expect a visit from one of your lot but I didn't think they'd send you. I don't really know why I'm surprised though. You probably volunteered. That is what you're doing here isn't it? They've sent you to run the rule over the place so you can be seen to be doing your job after that fat useless prick complained about us the other night.'

By sending an ageing, lazy, alcoholic detective Ævar had ensured that there would be no follow-up to concern himself with because there would be no investigation of any sort in the first place. His only faith in Grímur was that he was certain not to do his job properly and thereby would eliminate the need for any actual police-work in the near future. He knew that one way or another the problem of the American tourist and his complaint would simply disappear under the immense weight of Grímur's indifference.

'You and I both know that you didn't even have to come down here to take care of that particular problem so that begs the question, what the hell are you really doing here? Are you feeling a bit lonely tonight? Were you in the mood for some soft company? Or, did you just want a free drink or two?'

Grímur scratched his head and stared at the floor for a couple of seconds and then finally spoke up.

'Why don't I just get myself another drink and then get out of your hair? I'll tell them what they want to hear and that will be that.'

He tried a smile on for size but it slid down his face like a limp noodle down a wet wall.

'Sometimes I think you forget the dynamic of our relationship, Grímur. It is I that get to make those decisions. Not you. It is I that hold your career, or what's left of it, in my hand. And it is I that get to ask for favours. Not the other way around. You have a short memory when it comes to your mistakes. Perhaps that's why you've made so many of them.'

Janko turned and signalled to the bar. Less than thirty seconds later a drink appeared in Grímur's hand.

'Just remember who works for who here,' Janko said. 'If you're looking for a girl to make you forget how lonely you are, tonight is not such a good night.'

Janko smiled and took his hand off Grímur's shoulder.

'You might want to come back tomorrow after you've had the chance to do me your favour. That way I might feel like I owe you something no matter how insignificant that something might be.'

Janko turned and walked back to where the two men in suits were still talking to the girls. Grímur swore under his breath and downed his fresh drink in one go. If there was one thing he didn't enjoy it was being reminded of what he owed Janko. The Serb had a long memory.

Some time ago now Grímur had made a decision that had saved his career but which had lost him his soul. It was about this time that he had first met Svandís as well. The girl had obviously been struggling with a number of problems and it seemed that she was just one of these people who was addicted. To drugs, to booze and to the simple thrill of destroying herself piece by piece. He had asked her at the time how she had wound up in such a state and why she seemed to have no regard for her own wellbeing. She had laughed at him as if he were some sort of imbecile. He knew enough about her to know that she had good parents and hadn't had any sort of problems at school outside of her own making and yet she had somehow drifted off the road into a ditch she was unlikely to get out of again in a big hurry. There was something about her even then that had turned cold and nasty inside. She had sneered at him and told him that his life was nothing to get too excited about either.

'Don't judge me until you've spent some time in my skin,' she'd said. 'Life is complicated.'

He hadn't understood what could be so complicated about her life. She was young, pretty and had a loving family. If her life was complicated it was because she had made it so. After that last drink Grímur began to feel rather lightheaded and thought for a moment that he was going to faint. He exhaled heavily and wandered back to the top of the stairs. Whatever it was he'd been hoping to achieve by coming to the club he couldn't begin to understand.

He should have just stayed home and told Ævar he had been in for a look and that everything was above board. He wouldn't have known any better and it was unlikely he would have asked too many questions either. Staring down the stairs now he wondered if anyone would notice if he just never went back to see Ævar. Never went back to work. What if he just disappeared? Where on earth would he go though? Anywhere had to be better than where he was now. Trapped in a body that was falling apart. Trapped in a job that was making him a worse person instead of the better one he had hoped for when he'd started all those years ago. He weaved his way down the stairs and watched with surprise as the bouncer opened the door for him from outside. He must have heard him coming. He had never figured out how the guy knew you were coming no matter which side of the door he was on. He must have the keenest sense of hearing outside of the cat world. Grímur thanked him with a flick of his head and walked back down the street to his car. When he'd reclined the seat back as far as it would go he got himself comfortable and closed his eyes. He let the world drift around him as if he were the very centre of the universe. Behind his eyelids all he could see was the smug expression on Halldór's face and those terrible piercing eyes of Janko's and then without any further ado he fell fast asleep.

Sometime later he woke with a jolt. His calf muscles were freezing so he stretched them out as far as he could to try to bring some life back into his icy limbs. He rubbed his face and tried to guess how long he'd been asleep. However long it had been it was time to head home. As he put the keys in the ignition he saw the front door of the club fly open. Janko struggled out onto the footpath with Sóllilja, the girl from the park in his arms. She obviously wasn't very happy about the way she was being manhandled and was making life as difficult as possible for him. He was having none of it though and dragged her the short distance down the street to his car. She tried to escape as soon as he threw her onto the back seat but once he'd slammed the door in her face she couldn't seem to get it open again.

Janko sped off down Lækjargata in the direction of Hringbraut. Grímur's car was facing the wrong way so he made a quick U-turn at the intersection with Bankastræti and then did his best to catch them up without letting Janko know he was being followed. He tailed them onto Gamla Hringbraut and past the BSÍ Bus Station until they came to a stop at the traffic lights at Bústaðavegur. When Janko indicated he was turning right towards Öskjuhlíð and Perlan Grímur had no other option but to come up right behind them and wait in line for the lights. When they turned green the two cars turned onto Bústaðavegur and headed across the bridge. Grímur dropped back a little and watched Janko drive on ahead until he pulled over and parked near the foot of Öskjuhlíð. Grímur slowed down even more and pulled off the road as well. He turned his lights off and sat and watched as Janko got out and yanked the back door open. At first Grímur was unsure of what his next move should be but his mind was made up for him when he saw Janko pull a handgun from beneath his shirt and stick it into Sóllilja's ribs. As the two of them disappeared between the two rows of trees that led up the hill Grímur pulled himself out of his car and took a very deep breath. A strange sickly feeling had begun to settle in the pit of his stomach but it wasn't going to stop him doing what he had already decided to do.

CHAPTER TWENTY-SEVEN

Friday 6th February

Inga Lind looked up and down the street several times before reaching out and pressing the buzzer. She felt as if the eyes of every drunk that wandered past her were burning a hole in the back of her head. As if every rowdy group of friends knew exactly why she was standing there and what she was about to do even though to them she was just another face in the Friday night crowd. She had already double-checked the address on the building three times and was hoping she would relax a little once she was upstairs but she seriously doubted it. Margeir, the guy she had been messaging on Fetish World had talked her down from the original figure of 30,000 to 25,000 for the visit but still expected the same deal as they'd originally discussed. His argument had been that she was obviously new to the business otherwise he would have heard about her before and that once she'd gained a bit of a name for herself she would be able to charge whatever she wanted. He had obviously done his homework and knew that she wasn't really in a position to argue too much about the price. Most of the girls who did this sort of thing for a living were supporting drug habits or young children or, more often than not, both. Not that Inga Lind fell into either of these categories but she still wanted the job badly enough to not put up too much of a fight when Margeir decided to move the goalposts a little. In the end she'd agreed to the new price mainly because she had no intention of having sex with him anyway. Her plan was to interrogate him once he was tied up and get him to tell her exactly what she wanted to know. It had all sounded so easy when she'd talked herself through it step by step earlier in the day but now she was standing on the threshold of his building she was having second thoughts. And plenty of them. There was still time to chicken out. There was nothing stopping her from turning around and going home. Except the pressing need to know what had happened to Svandís that was weighing down on her and squeezing the life out of her. She knew that no matter her present doubts she had no choice but to go through with it now whether she liked it or not. She shook her head to clear it and took a deep breath before pressing the buzzer. She heard a click from the other end and without a word the door unlocked and she let herself into the building. She had been told in his last message to take the stairs to the top floor. By the time she'd reached the halfway point she was already breathless and wondering how she had managed to get so out of shape. Late nights full of cigarettes and vodka drinks flashed before her eyes and she made a silent vow to knock all that on the head as soon as she'd found out what she wanted to know. After a short break to catch her breath she finished the climb to the top. The door to his flat was already open. Not a lot, just a few inches. She reached out to push it but stopped just short of touching it. She called out to Margeir but when there was no answer she gave the door a little nudge. The warmth of the room spilled out onto the landing as she took off her boots and walked inside.

The sparsely-decorated living area was illuminated by tea light candles that sat in small coloured glass jars on most of the flat surfaces around the room. The curtains were wide open exposing large windows that looked out over a small car park to the rear of the apartments and the back of the shops on the main shopping thoroughfare of Laugavegur. Although she felt as though she was visible to everyone in the immediate vicinity the room was so dark that it was unlikely anybody would be able to see in. It was at once exposed and yet voyeuristic at the same time. Margeir emerged from his bedroom dressed in a silk Oriental robe and leather slippers. His pupils looked wide open in the candle-lit half-light as he carried a small tray towards to Inga Lind. He bowed theatrically in front of her and offered the tray to her. On it was a bundle of banknotes rolled up in a rubber band and two lines of cocaine next to a 5,000-krónur note that had been rolled up into a small tube.

Inga Lind smiled and then took the tray from Margeir and placed it on the coffee table in the centre of the room. She rolled the rubber band off the cash and counted it before pocketing the 25,000 krónur. She tightened the 5,000-krónur note until it was a tight little straw and snorted one of the lines. And then the other. Maybe she was going to like this guy after all. She didn't know what he did for a job but it had to pay well to have coke as good as that in his flat. While she'd been snorting it she'd noticed him looking her over. She had to get any ideas about liking this creep out of her head before they went about their business. There was going to be no room for sentiment once she started asking him questions.

'Have a seat and let's get comfortable,' Margeir said.

'Thank you.'

As she sat down she swallowed thickly as the cocaine numbed the back of her throat.

'You've counted your money?' he asked.

'Yes. It's all there. When do you want to start?'

Margeir smiled a sluggish and blissed-out smile.

'You're very eager. That's good but there's no hurry. We've got the rest of the night ahead of us. Let's get to know each other a little better and then we can have some fun. The more familiar we are with each other the better the sensations will be in my experience. Would you like something to drink?'

Inga Lind nodded. This was going to take much longer than she'd thought. If she was going to have to spend all night in his flat then she might as well get a buzz going. The cocaine was nice but it always made her want to drink. She looked around the room and smiled.

'Nice place. From what I can see of it. It's kind of gloomy don't you think? Do you always have it so dark in here?' she asked.

'I prefer it this way. Bright lights give me a headache. What did you say you wanted to drink?'

'Bourbon, if you've got it,' she said.

Margeir nodded.

'Of course. With a little cola perhaps?'

'No, just some ice, thanks. A double.'

Margeir made his way across the room to a bar that opened out from a wall cabinet next to the kitchen. He took two tumblers and filled one of them with ice. He poured a large bourbon into the glass with ice before getting himself a similarly-sized glass of golden-hued Mezcal. He took a seat and slid her drink across the table to her. Inga Lind smiled when she saw the size of the drink and took a large sip straight away to take the edge off her newly-acquired high. The liquor burned the back of her throat but nowhere near as much as it would have done without the drugs. It was warm and soothing as it made its way down her gullet. She had been watching Margeir as he moved around his living room and there was something about the way he looked at her that she didn't like very much. He seemed pretty spaced-out and she wondered how many lines and just what else he'd done before she'd arrived. He certainly seemed to be prepared for something of a party. He stared at her without blinking.

'Is everything okay?' she asked.

'Of course. You remind me of someone a little,' he answered.

'Oh?'

He smiled and shook his head.

'No one you'd know.'

Inga Lind nodded as if she understood completely. She'd taken her time getting her look as much like Svandís as she possibly could and even to her the likeness was unmistakeable. As she'd left the house she'd caught a glimpse of herself in the hallway mirror and had thought, just for the briefest of moments, that it had been her troubled sister staring back at her. The way that Margeir was looking at her now gave her some idea as to why Svandís had begun to feel so lost.

CHAPTER TWENTY-EIGHT

Sunday 1st February

As Svandís pulled the curtain across to seal off her tiny work space she felt the guy's hand on her thigh as it slid north across her lower back. She turned around and attempted to smile but it just wasn't a smiling day. She had been warned about this particular customer's wandering fingers as well as the fact that he would be wearing a mask and maybe a hood. It was late at the club and they were the only two left apart from Janko and Marta who'd stayed behind to do something in the office and Sóllilja and her friend Valdís who were just finishing up with their last clients of the night. Janko and Marta had made themselves scarce as soon as their special guest had arrived and were probably in Janko's office fooling around by now. The fact that Marta earned almost as much as the girls who tricked at the place was not lost on any of the other workers there and as a result she was far from popular. Not that she cared though. She'd arrived from Poland six years ago and was probably the highest paid barmaid anywhere in town now. There was nothing like keeping yourself in the boss's good books with a little extracurricular activity if you wanted to get ahead in life.

When Svandís let the hooded customer have one of her soul-withering stares he seemed to get the message albeit a little slowly and very reluctantly. He moved his hand away and sat back down on his stool again. This time she did manage a smile. At least he knew the rules, even if he chose not to play by them all the time. His identity, it had been repeated endlessly to her by Janko, was to remain a closely-guarded secret. No matter what. Svandís had listened to him go on about the guy's privacy ad nauseam but as usual she hadn't really been paying attention to a thing he'd said. Sometimes Janko got a tone in his voice that made her just switch off halfway through a sentence. She got bored easily if she didn't like the news.

Why these guys couldn't just go home and get their wives to fuck them whichever way they wanted was beyond her but she supposed it wasn't really her place to wonder about such things. If they could do just that then she'd be out of a job so she guessed she owed the uptight housewives of Reykjavík a favour of sorts. Even still, he could keep his hands to himself if he knew what was good for him. There was no room for compromise on that rule as far as she was concerned. At the same time though she needed to keep this guy happy so Janko would continue to give her jobs. Easy, low-risk jobs that kept her off street corners and out of crazy people's homes. If she had to sleep with guys to support her habit then this was the way she preferred to do it. In a controlled environment under the watchful eye of someone like Janko. She didn't have much time for the guy as a human being but she'd give him one thing. He ran his place with an iron fist. No one would ever think of stepping out of line in his club and she knew she was safe there. Otherwise it was outcalls to stranger's houses where she would have only Gylfi and her instincts to guide her and neither of them were as dependable as she might have liked. While Gylfi had nothing but the best intentions he just wasn't much of a deterrent. Sometimes he only made matters worse as he struggled to reason with guys who simply wouldn't be reasoned with. She shuddered when she thought of all the nights she'd spent running from one lousy job to another until she finally had enough to pay off her debts and get another score. Once the dealers around town knew how desperate she was they would fuck her around just because they could. Just because there wasn't a thing she could do about it. They were good that way. She had become a source of amusement to them. The sad little rich girl who could have gone back to her nice safe little home in the suburbs if only she didn't have such a giant monkey on her back. Sucking up her pride and plastering her best fake smile across her face she shimmied up to the masked man, grabbed his hand and put it back on her arse exactly where he'd just had it. He gave it a squeeze in silent appreciation and she could tell he was smiling now, mask or no mask.

He pulled her closer and she could smell the whiskey and tobacco on his breath. She swivelled slightly and sat on his lap. He pressed his face into her chest and held it there. His grip on her rear end tightened until she thought she was going to scream. She was just about to tell him to loosen his grip on her rear when she felt him bite one of her nipples through her top. She let out a piercing scream, leapt up off his lap and slapped him as hard as she could across the face.

'What the fuck is wrong with you?' she demanded as she clutched her chest.

His pale blue eyes with their dilated pupils stared up at her through the eye-holes of his PVC mask but looked straight through her and into the mysterious ether beyond.

'Well?' she wanted to know. 'Are you going to apologise or are you just going to sit there staring at me like some sort of idiot? That fucking hurt.'

He laughed the slow deliberate laugh of a deranged individual as she waited for an explanation. Svandís's patience with the world in general was at an all-time low and with this idiot in particular. His gaze returned from wherever it was that it had been but he remained silent. A small strand of saliva appeared at the side of his mouth and fell onto his trousers. He gave off the vibe of a brain-damaged animal at the zoo waiting to be fed. She no longer cared who this guy was. Her patience, such that it was, had finally run out and she grasped the hood just next to his left ear and pulled at it with all her might. As the material gave way and flew from his face he tried to cover his face with his hands. It was a futile exercise and his fury soon got the better of him. As he lunged at Svandís's neck she raised her hands to protect herself but was quickly overpowered. Before she knew what was going on he was on top of her and she was pinned to the ground. His left hand closed over her mouth and her nose to cut off her air supply while he fastened his right hand around her throat and squeezed. She tried in vain to suck air into her lungs but he had already cut off the supply.

She wanted to scream but all she could do was gurgle out of one side of her mouth. She was trying to suck oxygen into her lungs but the air just wouldn't flow and she knew it wouldn't be long before she blacked out. He waited until he could see her eyes rolling back in her head before he relaxed his grip and tore open her shirt and undid her jeans as she struggled to hang on to consciousness. Her breath was only coming in tiny gasps and he watched with glee as her eyes widened in disbelief at what was happening to her. It was important to him that she remained aware of her plight and yet unable to do a thing about it. If anyone he'd ever met was deserving of being taught a lesson then it was this uppity little bitch. Halldór Valdimarsson pressed her face against the floor as he forced himself into her and smiled his grisly drug-fucked smile. He waited until he'd ejaculated to tell her that now he was done with her they would have to get rid of her too.

CHAPTER TWENTY-NINE

Friday 6th February

By the time Inga Lind had finished her third drink and listened to Margeir talk about himself for close to an hour she was ready to be tied up and whipped herself. For someone who was supposedly into some pretty kinky stuff he was unbelievably boring. A banker by day he seemed to take the dullness of his pointless money-shuffling job and inject it into the rest of his life with consummate ease. She got the feeling she was expected to fill some role in his life other than just a call girl. He appeared for all intents and purposes to be genuinely lonely. And boring. It was as if he didn't get to talk to anyone in the course of his banking duties about anything other than work so when it came to conversations outside of the office he genuinely struggled to find anything else to talk about apart from his job. And himself. The problem was that outside of his work he didn't seem to have much in the way of interests or hobbies. Apart from the one he was indulging in tonight.

When she'd first sat down on his sofa and watched him she'd thought he was one of these weird silent types who thought just a bit too much and chose when to speak way too carefully but it seemed now that he had only been sizing her up because as soon as he was comfortable he'd started talking about himself and now just wouldn't shut up. She hadn't minded too much at first thinking that if this guy had been involved in Svandís's disappearance she would almost definitely hear him slip up at some point and give away some sort of vital clue. She strongly suspected she was reprising a role her sister had already played and felt as though she was walking in her footsteps. Or pretty close to them anyway. What she really needed to hear at some point in the conversation was confirmation he had kidnapped Svandís himself or had played some other part in her disappearance. If she could last that long.

After turning down another drink she politely suggested that they get on with what she had come over for. Margeir smiled and nodded that he understood.

'Of course, my dear. You are a businesswoman after all.'

Inga Lind smiled a little at that. She was no more a prostitute than he was an astronaut but she would happily let him think whatever he wanted.

'I'm a little undecided about what role you should play for me tonight. I'm a switch you see.'

Inga Lind nodded accordingly despite not having a clue what he was talking about. Was it something to do with turning her on? This guy would need one hell of a switch to do that anytime soon. Margeir stood up and pressed his hands together as though he had made a decision.

'We'll begin with some basic bondage. I assume you're familiar with these?'

He reached under the coffee table and pulled out a collection of straps, buckles and padded cuffs. Inga Lind had no idea what she was looking at but nodded again anyway. She dearly hoped there was a gag in there somewhere so she could shut him up until it was time for him to start answering her questions.

'Good. I'll start with the wrist restraints and then you can put the ankle ones on me too. We'll use the frame in my bedroom. Of course, you'll need to get undressed first,' he said with his rat-like smile.

Inga Lind took the restraints off him and put them on the table where she could get a better look. They were made up of nylon straps with leather straps and metal buckles at one end and padded cuffs with their own metal buckles at the other. She was dying to get a look at the frame he'd referred to and quickly stripped down to her black underwear. It was the exact same kind that Svandís had always worn. She prided herself on her close attention to detail.

Margeir smiled as he watched her undress and signalled that she should follow him into his room. She scooped the restraints up off the table and did exactly that. The bedroom was even more atmospheric with its equally minimalist approach to décor and its mood lighting. She had seen a few bachelor pads in her time but none of them had looked anything like this one. Behind the sliding doors of his mirrored wardrobes she could see the uber-tidy collection of suits, shirts, shoes and ties. There was a line of shirts, thirty or forty of them at least, and from what she could see, only three different kinds. Same with the shoes. Twenty pairs when two would have done as he only had two sorts. And the ties. At least thirty ties but as she leaned in a little closer to look at them she could see that the designs on them were all the same. Only the colours changed. They were all so neatly ordered that it looked as if someone came in every day to straighten them for him. She could only imagine the drawer where he kept his socks and underwear. Maybe once she had him tied up she would find it and investigate further. Just out of curiosity. She had read somewhere that being overly fastidious in the organisation of the mundane things in your life was a trait of potentially psychopathic people but had thought it sounded like a load of rubbish. Until now that was.

Her bedroom looked like a landfill site compared to his. She would have felt much more comfortable if she had been able to see just one thing out of place. A coffee cup with a stain down the side. A piece of paper out of place on the desk in the far corner of the room. A crease in his faultlessly made up bed. Anything at all. She stood and watched as Margeir worked quickly and efficiently first pulling the bondage frame down from the ceiling on a set of ropes and pulleys and then attaching the restraints to the impressively large black wooden frame. The bedroom was more solemnly lit than the living room by a small number of lamps with bulbs in them that flickered as if they were candles. She was a little disappointed he didn't have the real things so she could drip wax on his nipples once he was immobilised. That was one thing she had seen on the internet when she'd been doing her research.

When Margeir was finally happy with the alterations he'd made to the frame and had everything set up just the way he wanted it he turned to face Inga Lind once again.

'Where would you like to start?' he asked. 'It will be more fun if you undress me yourself. Then you can attach the restraints and we can get down to the business at hand.'

'Yes indeed,' she said as she started unbuttoning his shirt. 'Then we really can.'

CHAPTER THIRTY

Saturday 7th February

Ævar smiled as he took a seat opposite Knut in the interview room.

'I've just read the ballistics report from the shell casings found on Öskjuhlíð. We found six altogether, all 9mm cartridges, but it seems they were fired from two different guns. Neither weapon has been recovered so far but we anticipate that it's only a matter of time before we find them. Either you had two weapons or there was someone else with you.'

Ævar sat in silence as he waited for a response but there was none forthcoming.

'You probably own a gun or two in your line of business don't you, Knut?'

Knut smiled.

'You know handguns are illegal in this little backwater island nation of yours,' he said.

'Of course I do. But what I want to know is have you somehow come into possession of one anyway? Illegally perhaps. Despite the fact that the ownership of such weapons isn't allowed in this little backwater island nation of ours.'

Knut smiled again but said nothing.

'You think you're pretty clever but we will have the last laugh. I can assure you of that. The only way you can help yourself out here is by telling me who it was on that hillside with you. Grímur is going to do that for us soon anyway.'

'You sound pretty sure of yourself all things considered. What makes you so sure he even knows who shot him? That time of night it must have been pretty dark up there. I'd be surprised if he saw anything at all. Really surprised in fact'

'Either you shot him or you know who did,' Ævar continued. 'If you're protecting someone you're going to learn the hard way that it's not the smart thing to do. You will both get found out sooner or later. I think you lured Grímur to Öskjuhlíð knowing you'd be able to shoot him there and make good your escape in the dark. Unfortunately for you your gunshots were heard by a man walking his dog nearby on Háahlíð and he phoned us straight away.'

Knut grinned ever so slightly to himself and stared at his hands in his lap as he drummed his fingers on his thigh.

'And what if you're wrong? What if I had nothing to do with the shooting? What will your super-efficient police force do then? What if the real killer's already escaped while you've had me in your drunk tank? You're so sure you're right but what if you're wrong? What then?'

Ævar looked back at Knut trying hard to keep any trace of emotion off his face.

'If in the unlikely event that actually proves to be the case then we will of course release you and you will be free to return to Oslo. Although I think you and I both know that this is improbable at best. Whatever it is that you've been up to here in Reykjavík I know that it's been no good. We still have forensic experts going over the construction site where we found Óli Þór Sigurdsson and I am still very confident that we will find some trace of you having been there. I am totally sure you are responsible for that murder. One hundred per cent. There is no doubt in my mind whatsoever. You came here to settle a score with your Icelandic counterparts and Grímur has somehow found himself in the middle of it all. It still remains to be seen if he will recover from his injuries or not but in the meantime I will continue to put together the case against you and by the time I'm done I think you will find that there will be very few secrets left between the two of us. And that will be very bad news for you. Very bad news indeed.'

Knut stopped drumming his fingers on his thigh and let out a slow deliberate breath. A look of exasperation crossed his face and then disappeared again.

'I'm going to walk out of here a free man in the near future and that's whether your friend wakes up from his little sleep or not. You can sit there and talk all the shit you want. It's not going to change a thing,' he said.

Ævar shifted in his seat a little. He was itching to lay a punch on this smart-mouthed Norwegian. There was some truth in what he was saying but he knew deep down that it was nothing more than bravado that was allowing their suspect to put on such a brave face.

'There's a couple of things you should keep in mind. One is that I'm not the only killer you have in town at the moment. I'm not even the one you need to be worried about at the moment. You only want to nail me for this because I'm foreign and it's easier to go after me than it is to go after the problems that are a little closer to home. And the other thing is that there's probably a good reason why you haven't found any evidence linking me to these murders yet. I wasn't there for either of them. If you can get your head around that then you might be able get on with finding the guy you really want to catch. You've got much bigger fish to fry than me. You're just afraid to go after them because when you do the whole place is going to stink and it's going to stink like it's never stunk before.'

Ævar sat and stared at Knut then he stood up and pushed his chair back under the table. He opened the door and then turned to face the Norwegian again.

'We'll just see about that,' he said and walked out of the room.

CHAPTER THIRTY-ONE

Eight years ago

Lili Poursalami looked at her sister in the mirror they were sharing to put their make-up on. Nothing more than some eyeliner and a bit of mascara. They didn't need anything more than a little something to accentuate their incredible brown eyes. Lili would never say anything but Mariam was starting to look much older than she really was. The same could be said for Lili but for some reason she didn't see it in her own face. When they were done they turned to each other and smiled. They were so alike not even their mother would be able to tell them apart. God rest her soul. They had dressed in exactly the same outfits tonight as they did every other night. It was a game they'd played since they were little girls and it had become a tradition for them. Mariam was the one who'd insisted that it was more important that they keep it up now than ever before. Lili had disagreed at first but had seen her twin's argument once she'd explained herself. It gave them something to focus on rather than the mechanics of the night ahead. It also gave them the advantage that no one ever knew who exactly it was that they were dealing with. The girls were identical to the point that it was impossible for anyone in Iceland to tell them apart especially with their exotic Persian looks. They tended to stand out in the land of blonde hair and blue eyes. That was what made them so popular with the local men. They represented something the Viking descendants could only ever dream of otherwise. The girls hugged each other and said a short prayer. The same one they said every night. That their father would stay safe and be reunited with them soon. God willing. He was what their bosses held over their heads every day. If the girls didn't do what they were told they would never see their father again. They had fled Iran together with the help of some fellow Christians but as soon as they were out of the country things had started to go wrong. They had been separated from their father for the first time in their lives and driven across strange countries and through border after border, put on a ferry somewhere across a bleak and cold stretch of water and then flown from a Scandinavian airport to the frozen Icelandic capital. Along the way their names and papers seemed to change every time they had crossed a border or been stopped by police, outlaws or soldiers. By the time they were ready to leave Arlanda for Reykjavík they had become French nationals who could hold a reasonable conversation in English but had absolutely no French skills whatsoever. Luckily no one noticed. Their English skills had improved even further now as had their grasp of Icelandic and they were able to hold simple conversations with the men they came across in the course of a night's work. Some of their customers were foreign and used English but most of time they were locals and even though they had struggled with the difficult language initially their Icelandic had improved in time. Most of their conversations were about where they were from and how they had got to Iceland which they lied about repeatedly. Other than that there were the questions they asked their bosses regularly about their father but they were always met with stony stares and silence.

Every now and then one of the girls would disappear for an hour or two just to piss off the guys who were supposed to be keeping an eye on them. By the time the offending girl had returned their overseer for the night would be so angry they often looked like they might explode. If the offending girl waited for just the right moment to reappear it would be completely impossible for their supervisor to tell them apart thereby rendering any punishment he had in mind obsolete. After it had happened a few times the guys figured out they were being toyed with and it was both girls who were punished. One night after one prank too many three guys showed up to teach them a lesson. The men were all sick and tired of being made to look like fools and had simply had enough of the girls' childish antics. While one guy held Lili's arms behind her back the other two pinned her sister to the ground. Lili twisted this way and that but had no chance of getting free to help Mariam who was being held flat on her back on the floor by one guy while the other dealt out the punishment that was designed to break the will of any troublemakers who went too far. While her arm was held motionless by a heavy knee on her elbow a needle was inserted into a vein and she was given a ride she would never forget. Once Mariam had been dosed with heroin she was dragged to the corner of the room and left curled up in a bundle while the procedure was repeated on her sister. The girls didn't give anyone any more trouble that night, apart from a little vomitus that had to be mopped up, and never repeated their fun and games of running away and then pretending not to know which girl it had been. Ever again.

While under the influence of the powerful opiate for the very first time they were driven to a warehouse outside Selfoss and tied to chairs. When the drug had begun to work its way out of their system they were injected again and again until they'd been under its influence for three whole days. After that neither of them were the same ever again. Their only interest became scoring more drugs and shooting each other up before they went to work. They still dreamt of seeing their father again but with time he too, like the rest of the life they'd left behind, became more and more of a distant memory. And now as they readied themselves for yet another night at work they checked each other's make-up and then got to work with their other routine. Mariam divided the coarse brown powder into equal portions and put one half into a spoon. She mixed it with a little cold water and stirred it gently with a small piece of cotton wool. She then put a cigarette lighter underneath it and waited for the heroin to dissolve. Once that was done Lili stabbed the end of the needle into the cotton wool and drew the liquid into the chamber. They repeated the process and filled a second needle. Mariam found the silk scarf they used as a tourniquet and tied her sister's arm off. She patted the vein on the inside of Lili's elbow and slid the needle home. After drawing a little blood into the syringe she then fired the load into the vein and watched her sister close her eyes. Once the tourniquet had been removed she folded her sister's arm in half and told her to lie back against the wall while the drugs worked their magic. Mariam was always the one who administered the shots. Lili had never really mastered the skill and always seemed to miss the vein. Some people just didn't have the eye for it. Mariam did herself next and lay her head down on her sister's lap and sighed. A tiny slice of a smile passed across her face. Gone before it was even really there. For all their religious zealousness and constant belief that their father was still okay and would be with them again soon she knew it was no longer anything but an elaborate pretence. They would never know what had happened to him just as she was sure that they would never see him again. She would never say that out loud to Lili but she knew it in her heart to be true. Chances were he had been killed the same day they had been separated. He had possibly even known his fate and accepted it to get his daughters out of the country knowing that by giving them their freedom he was ensuring that he never saw them again. A tear grew in her eye and spilled down her cheek. It was probably just as well, she thought to herself. Only God knew what Dad would say if he could see them now.

CHAPTER THIRTY-TWO

Sunday 1st February

Svandís was about to scream when she felt the hand on her shoulder but when she rolled the look in Marta's eyes told her to be quiet. Svandís looked up at her and nodded that she understood but before she could even think about getting up off the floor she had to run her fingers down her ribs to see if any of them were broken. Halldór's post-coital punches had done some real damage and every time she moved in the slightest it hurt. Even breathing hurt. Especially breathing. He probably hadn't wanted her getting up again in a big hurry. Marta helped her to her feet but the effort made her double over in pain.

'You've really done it this time,' Marta said. 'He's in there talking to Janko. If I don't get you out of here right now you might not be getting out at all you stupid girl.'

Svandís grimaced as she took a step and then another but said nothing. Now was most definitely the time to be keeping her mouth shut even if it might just be for the first time in her life. From Janko's office behind the bar the two of them could hear raised voices as Halldór and Janko shared opinions on what had just transpired. Marta shook her head again and looked Svandís up and down.

'If I get fired because of this I'm going to kill you myself,' Marta said. 'This isn't funny.'

Svandís tried to smile apologetically but she was having trouble finding anything to smile about. She had spent her whole life getting in and out of stupid situations that were all of her own making and for the large part could have been avoided. So far she'd managed to escape most of them with nothing more than a few minor dings and scrapes but her luck was bound to run out sometime.

As the shouting from Janko's office continued Svandís and Marta hobbled arm in arm down the stairs to the front door. Marta let go of Svandís to unlock the door and then ushered her out into the night. Svandís turned to say something to her helper but Marta wasn't paying any attention to her. She was looking up and down Lækjargata for any late-night revellers who might have noticed Svandís leaving the club. Luckily the street was completely deserted.

'You're a very silly girl. You know that?' Marta said finally looking at her.

Svandís smiled. It wasn't the first time she'd heard those words.

'Thanks for your help.'

Marta shook her head and pointed a finger at Svandís.

'Don't thank me and don't ever show your face around here again,' Marta said waving the finger at her. 'You're living on borrowed time.'

Svandís took a step towards her to give her a hug but the front door had already closed in her face. Upstairs in Janko's office the initial tension had quickly disintegrated into palpable anger and loud threats. Janko was standing behind his desk with his hands up trying to placate his irate and increasingly difficult to reason with guest. Halldór was towering over the desk as if he were about to launch an assault on the other man.

'Are you listening to me?' Halldór asked even though it was more of a demand than a question. He was so angry that bits of saliva flew across the table as he spoke. The cool, calm and composed demeanour that he was famous for in the Alþingi had deserted him momentarily. 'Don't forget how much you have to lose too,' he shouted.

A cruel grin crept across Janko's face as he had finally had enough of the pompous parliamentarian screaming at him.

'Need I remind you,' Janko said leaning across the table himself now, 'that no one has as much to lose as you do. I'll do what you ask but there will be a price for you just as there would be for anybody else and don't think for a moment that any part of our deal includes you getting to tell me what to do. I provide a service for you as I do for many other people and nothing more. I do not at this point in time owe you any favours nor will I at any stage in the future. Do not confuse me tolerating your ridiculous behaviour at my club with me condoning it. I will give you a price tomorrow when you have sobered up and cooled down and you will pay it. Then the next day the job will be done and we will never ever talk about this again. Not ever. Not to each other and not to anyone else otherwise the next idiot I take care of will be the one standing in front of me right now. Have I made myself clear?'

Halldór attempted to restore some of his composure by standing as straight as he could and straightening his shirt. He took a deep breath and smiled. His eyes were still red-rimmed and almost glowing in the soft office lighting.

'I understand perfectly,' he said. 'And of course I look forward to hearing from you tomorrow. I'm sorry if I became overly animated in making my point but it is vital you understand the situation. Do it quickly and quietly and you will be rewarded handsomely. Fuck it up in any way whatsoever and I will see to it that you never make another penny on our little pile of rocks ever again. Just remember one thing though, Janko. It is not you who tolerates me but us who tolerate you, you insignificant fucking Serb.'

CHAPTER THIRTY-THREE

Friday 6th February

The wind blew hard and cold across Gísli Helgason's face as he stumbled across the jagged rocks. He wiped the saltwater spray out of his eyes and peered again towards where his expensive fishing rod had ended up. He'd been sea-angling along the coast at Álftanes just across the water from Borgarnes when he'd snagged his line on something and after a full thirty minutes of trying to free his equipment he'd given up and thrown his rod as far as he could through the air in a fit of anger. Unfortunately that had been quite a long way and now he was cursing himself as he clambered over the rocks trying not to turn an ankle or break a leg in the process.

At first he thought he'd caught hold of some submerged debris and had wiggled the line about furiously hoping that whatever it was would dislodge itself but his efforts had proved to be futile. Once he'd admitted defeat on that front he'd tried to break the line knowing that although it would take time and cost him some gear he could simply retie some new hooks and weights and get back to fishing as soon as that was done. After all, he hadn't come all the way out here to chase hooked rubbish about the place. He wanted some fish for his supper. But that proved just as fruitless because the line he'd set on his rod had been a heavy one just in case he'd come across something sizable swimming in the rough waters. He'd heard of monkfish and halibut swimming around these parts but they had been known to chew through even 100lb lines. All dreams of a giant wolfish and coalfish had disappeared now as he stared down at the mess of line and seaweed in front of him. One of his hooks had grabbed itself what looked like a clump of black material of some sort. He pulled a pair of work gloves from his back pocket and put them on determined to untangle the unwanted catch of the day.

He wrapped his fingers around the heavy-duty line until he was sure he had a good enough grip and then preceded to slowly winch it in. As he retrieved the length of line from the water his worst fears were confirmed. The black material was clothing of some sort just as he'd suspected. Unfortunately the poor girl was still wearing it even though she had obviously been in the water for days. Her face was pocked with small bite marks and her eyes had long gone leaving her staring soullessly up at the dismayed fisherman. He took a moment to compose himself and said a prayer for her that he remembered from his youth. She was beyond anyone's help now even His but she deserved to be laid to rest in the manner befitting any Christian Icelander. As he dragged her ashore he could see that one of her legs had been badly broken. He was pretty sure he knew who she was. He had seen the story on the news just a couple of days ago. She had disappeared from Borgarnes in the middle of the night and they had been looking for her ever since. At least now her poor parents could put their minds at ease about what had become of her. It wouldn't make the pain of losing their daughter any easier but it would remove the nagging doubts from their minds as to what had become of her. He'd heard many people say that the worst part was not knowing and he was sure they were right.

As he manhandled the body onto the uneven shore he started to feel his age. Her body felt twice what it must have actually weighed. She was the heaviest thing he'd tried to lift in the last twenty years or so and by the time he had her prone on the closest flat surface he was exhausted. He laid back on the rock next to her and sucked as much air into his old lungs as he could. When he'd caught his breath he pulled his phone from his jacket pocket. The one his niece insisted he took with him whenever he went out fishing these days. Today he was grateful for her concern for his wellbeing instead of just being grumpy at the fact that he was so obviously getting old in her eyes. He dialled 1-1-2 and waited for someone to answer.

'Hello? Emergency services. What do you need?'

'Hello. I've found the girl you've been looking for. She's dead but I've found her. You'll need to come and get her now. I've done my dash for today.'

'Who is this? Where are you calling from? Who is it you've found?'

'My name is Gísli Helgason. I'm on the rocks along the shore from Álftanes. She's been in the water a few days now I'd say.'

'Okay. Do you know what her name is?'

'I can't remember. There was something on the news the other night about her. I saw the picture on RUV. It's definitely her. She's a little worse for wear now though.'

'If you just stay where you are I'm going to send someone to you straight away.'

'Thank you.'

Ten minutes later he had recovered from his exertions sufficiently to tell his story to a couple of local police officers who were full of praise for his efforts. They had wrapped a blanket around him and untangled his fishing gear from the body. He called his niece and told her what had happened. He thought she might want to hear about it from him before she saw it on the evening news. As he warmed up again and the feeling came back to his fingers he realised that everything was under control. He would be able to relax now that he had done his good deed for the day. It might not have been the best day's fishing he'd ever had but he wouldn't be going home empty-handed. Not really. He had a tale the grandchildren would never forget. Neither would he for that matter. Not for a very long time.

CHAPTER THIRTY-FOUR

Friday 6th February

Inga Lind slapped Margeir across the face as hard as she could and then started crying. It wasn't the most sensible thing to do but it was the only thing she could think of. She wasn't sure but she thought he might have just had a heart attack. Or a stroke. She wiped the tears from her eyes and started undoing the buckles on the wrist and ankle restraints that were holding him in place. When he'd told her that he wanted to be tied up she thought all her Christmases had come at once. Not that she'd ever had any great desire to tie him or any other man up before but she thought that once he was naked and pinned to his big black wooden frame he would have little choice but to tell her everything she wanted to know.

It hadn't quite worked out that way though. At first he had been quite demanding and rather obnoxious if she was to be honest. He seemed put out that she didn't know every little nuance of his sordid peccadillos and her obvious distaste for some of his requests hadn't helped either. She began to find him quite tedious and soon took real pleasure in delivering the kind of punishment he wanted. It was when she'd decided to change tack and begin questioning him about other girls from the website that he had admonished her for stepping out of character and refused to answer a single question. She'd told him that if he didn't answer her questions she wasn't going to release him from his restraints and he could hang on his specially-built frame until such time as he'd changed his mind about cooperating. This had not gone down at all well. Margeir had started cursing her and threatened all sorts of bodily harm should she not let him out of his restraints immediately. She had thought such threats to be rather odd since they seemed to be designed to convince her that undoing his straps would be a good idea when it was blatantly obvious that it would not.

As she had tried to decide what to do next he had become increasingly agitated and the colour in his face has turned from red and simply flustered to a much more serious shade of purple. She had told him over and over again to calm down but he refused to listen and perhaps it had been the cocktail of booze and drugs in his system that had kept him in a state of constant agitation. When she'd started laughing, not so much at him but at the situation she had found herself in, he had lost all self-control and begun a tirade of abuse the likes of which she had never heard before. That had been about thirty seconds ago and now he was completely silent. Not because he had calmed down but because he had stopped breathing. She undid the ankle restraints first and then moved up to the ones on his wrists. When she had the last buckle loosened she watched helplessly as Margeir dropped to the floor like a sack of rocks.

She felt for a pulse in his wrist and then his neck like she had seen people do in the movies but could find nothing. He was gone. She could see it in his eyes. Whatever force it was that gave people the spark that was their life and soul it had left him and it wasn't coming back. She slumped on the bedroom floor beside him and let the tears overwhelm her. What on earth had she been thinking? That she would be able to solve the mystery of her sister's disappearance all on her own? Such foolishness had cost this strange man his life and she was now in some very serious trouble. Could she feasibly wipe clean any surfaces she had touched and leave? She thought hard trying to remember what she had touched since entering the apartment and realised that she had virtually no idea. She would have to wipe down every single surface in the place just to be sure. Then what? Let some unfortunate friend of his find him dead on his bedroom floor in a day or two? She didn't even know when someone would miss him and come looking for him. As much as the guy disgusted her she didn't hate him that much. On the other hand if she called the police she would have so much explaining to do that she may never get through it all. They would want to know what she had been doing there and any way she tried to explain it was going to look bad. Really, really bad.

Her mother and father would never be able to understand. They would think she was crazy and they would probably be right. What she had been trying to do would be seen as totally insane no matter how good her intentions had been. She even had his money in her wallet for God's sake. She pulled it out of her back pocket and thumbed through the notes he had handed her. She opened the top drawer of his bedside table and dropped them in with his underwear and socks. Just as she'd expected they were all the same. Dozens of pairs of underpants and dozens of pairs of socks. All identical and all folded and stacked neatly one on top of the other. Just like his shirts. Just like his shoes. Everything so ordered and organised that it creeped her out.

As she was closing her wallet again something caught her eye. It was the card Grímur had given her at the police station. Maybe this was the solution to her dilemma. She pulled it out and stared at it. This probably wasn't what he'd had in mind at the time when he'd slid the card across his desk but she was desperate. She grabbed her phone and dialled the number. It rang for what felt like an eternity so she just hung up. After looking around the living room and weighing up her options she decided not to give up that easily. She dialled his number again and waited. It rang and rang again and just as she was about to end the call for a second time it was finally answered albeit without anyone saying anything on the other end. Despite her pleas for help there was nothing but silence. In her frenzied state Inga Lind simply started getting things off her chest as fast as she could.

'I need your help, Grímur. All I wanted was to get him to tell me what had happened to Svandís but he must have had a weak heart or something. It couldn't have been my fault. Maybe he was using drugs. Yes, that's it. He was on drugs.'

There was a brief pause as Inga Lind waited for Grímur to say something but in the end she just ploughed on.

'I'm going to need you to come and help me. I'm in all sorts of trouble otherwise. Grímur?'

She started to lose her composure and the tears began to overwhelm her again. She hung her head between her knees and sobbed.

'All I wanted to do was help. Can you come and see me, Grímur?'

Still there was no answer.

'Grímur?'

Nothing.

She pulled her head up and stared at her phone. She put it back to her ear again and she could hear the line go dead.

'Fuck,' she screamed at the handset.

She dialled his number again but this time there was no answer.

'Fuck, fuck, fuck.'

She sat down on the bed and started to sob like a child until she was gasping for air with the effort of it all. After a couple of minutes she managed to regain a little composure and started to think about what she was going to do. Finding the truth behind her sister's disappearance now seemed a somewhat more distant concern than saving her own skin. It was just possible however unlikely that Svandís was still alive. Margeir definitely wasn't. And the longer she sat on the edge of his bed feeling sorry for herself the more likely it was that her own life would become unmanageable. Whatever she did next she would have to live with for the rest of her life and right now that felt like a very, very long time indeed. She tried to remember if anyone had actually seen her enter the building or Margeir's flat. Even though she had been pretty nervous on the way in she was pretty sure that no one had seen her.

That gave her options. Not many, but it gave her some. She thought back to how the two of them had got together. Even if she deleted her account on Fetish World there would still be a trail that led back to her somewhere. But only if they knew where to look in the first place. She had to take advantage of the fact that he lived on his own. She hunted hurriedly about the flat looking for his car keys. They were in a bowl in the kitchen next to the microwave oven. The next job was to find the car. It had to be parked nearby so she made her way back down the stairs being careful not to make too much noise even though it was unlikely that anyone would notice her over the racket coming from the street outside. It was late into just another party night in downtown Reykjavík and there were drunks staggering all over the place from one watering hole to another. She slipped out of the building and made her way around to the back where the small car park was hidden away from the street. It wasn't much more than a patch of gravel but it had room for a handful of cars. There were four flats in the building and three cars in the car park. There was one black four-wheel drive, one dark green Volvo and one metallic blue BMW. She stared at them a moment trying to guess which one was his and then pressed the key to see if any of them would unlock for her. As soon as she pressed the unlock button on the key the BMW beeped and flashed its lights at her. She breathed a sigh of relief and looked around to see if anyone had seen her but she seemed to be alone. Next to the cars was a door that led into the rear of the building. Inga Lind went through the keys one by one until she'd found the one she was looking for. The door was old and heavy and took some real effort to open but now she had decided what she was going to do she knew all too well that much more strenuous work lay ahead.

CHAPTER THIRTY-FIVE

Tuesday 3rd February

'Svandís sat on the end of Guðmundur's bed chewing her fingernails and staring at her feet. She couldn't understand what could possibly be taking him so long in the bathroom. She got up and made her way downstairs to the kitchen to get another drink even though there wasn't enough vodka in the world to get her excited about the prospect of getting into bed with this guy. She could deal with unattractive and even rude or a bit overly-physical but boring was another thing altogether. When she'd walked in through the front door she had been looking forward to having a bit of fun while Gylfi got some sleep in the car. Any hope of having a few laughs along the way had soon disappeared when she'd remembered just how dull this guy was.

She threw half a glass of vodka down her neck and poured herself another. She exhaled deeply as the burning liquid set fire to her throat and stomach. She could feel her head start to spin a little and decided it was time to get back upstairs just in case she needed to lie down in a hurry. Rather than holding on to any hope that she was going to enjoy herself she just wanted this over and done with now. Time had been dragging by ever since she'd arrived. It was almost as if he had been doing everything possible to drag the night out as long as possible. The silences were uncomfortable and the conversation, such as it was, left a great deal to be desired. The last thing she needed was some lonely git who wanted to talk to her as if they were friends but he hadn't even been talking all that much. She didn't know what was wrong with him. Back in the bedroom the phone on the bedside table rang just as she took a seat on the bed again. Guðmundur still hadn't reappeared so Svandís reached over and picked the receiver up. Hopefully this would be a good opportunity to get him out of the bathroom.

'There's been a slight change of plans,' the voice on the other end said before she'd even had a chance to say hello.

Svandís's face froze as she held the receiver to her ear. She recognised the voice on the other end of the line although she had no idea why he would be calling Guðmundur in the middle of the night. Or at all for that matter. She wanted nothing more than to slam the phone back down and bang on the bathroom door until Guðmundur told her what the hell was going on but she resisted the urge and bit her tongue. The voice on the other end didn't know it was her listening and she wanted to keep it that way.

'There's been a bit of a delay. I should be there in about forty minutes or so. Keep her there and keep her occupied and most importantly, keep her calm. If she suspects something's wrong there's no telling what she might do. I don't want any surprises tonight. Don't go doing anything stupid and everything will be fine. See you soon.'

The line went dead leaving Svandís sitting on the bed with her mouth hanging open. She could hear movement now from behind the bathroom door. She quickly replaced the receiver and walked back down the stairs as quickly and as quietly as she could. Behind her she could hear Guðmundur mumbling something or other from behind the bathroom door. From the living room she could hear the bathroom door open and Guðmundur call out her name. She looked about the room for somewhere to hide and then jumped over the back of the sofa. She dialled Gylfi's number on her mobile and prayed to anyone who might be listening that he would answer. The useless prick was probably stoned and sound asleep by now. As if to confirm her suspicions he sounded sleepy and disorientated when he finally answered the phone.

'They're going to kill me,' she whispered.

'What?'

She couldn't understand what part of that statement might have confused him and wished that he would get his cannabis-infused brain into gear. She wanted to scream at him but she knew she couldn't raise her voice or Guðmundur would be onto her in a flash.

'What's that again?' he said.

'I'm behind the sofa.'

'Behind the sofa? What the hell for?'

'He just called here. You've got to save me.'

'What? Who called? What are you talking about?'

'They're in it together. I can see that now.'

'Who's in what together? Can you speak up? I can hardly hear you.'

'If I'm still here when he gets here I'm dead. Do you understand what I'm saying?'

'No, Svandís, I don't understand what you're saying.'

'Just get here as fast as you can and get me out of here. I'm serious. If you don't you'll never see me again.'

There was silence on the other end of the line.

'Gylfi?'

Gylfi cleared his throat and sneezed.

'Okay, I'm coming.'

'Hurry.'

She could hear Guðmundur making his way down the stairs. There was no way Gylfi would be able to make it back to the house to help her in time even if he came as fast as he could.

Svandís froze as Guðmundur stopped at the bottom of the stairs and called out again. He mumbled something to himself and disappeared into the kitchen. While he was in there was her best and perhaps her only chance to get away. She stood up and looked towards the front door. From the kitchen she could hear the sound of ice cubes rattling in a glass and knew it was now or never. If she didn't take off now Guðmundur would stumble back out into the living room and catch her hiding like a thief behind his living room furniture. She couldn't for the life of her remember where she'd left her shoes and knew she'd have to do without them despite the temperature outside. She ran for the front door and grabbed at the handle. The door sprang open and without looking back she launched herself out into the freezing cold night. She looked one way and then the other before setting off towards the only set of lights she could see. She had to get help from somewhere and she had to get it now.

CHAPTER THIRTY-SIX

Thursday 12th February

Grímur opened his eyes and wondered for a moment where the hell he was. It didn't take long for it to dawn on him that he was in a hospital bed but exactly how he had ended up there was something of a mystery. He could recall trying to run across the ice on Öskjuhlíð and falling down. And getting up. And getting shot. And falling down again. He could remember the pain of the bullet hitting him and thinking he was surely about to die. A large white bandage on his torso gave away the location of the wound and his left arm was in plaster from his fingertips to his elbow. It was all coming back to him now. The collision of his wrist with the ice as he'd heard the dull snapping noise of the bones breaking. His phone skidding away across the frozen surface as he'd tried to get help. The sound of the gun firing. The sensation of being shot. He tried to piece together the moments after that but they were too blurred and scattered. What had happened to Janko and the girl? There were too many missing pieces and his head hurt just trying to think about it all. A nurse walked into his room and smiled at him.

'I've been wondering when you were going to say hello to us. It's good to see you back in the land of the living,' she said.

Grímur tried to speak but the pain made him grimace and gasp for air. The nurse reached out and pressed his head back into the pillow.

'Just relax and don't try to do too much. That includes talking unnecessarily. You're going to be very sore for a while. You'll find that if you stay perfectly still it will hurt the least. Let me get you something to take care of the pain. I'll do that and get the doctor and we'll both be back in just a minute.'

Grímur watched in silence as she hurried out of the room.

She hadn't been kidding. Every breath he took was a new adventure in pain that left his eyes rolling back in his head as if they were trying to find somewhere to hide until it was all over. Every movement no matter how tiny felt as if a knife had been left in his side and was being twisted slowly from side to side. He watched the doctor walk into the room and began to realise that he wasn't going to be able to do much of anything at all for quite some time. The doctor stopped at his bed and pulled out a syringe. He stuck it into the IV tube that was attached to Grímur's forearm and pressed down on the plunger. The cold liquid made its way into Grímur's vein and wound its way up his arm like a small cold snake. The relief he so badly needed flooded over him like a comforting blanket of snow.

'I will let your colleagues know you are back with us, Grímur. But first you must rest.'

They were the last words Grímur would hear for quite some time. The dark peaceful wave that had been threatening to wash over him in the moments since he'd been given the injection reared up off the ocean floor and swallowed him like a child. The next time he opened his eyes he saw Ævar sleeping in a chair next to his bed. Grímur stretched his right arm out as far as he could from his side and marvelled at the power of modern drugs. He took a drink from a plastic cup that was sitting on a tray next to his bed and drained it in one go. When it was empty he looked at his boss and tossed it into his lap. A broad grin grew across Ævar's face as he woke and their eyes met.

'Nice of you to finally make an appearance,' Ævar said. 'I was starting to think I'd have to move in here permanently but the doctor doesn't like me very much and my back's too old for this crap.'

Grímur smiled.

'It's good to see you too,' he croaked.

He tried to clear his throat but the effort involved was more painful than he would have liked. A concerned look passed over Ævar's face.

'They tell me you've got to take it easy. Really easy. They didn't say as much but I got the feeling that bullet got pretty close to signing you out permanently. I think you're in the lucky-to-be-alive club, Grímur.'

Grímur looked at the cup lying in his boss's lap. His mouth was so dry he could hardly pull his tongue from the roof of it. Ævar noticed what he was looking at and held the cup up.

'You need some more of this?' he asked.

Grímur nodded. Ævar thought his detective looked pale and fragile and very unlikely to be answering too many questions in the near future. As soon as the nurses heard that he was awake again they would swoop into the room and shoo Ævar away like a bothersome child as they'd tried to do a hundred times already.

'I'll get this filled for you in just a second but I just need to clear one thing up first. Those nurses can be a real pain in the arse when it comes to having me hanging around this place.'

Ævar stood up and leant over the bed. Grímur could feel his chest tighten as if giant hands were closing around his ribcage.

'Who was it that shot you?'

Grímur blinked once and then closed his eyes. Visions of shadows on ice flashed behind his eyes. The noise of the gunshot on Öskjuhlíð rang in his ears and he flinched as he felt the bullet hit him all over again. The painkilling injection the doctor had given him was starting to wear off in a big way. He could feel an invisible fist squeezing the breath out of his chest and he gasped for air sending a look of grave concern across Ævar's face.

'I really need to know. We've got that Norwegian in custody but I need you point the finger at him or we're going to have to let him go. Just nod your head if it was him. You know the guy I'm talking about. Vigeland.'

Ævar started nodding his head as if by doing so he would be able to coerce the desired response from Grímur but all the injured detective could do was reach out for his water cup even though he knew it was still empty. Ævar continued to stare at Grímur for some sign that his suspicions about Knut Vigeland were correct. As the doctor entered the room the look on his face changed from one of a calm and content man to that of an irritated one as soon as he saw Ævar towering over his patient. From his angle it looked as though Grímur was reaching for the water and Ævar was refusing to give it to him. He walked up behind Ævar and placed his hand on his shoulder.

'It is probably time you left him alone now, don't you think?'

It was an order to leave. Ævar was ready to argue his point with him but the look on the doctor's face dissuaded him from doing so. The doctor took the empty water cup from Ævar and moved in between the two men to examine Grímur. Ævar took a few steps back from the bed as he admitted defeat momentarily. He would be back soon though and he would get his answers no matter what this irritating doctor said. He had no other choice.

'I was just leaving anyway,' Ævar said. 'You'll let me know as soon as he's well enough to talk to me, won't you?'

As Ævar walked away from the bed the doctor pulled another syringe from one of his pockets and administered the painkiller into Grímur's IV. He then addressed Ævar without turning around to look at him.

'In a moment your friend will sleep again for a considerable time. I suggest you get some rest yourself and come back in a day or two.'

Ævar stared at the doctor's back trying to discern if he was kidding or not. He hadn't detected any trace of humour in his voice whatsoever but had to assume he was joking.

'I am presently conducting an investigation into the shooting of this police officer and the murder of another man. I'm not sure we have a day or two to spare.'

The doctor turned around to face him and spoke quietly but firmly.

'Your friend has been shot at close range in the chest. The bullet couldn't have done any more damage without actually killing him. He is alive right now because he is a very, very lucky man. Without the proper rest and care that luck could easily still run out. Your expectations of quizzing him about what happened are utterly unreasonable. By all rights you should be arranging his funeral right now instead of talking to me.'

As he paused to let his words sink in a smile appeared on his face again. Not the friendliest smile in the city on this or any other given day but a smile nonetheless.

'You need to give him sufficient time to heal. Then, and only then, will he be in a position to help you. Bringing his assailant to justice will be all the more satisfying if he lives to see it, don't you think?'

CHAPTER THIRTY-SEVEN

Wednesday 11th February

Auður Jökulsdóttir looked at the plain white A4 envelope on her desk and wondered if it was what she'd been waiting on for almost two weeks. She had received a cryptic text message last night from Halldór and now here it was. A mysterious sealed envelope left for her without so much as a name typed on the front of it. She smiled to herself and hung her coat on one of the hooks on the wall. If this was as big a deal as Halldór had been making out then this was indeed a moment to be savoured. She sauntered down the corridor to the lunch room nodding hello to a few colleagues along the way and poured herself a mug of coffee from the thermos. Part of her was excited about what the envelope might contain but part of her was sceptical too. Halldór was an old and dear friend but he was a politician first and foremost and as such couldn't be trusted.

As she made her way back to her office there was one question burning bright in her mind. What was in it for him? There had to be an angle of some kind he was working and more likely than not he was expecting her to do his dirty work for him. And if that was the case then the next question had to be why was she being given the dubious honour of uncovering this story? After sitting down at her desk again she stared at the envelope for a full minute as she waited for the answers to form in her head but soon realised they weren't going to come. No amount of intuition would help her out here. She pulled a small knife from her top drawer and slit the envelope open. Inside was a series of photographs of Jón Egill Hafsteinsson, the Prime Minister of Iceland at a meeting with several other men whose faces she knew also. They were known colloquially as the 'Quota Mafia'. The men behind Iceland's biggest industry – fishing.

The most valuable commodity in all of Iceland was the elusive fishing quotas. The licences without which you were not allowed to fish in Icelandic waters. They controlled the boats that were allowed to drop their nets off the coast of Iceland and the amount of fish they were allowed to land. Without these precious pieces of paper no one was allowed to take part in the most productive gold rush Iceland had ever experienced. For the people who owned them they were licences to print money but the men who had them weren't satisfied with that. They wanted more as greedy men always did. They spent entire days looking for and exploiting loopholes in the tax legislation of Iceland, as well as every other country they dealt with, to find ways to not pay their fair share. And they were good at it. They ran a multitude of businesses across Europe and Asia that somehow made little or no money and yet these men were the richest men in Iceland. And that was because they had help from above.

They greased the palms of those in power and then looked on as those whose job it was to hold everyone equally accountable turned a blind eye. The closer to the top you got the more twisted it became. And now she had something in her possession that was going to blow it wide open. Along with the photographs were three mini-cassettes. The sort used in Dictaphones and small portable recorders. It didn't take a Pulitzer Prize winner to figure out what she was going to hear on those tapes. The suspicions of the nation were about to finally be proved beyond any reasonable doubt. She slid the photographs back into the envelope and locked them in the bottom drawer of her desk. Taking a quick look around to make sure no one had been watching her she finished her coffee and put the tapes into her jacket pocket. She had a portable voice recorder at home which played that particular size of tape and as far as she was concerned the rest of the day was now hers to take off. She stopped briefly at the front desk to let the receptionist know she wouldn't be back and that if anyone wanted her they could get her on her mobile. She was going to be busy though and didn't want to be disturbed unless it was really urgent. She would be at home working on a new and very special project.

CHAPTER THIRTY-EIGHT

Tuesday 3rd February

As Svandís approached the house she tripped on a rock in the dark and cried out in pain. She was making very slow progress without her shoes and now she had hit one of her toes so hard it felt as if it was broken but she had no choice but to keep on going. When Guðmundur discovered she was gone he would be furious. She'd half expected to see his headlights in the darkness as he searched for her but so far there had been no indication that she had been followed. Not yet anyway. Gylfi would be looking for her too. He would be on his way to Guðmundur's house with any luck and hopefully he would distract him long enough for her to get away.

The last part of her journey threatened to be the hardest. Every step she took over the rough ground did more and more damage to her feet and her toe was so sore now she doubted if she could actually continue. All she wanted to do was stop and rest but she knew that wasn't going to help her escape and the alternative didn't bear thinking about. There was no choice but to soldier on. By the time she got to the front door she was ready to collapse so that's just what she did as soon as she'd announced her arrival with a few frantic knocks. She was too exhausted to even look up when the door finally opened but when it did she grinned like a small child and tilted her head towards the all too familiar voice.

'Svandís?'

She stared up at the disbelieving face of Jón Páll Sigmundsson.

'Jón Páll. I can't believe I'm actually happy to see you again. Since when do you live all the way out here?'

'I'm semi-retired now and I prefer the peace and quiet of Borgarnes. Why is it that every time I see you there's something wrong with you? Can I at least help you up?'

Svandís told him that he most certainly could and then allowed him to pick her up by the armpits and drag her into the house. When he'd deposited her on the sofa he went back to close the front door and then headed to the kitchen to make them both some tea. Once the water had boiled he made his way back to the living room with the cups and put them down on the table. He folded his arms and cast an appraising eye over his guest.

'You're in quite a state my girl. Sadly it looks as though my prediction about our next meeting couldn't have been much closer to the mark if you'd tried to do this to yourself. Where on earth are your shoes?'

'I need your help.'

Jón Páll scratched the grey stubble on his chin.

'Yes. It would seem so.'

He bent down to give the teabags a stir and then busied himself squeezing them, dumping them on a spare saucer and then adding a little milk.

'Please don't give me one of your sermons. Someone's trying to kill me,' she said.

'For God's sake, Svandís. The stories you come up with you'd think your life wasn't dramatic enough as it is.'

A mobile phone in the kitchen started ringing and vibrating against the hard bench surface. Jón Páll handed Svandís one of the cups and looked over his shoulder in the direction of the noisy electronic interruption.

'Now what? Excuse me, I won't be a minute.'

He turned and walked back into the kitchen to answer the phone. From where she was sitting Svandís could only hear one side of the conversation. But it was enough.

'Hello. What do you want? … Yes, of course I understand but…'

Jón Páll's head suddenly appeared around the corner from the kitchen and then disappeared just as quickly again. Svandís could hear the kitchen door closing behind him but his voice could still be heard behind it even if it was a little fainter now.

'You can and will do whatever you want the vast majority of the time but not in my house,' he said.

Svandís sat upright. Her confusion as to who could possibly being calling Jón Páll in the middle of the night turning to terror as it sank in as to who was on the other end of the line. She looked down at her sore, damaged feet and swore.

'I agree completely but remember what I said,' came Jón Páll's voice from the kitchen. 'Not in my house.'

Svandís was up on her feet and wincing in pain before Jón Páll had even ended the call. By the time he'd reappeared from the kitchen his front door was wide open and she was gone. Back out into the cold dark night once more. Limping badly and lost almost as soon as she'd taken her first steps she could feel tears welling in her eyes as she started to realise just how desperate her situation really was. The night seemed almost unbelievably quiet but somewhere in the distance she could hear the ocean. Waves breaking against the shore just beyond her somewhere in the dark.

CHAPTER THIRTY-NINE

Friday 13th February

Grímur found that his eyes were opening and then closing again without his consent and with alarming regularity. It was impossible to tell what time of day it was or even what day it might have been. Each time he woke he noticed slight changes around the room. His water cup would be missing and then the next time it would be back in its place next to his bed. Sometimes full and sometimes empty. Occasionally he could hear voices from the corridor outside and other times it was so quiet that all he could hear was himself breathing. It sounded like the sawing of wet stubborn wood deep down in his chest. And it hurt. Every breath he took hurt. Sometimes the smell of hospital disinfectant would be nearly overpowering and then other times there would be just the faintest trace of perfume in the air as if one of his guardian angels had just left the room before he opened his eyes.

During one of his more lucid moments he noticed that the television set in the corner of the room was turned on albeit with the sound off. The evening news was on and the news was big. The scandal everyone had been talking about under their breath for the last ten years had finally dug its way to the top and broken through the winter ice. The Prime Minister had finally been caught with his hand in the biggest cookie jar of them all, namely the illegal allocation of fishing quotas to companies owned by friends and by friends of friends of his and his newspaper-owning buddies. Instead of just whispers around the corridors of power there were now recorded phone calls and secret video footage too. It had been revealed after a secret year-long undercover investigation and the shit had really hit the fan. This time there would be no cover-ups, pay-offs or hiding behind powerful friends. This time the prosecutions would stick and some very wealthy people would be going to jail.

The nation's most lucrative industry had been used to make a huge amount of money for a tiny percentage of the population for a long time. That had never been much of a secret. It was the lengths they had gone to in order to avoid paying tax in their native land that had thousands of people protesting outside the Alþingi today. Companies had been set up to organise the transportation and distribution of Icelandic fish out of the country and around the world and somehow nearly all of them managed to run at or very close to a loss. The fish would then be sold on to other companies that were owned by Icelandic concerns but which all also ran at carefully-supervised losses or made extremely small profits. It wasn't until the fish reached their final destinations whether that might be in Russia or China or elsewhere that a profit was finally made. And it was normally a huge one that went virtually untaxed in deals that had been thrashed out with the local governments of the countries involved. Where exactly that money went to no one was sure yet but the hunt was well underway to find it in Caribbean and Swiss bank accounts.

It had all been done with the complicity of the Prime Minister so he and his friends could also become wealthy beyond their wildest dreams while the rest of the country struggled to pay back the mortgages and loans that had been hanging over their heads since the crash of 2008. The crowds gathered in Austurvöllur Square were demanding the removal of the entire government but were unlikely to get their wish. As far as anyone could see at this point in time he had acted alone and without the knowledge of his fellow MPs. Jón Egill Hafsteinsson had resigned amid the furore and was now presumably laying low and planning his next move. There had been no delay in appointing his successor.

His resignation had been announced at midnight and by nine o'clock the next morning Halldór Valdimarsson had stepped into the breach for his party and his country. The face of the ex-Minister of Finance and Economic Affairs beamed through the television sets of nearly everyone in the land. The smile on his face said it all. The cat had cream all over his whiskers.

He had wiggled his way to the very top and was now basking in the glory of what would undoubtedly be a brighter future. For him, not Iceland. The fishing companies would be taken apart and resold but chances were he and his friends would know the new owners and probably know them very well. The Quota Mafia would live on in Iceland no matter who was in charge of the country. The money involved was such that governments could be bought and sold with it. One kingpin was simply being replaced by another. In a few days' time the crowds in Austurvöllur Square would dissipate and business as usual would resume in the back rooms of the Alþingi. One naughty boy had been caught cooking the books and another was waiting in the wings until no one was looking and then he would be at it too. Grímur closed his eyes again and wondered what the country was coming to. If this was all they had to look forward to then he wasn't at all sure if he wanted back in the game. Sometimes it felt as if the match was fixed before you even took to the field.

CHAPTER FORTY

Friday 6th February

Despite being a rather slight individual Margeir weighed a lot more than Inga Lind had bargained for. She'd removed the dog collar and redressed him but that had been the easy part and now his body felt as if he was made of clay as she dragged him across the living room floor. She had tried rolling him up in the expensive-looking rug that decorated his bedroom floor but there had been a couple of issues with that idea. It was what she'd seen people do on crime shows from America but it wasn't as practical as it looked on television. First of all she had to lift the corner of the huge bed to get the rug loose and then when she finally had him rolled up in it he was just too big and too heavy to lift. On top of that she didn't have any idea what she'd do with the rug once they'd reached their final destination. So the rug went back where it'd come from and she resorted to the old-fashioned approach of picking him up by his armpits and dragging him backwards down the stairs like a stubborn old sheep.

By the time she'd reached the bottom of the stairwell she was exhausted and dripping with sweat. All she wanted to do was sit down and get her breath back but she had a body to hide and the quicker it was out of the way the better. Leaving Margeir momentarily at the bottom of the stairs Inga Lind peered out the door to ensure no one was around to see the last leg of his journey into the back of the BMW. It would be just her luck that at the exact moment she decided to drag him to the car some drunk would take the opportunity to relieve himself on the back wall of the building. She had already heard one group of guys doing just that as she made her way down the stairs with her reluctant cargo. The amount of noise they made suggested they didn't care who saw them pissing all over the place like a bunch of animals.

Once she was convinced there would be no such interruption she opened the back of the BMW and dragged Margeir across the gravel. It took her three goes to get him into the boot and she was sure she was going to get caught but she finally managed to tuck his knees up and slam the boot shut. She was beginning to feel a little sick. Not just from the fact that she'd just dragged a body down three flights of stairs but the realisation that what she was doing was so very, very risky. She dashed back upstairs and grabbed the bottle of bourbon from the drinks cabinet and took a slug. She was going to need something to calm her nerves when this was all done and dusted, if not a little sooner, so she decided to take the bottle with her.

Inga Lind took care not to break the speed limit at any point on the way out of town. The last thing she needed was to be pulled over by some zealous cop with nothing better to do on a Friday night than hand out tickets. She headed up Hverfisgata and turned onto Snorrabraut before following Miklabraut all the way out of town. She tried not to think about what was in the boot but it was hard and the more she tried not to think about Margeir the more she worried about what would happen if she had an accident or engine trouble of some sort. It was impossible to relax so she helped herself to some more bourbon and hoped for the best.

By the time she'd taken the turn-off just past Mosfellsbær she began to feel more relaxed and was starting to believe she might just get away with it after all. She'd done a pretty good job of wiping down the surfaces she knew she'd definitely touched at Margeir's place and had washed and put away the glass she'd drunk from. She hadn't bothered hiding the drugs because she thought they would only help add to the picture of the despairing loner she was hoping to paint for those who would eventually force entry into his flat to investigate. The more troubled and drug-fucked he appeared to have been the easier it would be for people to believe how he'd met his end. That was the plan anyway and she was feeling confident now that it would work. As she cruised past Þingvallavatn she even put some music on the stereo. As she switched the CD player on the Kings of Leon blasted out of the surround-sound speakers at her making her jump a little. When she'd got the volume under control she started enjoying herself and was soon tapping on the steering wheel along with the songs. Before she knew it she was turning right into the lower car park at one of the country's most popular tourist attractions. As she stepped out of the car and stretched her tired limbs she could hear the roar of the mighty Gullfoss in the background. It wouldn't be long now and it would all be over. The worst night of her life so far, and hopefully ever, would be behind her. The thought almost made her smile as she opened the boot and lifted Margeir by his armpits once again. She wasn't going to miss lugging his dead weight around that was for sure. She struggled across the car park and over the small fence to the edge of the ravine that contained the Hvítá River and led from the falls a full fifteen miles all the way to the Atlantic Ocean on the south coast.

Many a lost soul had thrown themselves off these cliffs into the fury of the river just below the falls knowing that they would never have to deal with their lives ever again. This was what she was counting on people believing when Margeir was eventually found. It normally took a few days before bodies showed up such was the power of the river. She huffed and puffed over the final few yards until she was so close to the edge that she feared for her own safety. She almost felt as if she should say something before dropping the lecherous creep over the edge but the right words eluded her and she decided he could make the trip without a send-off. She had nothing nice to say about him anyway. With one last almighty effort she lifted the top half of his body and prepared to drop him over the edge but as she pulled with all her might Margeir somehow got caught on her shoe. She looked down expecting to see that she had inadvertently stood on his trousers without noticing but got the shock of her life when she saw his hand slowly tightening itself around her ankle. His eyes were wide open and he was reaching out to her with his other hand while trying to say something but failing. His lips moved but all that came out was an intermittent wheezing. His face contorted in pain as though he had been stabbed. Inga Lind screamed and dropped him onto the ground. She tried shaking his hand off her ankle but he refused to let go. The hideous wheezing continued as he continued to attempt some form of speech. Inga Lind looked around the car park and across the huge divide to the falls beyond and made her decision quickly. She prised his fingers off her ankle one by one and stood on his hand until he had little choice but to ball it into a fist. Standing well away from his hands and as close to the edge of the ravine as she dared Inga Lind grabbed Margeir by his shirt collar and pulled him towards the chasm. His weight crunched against the gravel as he inched closer to the edge. He'd given up trying to speak and his concentration was on getting his fingers working again.

As she pulled him the last few inches towards the edge and beyond the event horizon of his life he flailed about trying to grasp onto something and his balance shifted slowly but irreversibly. Inga Lind let go and stepped away from the edge. She held her hands to her chest and let gravity do the rest of the work for her. Something dark and panicked clicked in Margeir's eyes as he realised that the earth was no longer where it should have been beneath him and his mouth opened as if he were about to scream. As it was not a sound escaped him as he tipped over the edge and plummeted towards the cliff face and the icy torrent below. Inga Lind peered over the cliff to see where he'd gone but he'd vanished without a trace through the dark and onto an icy ledge some sixty feet below. He made a dull thud as he hit the ice and slid into the river beyond. She crossed herself and said a little prayer that she might be saved the worst of what was on offer where she was now headed in the afterlife. She was still convinced that he knew what had happened to Svandís and nothing was going to change that. Men like him deserved everything they got. He had been a vile despicable human being and she wasn't going to lose too much sleep over what she'd just done. She was going to the same place he would wind up though. She was in no doubt about that.

Without waiting around a minute longer than she had to Inga Lind got back in Margeir's BMW to drive it back to Reykjavík. She still had about an hour and a half left to go before this nightmare was over. She would have much preferred to leave the car at the scene but that would have left her stranded in the middle of nowhere very much in need of a lift home. She was better off taking the car back to his building's car park and leaving it there. Let the police worry about the finer details of his suicide. As she put the car into gear and turned the stereo off so she could have a bit of peace and quiet on the way home her phone rang. It nearly made her jump out of her skin. Who could possibly be calling her at this time? She scanned the car park for any other vehicles but knew she was alone even if it now felt as if someone had been watching her all along. An overwhelming feeling of guilt began to wrap itself around her as if someone had just thrown a net over her head. She turned the car's interior light on and fumbled about on the passenger seat for the phone. Although she had no intention of answering the call she needed to see who the caller was. Just a quick look at the caller ID and she would be on her way. It was a ridiculous time to be calling and whoever and whatever it was could wait until morning. She was going to need some sleep before she would be able to deal with anybody. Once she'd extracted the phone from her handbag she turned it over in her hand and checked the screen. It was Guðrún, her mother. Alarm bells rang in her head. She had never called at this hour before. Ever. Something was wrong. Really wrong. She answered the call trying not to sound panicked.

'Hello?'

'They found her body. I'm so sorry to wake you with this but I didn't want you to see it on the news in the morning. A fisherman found her in the water somewhere near Borgarnes. Your father's identified her. It looks like she hurt her leg badly and drowned. I don't know what else to say. I'm so sorry to do this to you. I didn't want to but the thought of you finding out from someone else made me pick up my phone.'

Inga Lind became aware of just how quiet the world was. On the other end of the line she could hear her mother sobbing into the phone. She wanted to be able to say something that would comfort her but the words she needed to find were lost in the jumble in her head.

'Mum. It's okay. I'm glad it was you who told me. I know how difficult it must have been for you to call. I'm so sorry too, you have no idea.'

Inga Lind burst into tears.

'I thought someone had killed her,' Inga Lind sobbed.

'They're saying she drowned. She broke one of her legs somehow.'

'Do they know how it happened?'

'No. Your sister lived her life the way she wanted to and we always knew something like this might happen. I've been waiting for it for a long time but it's still a shock. Go back to sleep now and come to see us as soon as you wake up. Your father's very upset.'

Guðrún's voice tapered off into silence that was only interrupted by the occasional sniff. Inga Lind wanted to say something comforting but all she could think about was confessing her terrible act of stupidity and this was definitely not the time to be doing that.

'I'll be over soon. I doubt I'll be able to sleep now anyway. We'll get through this together.'

'I'm going to go now. I'm completely exhausted and he'll be home soon. I don't know what's keeping him at the morgue. I'll go put some coffee on and I'll see you soon. You will be okay won't you?'

Inga Lind turned and looked out over where Margeir had disappeared into the darkness.

'I hope so, Mum.'

CHAPTER FORTY-ONE

Tuesday 3rd February

Svandís cursed as she hobbled over the uneven ground and away from Jón Páll's house as fast as she could. It wasn't long before she reached the water's edge and had to stop dead in her tracks. She hadn't really been paying attention to where she was going and now she had come to what amounted to a dead end. Getting as far away from Jón Páll's place as quickly as possible had been her only priority but now she was faced with a whole new conundrum. To each side of her was a rocky, inhospitable shoreline and in front of her an ocean cold enough to kill her in minutes should she be stupid enough to get into it. The rocks on either side of her were all different shapes and sizes. Some jagged and rough and some worn smooth by centuries of hammering swells and tides. She felt her way across them in the dark using her fingers to judge which ones would be safe to clamber across and which ones wouldn't. She climbed up onto one of them and found that it was much easier to stand on than the rough ground she had been limping across up until this point. She clambered from rock to rock wondering where it was exactly she was heading and whether she should call Gylfi again and try to describe to him where she was. That would be something of a long shot as she didn't have a clue how she'd got where she was and trying to describe it to him would be endlessly frustrating for them both. He would be looking for her by now but would have no chance of finding her without real directions. He would have received no cooperation from Guðmundur whatsoever and probably wouldn't have the first clue where to look for her after that.

Svandís pulled her phone from her pants pocket and just as she was about to dial she slipped. The phone went flying from her hand as she tried to break her fall. Her hands hit cold stone and she slid sideways down between two of the enormous boulders.

She flailed about with her arms as she tried to grab onto something but she was surrounded by nothing but cold dark air that whistled past her ears as she fell. As she twisted sideways her right leg hit something and snapped. She didn't hear it break but she could feel the bone give way just above the ankle and force its way through the skin like an old rough knife. Her scream was lost in the spray of a wave breaking against the rocks. She came to rest with her disabled leg wedged between the two boulders and the rest of her hanging upside down into the crevice below. She was trapped and in more pain than she'd ever been in before in her life as the blood rushed to her head and pounded behind her eyes. She reached out in the dark for the one thing that could save her life but her phone was gone and with it any hope she might have had of surviving the fall.

Wave after wave crashed against her face as she was slowly pulled one way and then the other by the surge of the tide. Her screams became sobs and then the tears came in silence as she embraced the knowledge that she was going to die. Her luck had finally run out and there was no one to rescue her this time. A jarring pain tore through her whole body as the surf finally worked her loose and she was sucked under the water as it ran between the overhanging rocks and back out to sea.

CHAPTER FORTY-TWO

Two years earlier

Fatima Mohammed Abdullah sat staring out the window at the snow starting to drift across the city skyline. It occurred to her that despite the horrid cold and the disgusting job she had been given in order to pay for her food and board she had a feeling she was going to miss something about the place. If you had asked her what it was exactly she would have shook her head and laughed at you.

'I don't know for the life of me,' she murmured to herself. 'What could I possibly miss about you?'

She shook her head to clear the thought and went back to what she had been doing before being so rudely interrupted by such sentimental notions. She unwrapped the third tiny package and let its contents slip onto the table in front of her. She had more than enough to do the job now. While there might just be something she was going to miss it would be fair to say that this place had not turned out the way she had hoped. Instead of setting her soul free as she had hoped it might it had only put more pressure on her heart than it could bear. More than she was any longer willing to take. The hope she had arrived with had somehow slipped through her hands and settled in its own dark place. That was what she was about to do now. Settle in her own dark place. She heard Moli's bell ring and the next thing she knew his head popped through her open bedroom window and he climbed through onto her windowsill. Moli was her only friend. An elegant slender cat with a short off-white coat and a pale grey face and paws. She spent what little money she had left over from her food shopping to buy harðfiskur to feed him. He loved the horrible smelly stuff and would chase her around the room relentlessly to get his paws on it. Not today though.

She didn't have any to feed him today so he just sat on the windowsill and watched her go about her business. She looked up at the plastic clock on the far wall and watched the slowly creeping hand come around one more time. She cooked the three packets in a little scoop of tinfoil and loaded the syringe. The same one she'd been using for the last two weeks. She hadn't bothered with any precautions lately and would have caught hepatitis or worse sooner or later. She tied her arm off and looked back at the clock on the wall. The hand fell and fell, tumbled down the face only to rise again once more up the other side. Soon enough, she thought. Soon enough it comes around to weigh us further down. That was what had happened to her. She had simply started to carry more than she could bear. Some loads were easier to maintain than others. At first all she had wanted was to get as far away from Mogadishu and the horrors of the militias there as she could but her saviour had become her jailer and it wasn't long before she wanted to go back home. By then of course it was too late. She had run too far and put too much distance between where she had been born and where she was now destined to die. By the time she'd changed her mind she could beg them all she wanted to send her back home, it was never going to happen. Not in a hundred years. She had got exactly what she wanted and now all she wanted was to die.

Even though she was still able to force a smile across her face a tear rolled unassisted down her cheek. She couldn't have felt like more of a failure if she'd tried. Moli turned his attention away from the snow falling in the garden and looked down at Fatima as he heard a sob that broke the precious silence of the room. He jumped down from the windowsill and sat on the table as she slid first to one side against the empty bookcase and then fell gracelessly to floor. The world had finally stolen all it could from her.

CHAPTER FORTY-THREE

Saturday 14th February

Ævar looked across the interview room at his unexpected visitor. He took a seat opposite him and shook his head rather than starting off the conversation with words. The guy's name was Aron Matthíasson and he looked as though he had missed a few nights' sleep of late. Every night of every week for the last month or so. The big black rings under his eyes only accentuated the bloodshot sclera. He was a part-time receptionist and barman at the hotel where Knut Vigeland had been staying when he'd been arrested. He had come forward out of the blue sky this morning with some news for them relating to the cases they were presently investigating.

All through his interrogation Knut had said nothing about what he'd supposedly been doing the night Óli Þór had been murdered and Grímur had been shot and now, from out of nowhere, a witness had come forward to give their only suspect for those two crimes an alibi. Ævar couldn't help but think that the whole world was conspiring to drive him crazy. If this strung-out excuse of a man stuck to his ridiculous story then the whole investigation would grind to a halt and there would be some nasty ramifications for Ævar if that were to happen. First off they would be obliged to release Knut from custody and then it would quickly become apparent that Ævar had put all his eggs in one basket. He had no other suspects for either crime. He had been convinced, and still was for that matter, that Knut Vigeland's arrival followed one week later by two of the most astonishing crimes the city had ever seen were events that were linked by the same motive. The Norwegian had come here with a specific task to carry out. The death on the building site had been the first item on his agenda but there were still pieces of the puzzle to be put together regarding Grímur being shot.

He had been sent out that night to investigate a completely unrelated crime and had somehow got caught up in the perfect storm that the Norwegian's presence in the city had created. Ævar wasn't sure what the connection was but he was sure that one existed. And now this scrawny little bleary-eyed prick was going to fuck everything up because someone had made him an offer he just couldn't turn down. They had either offered him a truckload of money or threatened him with a beating he would not walk away from. Either way he was on the verge of royally screwing everything up for the police and Ævar in particular. Letting Knut walk free would not only be a personal affront but would put the skids well and truly under his career. It was the last thing he needed right now and Aron Matthíasson was about to cop the full brunt of his frustrations. He slapped a typed statement down on the table with the palm of his hand as hard as he could next to a photo taken of Knut just after he was arrested and watched Aron jump a little in his seat.

'Do you seriously expect me to believe this shit?' Ævar yelled.

Aron stared back across the table at him but said nothing. He looked like he could quite happily fall asleep right there and then in the interview room. Ævar wanted to reach across the table and slap him across the face. He was on the verge of making Aron submit a blood and urine test for analysis such was his conviction that the guy was high on drugs of some kind or other.

'If you think I'm going to believe that one week after these crimes were committed, crimes that everybody in the country heard about on the news at the time, you've just remembered the guy we've been holding all this time was in your bar that night then you must be more stupid than you look. And that prospect boggles the imagination. How on earth do you expect anybody to believe that it's only just occurred to you to mention this to us?'

Aron fidgeted with his hands in his lap and rubbed his eyes to wake himself up.

'I heard about it at the time but didn't really think too much about it. The photos they had on TV weren't of the guy you were holding they were of the guy who was shot and the other guy who got burned. They were the faces everyone saw. Not this guy.'

He pushed the photo of Knut across the table towards Ævar a little way and then thought better of it and pulled it back to its original position.

'I know this is a real pain for you guys but you don't want an innocent guy to go to jail do you?' Aron asked.

Ævar studied Aron's face for any hint of a smile but luckily for Aron he couldn't find one.

'This guy's no more innocent than Charles Manson was. And twice as dangerous. You saw what happened to that guy on Einholt. He was tied up and barbequed in an oil drum.'

Aron shook his head.

'It wasn't him.'

'It wasn't him?'

'What I mean is, it couldn't have been him. He was in the bar.'

Aron shook his head again but couldn't lift his gaze from the table top. Ævar thumped the table so hard it actually leapt off the ground a little.

'Look at me when you tell me these lies,' he yelled.

Aron looked up at Ævar and shrunk back in his chair as far as he could without pushing it backwards. The fear was written large across his face. He looked disgusted at something and Ævar was guessing that it was probably himself. The only hope he had of getting this idiot to tell the truth was to make him more afraid of Ævar Rafnsson than he was of the thugs who had put the fear of God into him but it was a big ask and he knew it.

'Listen. I know you've been put under enormous pressure to come forward and make this statement,' Ævar said as he flicked at the printed statement with one of his fingers. 'If you've done this against your will we can easily take that into consideration as soon as you tell me that your statement is made up and that Knut Vigeland wasn't in the bar in your hotel on the night in question.'

He waited for a shake of the head or some form of tacit agreement but there wasn't one forthcoming.

'The easiest thing for you to do right now is what you're doing and I can't blame you for that but there are a few things you need to understand. By doing this you are compromising an extremely serious investigation. And I can't stress that part enough. A police officer has been shot and another man has been attacked, set alight and burned to death. These are not minor crimes and the investigation into them will not just go away because of your statement no matter what you or your friends think.'

Aron shuffled his feet and looked back down at the floor again. For a moment he looked as if he was about to say something but in the end he kept whatever it was to himself.

'So you're sticking to this ridiculous story then?'

Aron nodded without looking up from the floor.

'I said look at me when you answer me,' Ævar screamed.

He stood up and grabbed the table with both hands and shook it with all his strength. That got Aron's attention and a look of fear and confusion passed across his face. It didn't last long though and was slowly replaced by one of a slightly shaken but growing confidence.

'You shouldn't be doing that. I've every right to come forward and make this statement and not have to fear for my personal safety,' Aron said.

'Did they tell you to say that too?'

'Who?'

'Whoever it was who put you up to this,' Ævar shouted even louder than before. Rather than tempering his anger as he knew he should he seemed intent on letting it boil over. 'You didn't come up with this late-breaking news story all on your own. We're going to talk to every guest who stayed at your hotel that night and see how many remember seeing your Norwegian friend in the bar. My guess is that not one of them will recall seeing him there and that's going to make your story look like what it really is. A load of horseshit.'

Aron shook his head.

'No. No it won't. I think you'll find that someone is going to remember him sitting there drinking on his own all night and I think that will make you look pretty stupid, not me. You're just going to have to face the fact that you've got it all wrong on this one. You shouldn't be getting angry with me because you've arrested the wrong guy. People make mistakes all the time. Why can't you just admit that you've made one here?'

Ævar felt as though his head was about to explode. Who did this cocksure kid think he was?

'I'm going to make you regret this, Aron. I am going to take a personal interest in you from now on and that means I won't be leaving you alone for one second and I can guarantee that you're not going to enjoy that one bit. I don't know what these guys offered you or threatened you with but whatever it is you're going to wish you'd never agreed to it. I couldn't care less about some small-time drug dealer getting his head split open and set alight but one of my officers has been shot and the guy who did that is not going to get away with it. There is no chance of that happening and you're not going to get away with this either. You're going to wind up in Litla Hraun with your Norwegian pals. It'll be a reunion you won't forget for a long time that's for damn sure.'

Ævar paused to take a much-needed breath and then tried as hard as he could to smile at the now rather troubled-looking Aron. His arrogance had finally deserted him and after feeling quite sure of himself up until this point he now looked deflated and nervous. You could almost see the wheels turning over in his head as he played out all the worst-case scenarios in his mind.

'Well that's all for now but I wouldn't get too comfortable if I were you. We've got quite a bit of work ahead of us if we're going to track down all these guests of yours so I suggest you take some time to reflect on what your life is going to be like if none of them share your recollection of that night. Because if they don't then you and I are going to get to know each other even better than we do right now and I can assure you that will be much more fun for me than it will be for you. It's time for you to weigh up the options you have left in front of you and decide which one is going to be the least unpleasant for you because that's the only sort of choice you're going to get to make from here on in.'

CHAPTER FORTY-FOUR

Saturday 7th February

Inga Lind had started crying as soon as her mother wrapped her warm arms around her. The tears poured out of her and down her mother's cheek in a gentle warm stream. Guðrún comforted her the only way she knew how. With a mother's unconditional love and soft words in her ear. She knew all too well that the girls had had their differences in the past and plenty of them but losing her only sibling was going to be tough on Inga Lind. Svandís hadn't exactly been an ideal sister or daughter but she had been all that they had had.

When the two of them had composed themselves a little Guðrún went to make them all something hot to drink. Coffee for Finnbogi who had sat as silently as ever since coming home from seeing their other daughter's body in the morgue. He had been so upset that he hadn't been able to get to sleep and was now exhausted. Tea for herself even though she hardly ever drank the stuff. Her logic was that it would help calm her down and that she would need to get some sleep later on even if it was only for a few hours. Someone was going to have to keep the family together in the coming days and that job would undoubtedly fall to her. She was going to have to be the captain of this troubled vessel and to do that job she was going to need her rest. That way even if Finnbogi and Inga Lind couldn't face the world she would be able to do it for them. That's what mothers and wives were for.

Inga Lind didn't want either coffee or tea and asked for something stronger. Guðrún baulked at the idea of alcohol being consumed at such a time, she held it responsible for the beginning of Svandís's decline, but relented when she saw just how upset her daughter was. She warmed some brandy and added a little honey and a slice of lemon to it along with a dash of tea for good measure. She had heard a friend talk of such a drink.

Despite his cup of coffee Finnbogi didn't last long. His night had been a long and arduous one. All he'd said to his wife was that no one should ever be expected to do what he had done that evening. Parents weren't supposed to have to bury their children, it was one of those unwritten laws that when broken left you angry at the one who made those laws in the first place. He was angry at the man who had called him and asked him to come down to the morgue. He was angry at every lowlife scumbag who had ever sold his daughter drugs. He was angry at whoever she had been running away from when she'd fallen into the freezing water at Borgarnes. But most of all he was angry at God. He was the one who was supposed to make sure things like this didn't happen to good people. That probably wasn't the case but Finnbogi felt that if you went to church and lived a wholesome and virtuous life then you should be spared days like today. Without a word he got up and went to bed leaving Guðrún and Inga Lind to their own devices. He'd simply had enough for one day.

Inga Lind finished her brandy and went into the kitchen to pour herself another. In the living room Guðrún was trying to busy herself tidying this and that but Inga Lind could see that she was just doing her best to keep moving rather than face up to what had happened to her family. Inga Lind downed her drink and went back out into the living room. She pulled Guðrún away from what she was doing and gave her a hug.

'Go to bed, Mum. You've done enough for today. Go get some rest and I'll see you in the morning.'

Guðrún buried her head into her daughter's neck and nodded. Inga Lind could feel her mother's silent tears rolling down her chest.

'You're right. I'm not doing anyone any good staying up this late. We'll have a lot to do tomorrow I would imagine.'

Guðrún pulled away and tried to put on a brave face. She didn't look very brave though. She looked broken. As much as she had been trying to prepare herself for the worst, the news that Svandís's body had finally been found had hit her hard. All of them had seen it coming for quite some time now but it didn't make it any easier to take when it finally arrived. The girl had put them all through more hard times than any of them cared to remember. She seemed to hit the self-destruct button early in life and it seemed at times that it was almost a race to the finish line for her. A race she had now won.

Inga Lind watched as her mother nodded again and held one of her hands up in an admission of defeat albeit a temporary one. She'd be back to fight another day just as soon as she'd recharged her batteries. In the coming weeks and months she would have to hold the family together as it creaked and groaned at the seams and joins as it tried time and time again to pull itself apart. She would be the glue, the bind and the nails but right now she needed her rest just like everyone else so she hung her head and said goodnight to Inga Lind before heading off to join her husband.

Inga Lind was in no mood for rest even if her body was exhausted to the point of breaking and she was ready to collapse in a heap on the floor. She was trying to get to grips with too many things at once and she didn't know what to feel bad about first. On the one hand she was trying to understand the grim fact that she would never see her angry, troubled sister again and she just couldn't imagine what it was going to be like not having her around any more. The girl who had been there her whole life. Through the good times as well as the bad even though it had to be said that of late there had been a lot more of the latter than the former. The shock had hit her but the reality was yet to sink in. Her sister was dead and their family was now changed forever. Svandís was gone and there was now a hole where there used to be a somewhat complicated puzzle. The rest of their lives would be defined by this event. There would be before this day and after it.

No one had ever known how to deal with Svandís and that was perhaps part of the reason why she hadn't so much slipped off the rails but had thrown herself off them into every available ditch along the way. She had been determined to live life her own way and unfortunately that had involved dancing as close to the edge as she possibly could. Eventually she was going to topple over it and that was exactly what had happened.

And on top of all this she had killed a man. She was going to have to figure out how to live with that too. She had given herself something of a mountain to climb.

When she woke in the morning it was with an overwhelming sense of regret. Or regrets was more like it. There seemed to be so many now she could hardly keep up with them all. She rolled over on the couch and wondered why she hadn't just got up and gone to her own bed. As soon as she looked around the living room she understood why that hadn't happened. Not only had she finished off the bottle of brandy which now lay empty on its side in the middle of the living room floor but she had opened and half-finished a bottle of wine she had found somewhere even though she couldn't for the life of her remember where it had come from. It also lay on its side next to the sofa and had emptied most of its contents all over the carpet which was now sporting a large red stain the size of a football. Inga Lind groaned as she sat upright and held her throbbing head in her hands. What had she been thinking? What other stupid things had she done that she couldn't remember? Somewhere in the back of her mind she had a troubling vision of her mother's face. She could clearly remember her saying goodnight and going to bed though. If that had been the case, and she was pretty sure it was, then she must have got out of bed again. Maybe she had come back to see if she was still up. But if that had happened then surely she would have picked the bottles up off the floor. Inga Lind grimaced. It hurt just trying to think.

'What happened here?' Guðrún exclaimed from somewhere behind her.

Inga Lind turned to see her mother holding her hand over her mouth and staring at her defiled carpet. Inga Lind reached for the wine bottle and righted it as if that was somehow going to change the expression on her mother's face or fix the horrible stain it had left behind.

'Inga Lind. What on earth have you done? I knew I should have got up again. Well?'

Her mother looked pale and tired as she bent down to examine the mess more closely.

'Your father is going to have a fit when he sees this. What on earth were you thinking? Just how much did you have to drink last night and what was that nonsense you were talking about in the middle of the night?'

'What nonsense?' Inga Lind asked already dreading the answer.

She couldn't remember disturbing her parents in the middle of the night let alone talking to them. She desperately wanted to know what she'd said. Or rather how much she'd said.

'That nonsense about throwing someone into a river. You must have been plenty bombed to come up with something like that. I knew I should have got up and taken whatever it was you were drinking off you. Now look at this. How could you be so stupid? We're going to have to get this cleaned and you're going to pay for it. You need to learn to be more responsible.'

Inga Lind didn't answer. Her head was miles away. At the foot of the Gullfoss falls to be precise. Margeir's wide-open eyes flashed before her own as his face first appeared and then disappeared again back into the inky void it had come from. She looked up at her mother who was now standing with the empty brandy bottle in one hand and the almost-empty wine bottle in the other. Guðrún inspected the remaining wine as though it also contained the answers to all the questions running around in her head and looked down at the stain on the carpet again.

'Maybe I should have thrown you in the river instead,' she quipped and shook her head and walked off into the kitchen.

CHAPTER FORTY-FIVE

Saturday 14th February

Ævar couldn't believe what he was hearing. If there was a way for this day to get any worse than it already was he couldn't for the life of him imagine what it might be. He'd thought that in the worst-case scenario Grímur might have trouble remembering a few of the more minor details about the night he was shot but nothing on the scale of what he was listening to now. For most of the last week Grímur had been under some pretty heavy-duty medication and while everyone was aware that the man was very lucky to be alive there was now an underlying sensation of anger somewhere inside Ævar that he just couldn't shake. If he hadn't know better he would have sworn that Grímur was deliberately trying to sabotage the investigation even though to do so would be completely illogical. Even keeping their recent falling-out in mind. They were after all trying to jail the man who had almost cost him his life. Surely that was something he would want to help with as much as he could but instead his memory seemed to be deteriorating with each passing minute.

'Okay. So let me run through this one more time just to make sure that we're on the same page here. You'll excuse me if I seem to be repeating myself but some of this just isn't adding up. After you left the club you sat across the street and kept an eye on the place?'

Grímur nodded from his semi-upright position in his hospital bed. After a week of complete rest apart from the occasional interruption from Ævar he was starting to feel a little stronger.

'Yes, but I fell asleep for a while.'

Ævar's constant questions were a never-ending source of irritation but he'd found that if he just faked tiredness and pretended to fall asleep that his boss would eventually go away.

Then the next time they saw each other he would apologise and blame his lack of energy on all the drugs the doctor had been pumping into him. It was a pretty good excuse after all. Most of the time he was actually pretty zoned out with the sedatives in his system. Even when he was awake he had trouble focusing on anything for too long. The drugs were designed to make sure that he got as much rest as possible but they left him feeling drained and exhausted. Ævar would then mumble something along the lines of it was only to be expected and that he shouldn't worry about it and then they would get back to the questions until Grímur got tired of answering them and he would close his eyes and drift away once again. With not being able to get out of bed and walk away when he began to feel irritated and tense it was the only way he could get some peace and quiet so it was a trick he deployed with increasing regularity until Ævar started to become noticeably irritated. Today his boss had a particularly determined air about him and was unlikely to settle for anything less than a set of full and honest answers. He could understand the man's vigour at trying to solve both the cases they were dealing with but the truth of the matter was that the straightforward answers he was looking for might just not exist. Nothing was ever as simple as you wanted it to be.

'When did you wake up again?' Ævar continued.

'I don't remember what time it was but when I looked across the street he was pulling the girl out of the club.'

'Sóllilja?'

'Yes. Sóllilja. And no, as I've already told you, I don't know her father's name or where you can find her. As far as I know she's homeless and has been on the streets and in and out of shelters for quite some time.'

'And then you followed them?'

'Yes, I followed them to Öskjuhlíð where they stopped and got out of the car.'

Ævar was reading his notes as he listened to Grímur go over the story for the umpteenth time. He wasn't sure if he was being lied to exactly but he definitely wasn't being told the whole truth and as a result he was making Grímur go over things time and time again to see if he could trip him up on something. Anything.

'And you didn't think at any point that it might be a good idea to call headquarters to tell them that you might need a hand? If you had any reason to believe that either your life or Sóllilja's was in danger the first thing you should have done was call it in. I know we've been over this a few times but I still can't understand why you didn't just stop and take a minute to make a call.'

Grímur took a deep breath and tried to relax as much as possible given the circumstances. He got the distinct impression that Ævar would continue with the same questions over and over again until he got the answers he was looking for.

'I didn't stop because I thought that if I didn't keep an eye on them she would just disappear.'

'Sóllilja?'

'Yes. I wanted to keep them in sight so I had to follow them as quickly as possible and I didn't see the gun until we were halfway up the hill,' he lied. 'Then I got my phone out but as soon as I did I fell. My phone disappeared and by the time I got my hands on it again you called and as soon as he heard the phone ring he knew exactly where I was and that's when I got shot.'

'And you're sure it was Janko who shot you?'

'There wasn't anyone else there. Except for Sóllilja and I'm pretty sure it wasn't her. If you hadn't called just when you did he wouldn't have seen me or have known where to shoot.'

Ævar looked at Grímur trying to figure out if he was blaming him for getting shot. He didn't really think so but something was causing Grímur to be especially stubborn about being questioned.

'The problem with that version of events is that we found casings from two different guns, neither of which we've been able to locate. On top of that Janko's disappeared into thin air. He hasn't been seen at his club since that night nor anywhere else for that matter. We've been keeping an eye on one of the girls he's close to at the club but she doesn't appear to have had any contact either. I have Vigeland in custody at the moment but if I can't come up with a more convincing reason why he should stay there than, "I'm pretty sure he did it", they're going to let him go. We're sure he's the one who set the guy on fire at the building site but there's no actual proof apart from a spray-painted message on a wall and that could have been anyone with a basic understanding of Norwegian as far as the prosecutor's concerned.'

Ævar took a deep breath. The strain was visibly starting to take its toll on him.

'If I don't make something stick pretty soon I'm out of a job. That's the bottom line here. I know you and I haven't exactly seen eye to eye of late but as you know that wasn't my fault. We need to put all that behind us and help one another out here.'

Ævar was beginning to sound desperate and Grímur was enjoying watching him squirm. It was nice not being the one under the spotlight for a change and he was damned if he was going to fabricate a story just to help his boss out. He had been dragged off Svandís's case and now she was dead. Not that there would have been anything he could have done about that but it still left a bad taste in his mouth. It was thought she had become disorientated in the dark and fallen into the freezing water injuring herself badly in the process. Why she had run off from Guðmundur's and then

Jón Páll's in quick succession was still a mystery and one they might not ever solve.

'What exactly do you mean by "help one another out"?'

'Look, some people see what you did as heroic and there's even been talk of a commendation coming your way but not everyone sees it that way. The knives were out for you before you went running around in the dark after Janko and believe me they're still out. Some say the axe is ready to swing and that the department is ready to cut its losses with you. Do you understand what that will mean in real terms for you, Grímur? Maybe that's exactly what you've been waiting for. I don't know.'

Maybe that was exactly what he was waiting for. He'd never been so tired in his life and it wasn't just the shooting and all the sedation. He had been a police officer now for over forty years and the thought of going back to work now filled him with a fear he'd never felt before. If he were to be thrown off the force now would it really be the worst thing that could happen to him? He just didn't know. He wasn't even sure if he cared or not.

'I know why you arrested the Norwegian and I'm not going to just "remember" something to help you keep him in custody. If you don't have the evidence to charge him with these crimes then you're going to have to let him go. They're the rules.'

Ævar gritted his teeth. If he was going to be honest he was right at the top of the list of people who thought Grímur had long since passed his 'best before' date. It was a long time since they'd seen eye to eye on anything.

'There's one other thing too. It's probably unrelated but it's worth mentioning all the same. There was a body found four days ago in the Hvítá River downstream from Gullfoss. It looked like just another suicide at first but there's a couple of things that don't quite add up so we're still taking a look at it. What was interesting was that his car wasn't found in the car park where we'd expect it to be. It was still parked outside his flat on Hverfisgata so how he got himself all the way out to Gullfoss is yet another puzzle we're trying to solve. We've checked with the taxi companies and he didn't get a ride out there with any of them so he either got a lift from someone or walked just over a hundred kilometres to kill himself.'

'I understand that this is all very interesting but why exactly are you telling me this now? Couldn't it wait until I'm back on my feet again?' Grímur asked not even trying to hide his exasperation.

'I'm telling you this because when we searched the guy's flat we found one of your business cards on his living room table. Margeir Hallgrímsson's his name. Does that name ring any bells?' Ævar asked as he handed the slightly-crumpled card to Grímur.

Grímur shook his head and tried to look as tired as he possibly could. He didn't know any Margeir Hallgrímsson and couldn't have cared less how he had come into possession of one of his cards. He let out a sigh and closed his eyes. He'd had enough for now.

'I don't know who Margeir Hallgrímsson is.'

'Okay,' Ævar said. 'We'll leave it at that for the time being then. I can see you're still tired but before I leave you alone I want you to think about this. If I'm unable to obtain a conviction for either the murder of Óli Þór Sigurdsson or the attempted murder of yourself it's going to damage my career. There's no way of getting around that. But keep one thing very clearly in mind while you're recuperating. If I find out you've been hiding anything from me, for whatever reason whatsoever, I will end yours.'

And with that Ævar turned and walked out of the room leaving Grímur to close his eyes and wonder what it was he'd done to deserve all this. He didn't think he could take much more of the kind of life he'd been living. When he'd recovered from his injury he was going to have some decisions to make but for the time being he just wanted to rest. And think. How on earth had a suicide-jumper ended up with one of his business cards? The only one he could remember giving out recently was the one he tried to give to Svandís's parents.

Their other daughter Inga Lind had picked it up if he remembered correctly. If it was indeed the same card he would have to find out how it had ended up in Margeir's living room. He made a mental note to check up on that when he was feeling better but for now all he could do was close his eyes and try to forget about everything.

CHAPTER FORTY-SIX

Tuesday 10th February

Sitting and watching the evening news together was something of a long-standing tradition for Guðrún and Finnbogi and although each set of daily events had a tendency to blend into another this was one they weren't going to forget in a hurry. The lead story on tonight's news was the discovery of a man's body in the Hvítá River quite a way downstream from Gullfoss. The name of the man wasn't being released at the moment. Either they didn't know who he was or they were still trying to locate a next of kin. There was an interview with an Australian backpacker. He was the one who'd found the body and was very animated in his description of exactly how he and his mates had come across the corpse. This was one adventure they hadn't been expecting in Iceland. They had been well-prepared for glaciers, volcanoes, geysers and even hidden people but no one had mentioned corpses floating in the Hvítá. As unfortunate as it was for the deceased and his family and friends this was going to make for one of the all-time great backpacking stories. Better even than running with the bulls in Pamplona and walking the El Camino de Santiago. At one point the reporter actually had to remind the excitable Australian that a man had lost his life which he quickly recognised and tempered his enthusiasm accordingly. It was after all a tragedy that he and his friends had stumbled upon.

Guðrún didn't know what to make of it. She'd forgotten about her daughter's drunken ramblings because she hadn't wanted to think about them. It was the last thing in the world she wanted to deal with on top of everything else. Was her remaining daughter mixed up in something? She couldn't believe that she was yet there was an uneasy feeling settling in her stomach and it felt like that kind that shouldn't be ignored. One of those ones.

In all likelihood the guy had simply slipped and fallen into the river or had thrown himself into the falls like so many other lost souls before him. Inga Lind's drunken revelation had been nothing more than a weird coincidence. Guðrún looked across at Finnbogi to see what his reaction was but he had his nose in the newspaper and wasn't paying any attention to the television whatsoever. Despite her unsettled stomach Guðrún wasn't prepared to entertain the notion of there being any connection with Inga Lind babbling about throwing someone in the river and this guy on the news, not even for five seconds. It would simply be more than she could bear. She had just lost one daughter and there was no chance in hell that she was going to lose the other one. None whatsoever. She glanced back across the room at Finnbogi. He was transfixed on this morning's copy of Fréttablaðið. The news of the body in the river was just another news story to him. Slightly more exciting than the ones from the day before but nothing more than that. Good, she thought to herself. There's nothing to worry about then is there?

CHAPTER FORTY-SEVEN

Monday 9th March

The first day back on the job was never going to be an easy one. As Grímur arrived at police headquarters on Hverfisgata he couldn't have possibly anticipated who would be waiting for him at the front door. Knut Vigeland lit a cigarette and stared at Grímur as he approached the steps at the front of the building. Although they had never been formally introduced Grímur knew exactly who he was looking at. The guy's mugshots from the Norwegian police had been plastered all over the office noticeboards for a week before he'd arrived in Iceland. They had been notified as soon as his name had shown up on a flight manifest from Oslo and they'd been expecting trouble. And true to form they'd pretty much got what they expected.

The instinctive reaction to a violent and disgusting murder, an attempted murder of a police officer and two disappearances shortly after his arrival in the city, had been to blame it all on him. Too many of the police saw it as just too much of a coincidence for it to have been anyone else. If they could hang all the blame on one perpetrator then it would look as if they'd done their job and suggest that everyone was safe again. Put the bad guy away and all your problems are solved in one fell swoop. That was the theory anyway. Unfortunately, looking for such an easy solution inevitably led to problems. The main one being that while they were trying to connect everything to Knut Vigeland they hadn't bothered looking at any other possibilities. If it then turned out that he wasn't responsible for the crimes then whoever was got a free pass. Ævar's prediction that this was going to hurt his career was certainly coming true. Never before in the history of the Icelandic police had so few answers been available for so many questions. The one saving grace perhaps had been the Prime Minister's resignation amid a scandal of his own. An erupting volcano to distract people from the burning house.

It had given the police some breathing space but it wouldn't last forever and when the new Prime Minister got around to taking a good hard look at the situation there was a consensus that heads would roll. There was a good chance Ævar was loosening his collar already for when the axe came swinging his way.

'Good morning,' Grímur said. 'I see they've let you out for a cigarette break.'

'They've let me out full-stop. By this evening I'll be back in Oslo.'

Grímur was genuinely surprised. There was a detectable look of smugness on Knut's face and as he finished his cigarette and flicked the butt down the stairs he actually smiled. It almost made the guy look like a regular human being.

'How are you doing?' Knut asked.

'Better,' Grímur said. 'I thought I was history there for a bit.'

'You almost were.'

Grímur smiled too. In his head now he could picture exactly where the final two shots and the extra bullet casings had come from.

'You know, it's probably better if we never see each other ever again,' Grímur said.

Knut nodded and motioned towards a dark-coloured sedan that had just pulled up outside the station. The driver reached across and opened the passenger door and then motioned for Knut to hurry up and get in.

'You won't get any arguments from me on that score. If I never see this fucking town again it will be a week too soon.'

Grímur chuckled quietly to himself.

'You'd better get going before we change our minds then,' he said.

Knut held his hand out for Grímur to shake. He did so and the two men parted company.

'See you later copper,' Knut called out over his shoulder as he got into the waiting car.

Grímur hoped that would be the end of it but something told him it wouldn't be the last he saw of Knut Vigeland. Some people kept rolling back into your life like bad pennies. He didn't know when or where their paths would cross again but it felt inevitable that one day they would. It was only now that he truly understood how he had managed to get down off Öskjuhlíð alive when he had passed out in the freezing cold and was lying at death's door waiting for it to open. He was lucky to be alive but it seemed that there was more to luck than just being in the right place at the right time. Sometimes you needed an angel looking over your shoulder. Even if that angel came from the last place in the world you might expect it to.

CHAPTER FORTY-EIGHT

Sunday 5th April

Gunnar and Egill had borrowed the bolt cutters from the garden shed belonging to one of their uncles although borrowed wasn't exactly the right term if the truth be told. If he discovered they were missing before they returned them there would be hell to pay. The thought of the punishment that awaited them if they messed up wasn't enough to put them off though. They were just too curious about what lay within the old black barracks hut. The outside of the perfectly semi-circular corrugated iron construction still looked to be in near perfect condition with its fresh coat of matte black paint so they figured there had to be something important inside.

The chain securing the main door gave them some solid resistance at first but once they'd figured out how to get one of them on each handle of the bolt cutters and push as a team it soon gave way. A look of surprise passed between them as the chain flew free of the handles and they realised what they'd actually achieved. They unwound the loop of chain from the handles and opened the door ever so slightly. The boy holding the flashlight pushed his smaller companion out of the way and strode inside to give the impression that he wasn't concerned in the slightest by anything that might lay in wait for them. Not wanting to stand around in the dark on his own the other boy followed him in. The smell of the horizontal tin can was stale and sweetly pungent. It could easily have been used by some homeless person until someone had come up with the idea to chain the front door up. There was a faint yet distinctive odour of human waste in the air. It could have been some time since the place had been used by the homeless to shelter from the freezing city streets outside.

'I told you there'd be nothing in here,' Egill said.

'There's no need to sound so pleased with yourself,' Gunnar said. 'I know you just want to get home as soon as you can.'

In one corner of the old military hut a section of the wooden floor had been pried loose and lifted away. Apart from that there wasn't much else to see. The floor, walls and ceiling had all been stripped of electrical devices with the lights missing and even the switches gone. It even looked as if someone had gone to the bother of removing the wiring as well. Whoever had been in there last hadn't wanted to leave anything behind that could be reused or sold on. Gunnar let out an exasperated sigh.

'I hate to admit it but you might just be right. This time.'

Egill was unsettled by the unexpected compliment. It was unlike his friend to give him any sort of encouragement even jokingly. He smiled to himself and went back to studying the patch of bare earth where the floorboards had been removed and tried to get a better look. As soon as his friend saw what he was doing he wanted in on the action as well. It wouldn't do for a little pipsqueak like Egill to be getting the glory for finding any treasure that might still be hidden in there.

'O boy, did you take a bath today?' Gunnar said. 'Or did you forget again?'

Gunnar's laughter echoed around inside of the tin can. The metal roof and walls made it sound as if everything was just a little bit too close for comfort.

'Because you sure smell funny,' Gunnar continued.

He was just kidding around but the funny smell in the tin can building was no longer a joke and the closer they got to the upended floorboards the more pungent it became.

'I don't know about this,' Egill said.

'I knew it,' Gunnar spouted. 'You are too scared to have a look.'

He barged passed Egill to take control of the situation and put himself in a position to take the credit for anything they might stumble across. He peered down into the crawlspace under the floorboards and flicked the flashlight's slender beam from side to side but it looked as empty as everything else did.

'What a waste of time,' he sighed. 'This was a stupid idea of yours.'

Egill bumped into Gunnar as he tried to get closer to the hole in the floor which made his much bigger friend flinch noticeably in the darkness. Gunnar turned and swatted at Egill's head with his free hand but missed the target.

'Watch what you're doing you smelly little git,' Gunnar said.

'Shine the flashlight in that far corner again,' Egill said pointing to the spot furthest from them right up against the wall.

'What do you think you can you see down there that I can't?' Gunnar asked as he swung the beam where he'd been directed. Egill got down on his hands and knees and pointed at something.

'Right there,' he said.

'I still don't see anything,' Gunnar said.

Egill reached back over his shoulder and motioned for Gunnar to hand him the flashlight.

'Give me that and I'll show you,' he said.

Gunnar was a little reluctant to comply with the request but after a little hesitation he handed over the flashlight and put his hands on his hips.

'This had better be good,' he mumbled just loud enough so that Egill could hear.

Egill took the flashlight and focused its beam on the section of dirt that had grabbed his attention. He leant over and brushed some loose earth out of the way.

'There's nothing there, you're seeing things,' Gunnar protested.

'Yes there is. Here, take this again,' Egill said and passed the flashlight back to Gunnar. 'Shine it over here so I can clear this dirt away.'

Once he had both hands free again he got down on his stomach and reached across the gap to the small mound he'd found. As he scraped away at the loose dirt something did in fact start to materialise before their eyes. There was something buried under where the missing floorboards should have been. As he brushed away layer upon layer of dirt the boys could see what it was that had been producing the odd smell that was hanging around in the enclosed space. The outline of an ear and then a nose was revealed as the profile of a man's face emerged before their eyes. His eyes were still open but clouded by death and flecked with dirt and water giving him the look of a long-neglected museum piece. Egill squealed like a child and backed up hard into Gunnar's legs. The older boy had also seen the face in the ground and dropped the flashlight and the bolt cutters as the two of them turned and fled from the hut as fast as their legs would carry them.

CHAPTER FORTY-NINE

Monday 6th April

The area around the back end of the domestic airport along Nauthólsvegur and all the way down to Nauthólsvík had been transformed into a giant crime scene. Once the terrified boys had made their discovery known to a passing motorist the police had descended on the abandoned hut en masse. It was exactly the kind of thing Ævar had dreaded happening and now that it had come to pass the fallout had been swift and brutal. The axe that had been hanging over his head had fallen and he had been replaced pending an investigation into the crimes and how they had been allowed to go unnoticed for so long. The corpse of Janko Kovaʔeviʔ was fresh and had been the one the boys had unearthed but some of the bodies had been in the ground for a considerable amount of time and questions were being asked in the Alþingi about how these women could have disappeared from the streets of Reykjavík without anyone noticing. Or caring. The champagne club on Lækjargata had been raided immediately and the work permits of everyone on the premises inspected. Unsurprisingly many of the girls working there had been doing so illegally and were arrested. The murmuring that had been going on for quite some time about what went on behind closed doors, or drawn curtains as the case may be, in these clubs had become a scream for action and action was what they were going to get. The first head to roll had been Ævar's. He had feared that anything even resembling a botched investigation this time around, let alone the discovery of six bodies hidden in plain sight in the city centre, would cost him his job and he had been right. He was replaced immediately by Haukur Hauksson who was making a habit of leapfrogging men who had been around much longer than he had into positions many others would have coveted. Their mistakes had become his stepping stones.

Before his dismissal Ævar had insisted on Grímur receiving counselling to help him with his recovery. He had attended the first two sessions but soon gave up on the idea convinced that the only person capable of helping him through the trauma was himself. At the same time that Ævar was given his marching orders Grímur was handed the option of an early retirement package. It was the most polite way that the upper echelon could come up with to get rid of him. They wanted him out the door more than ever after the shooting incident but couldn't risk incurring the wrath of public opinion by firing an officer just after he'd been shot in the line of duty. It wouldn't do to be seen to be that cold-hearted.

Björn Magnússon and Kristinn Gunnarsson became the two most sought-after interview subjects in Iceland. Björn's busiest day on the job up until now had involved at most two bodies to uncover and identify. As one by one the bodies in the tin hut were revealed it soon became apparent that the scale of the crimes committed far outdid anything the country had seen before. Five more bodies were unearthed once the remains of Janko Kova?evi? had been removed. Night after night Björn patiently answered the press's questions. All five were female and had been deposited at the site over a considerable period of time. The oldest somewhere between eight and ten years ago was his best guess.

Björn found the whole process draining from the initial exhumations of the dead women all the way through to the questions he received every night and you could see the tiredness slowly etching itself into his face. After three days Haukur told him he didn't have to do the press conferences any more but Björn insisted that they were part of the job and he was willing to continue with them. They did seem to be taking their toll on him though and not just him but Kristinn also. He found many of the questions unnecessarily invasive and simply didn't have all the answers they wanted. For some of the girls it would take weeks or even longer to identify them. They had not been missed thus far and were the long-forgotten children of as yet unknown souls.

Most of the questions directed at Kristinn were to do with the cause of death of each victim. As he explained over and over again some were much easier to determine than others. Some had been in the earth so long that there was virtually no chance of determining the cause of their demise and with others it was painfully obvious. Two had broken necks while another had obvious knife marks on her ribs where she had been stabbed but with the other two there were no obvious injuries and with the advanced state of decomposition it would be little more than guesswork as to what had killed them.

Every day the journalists filed into the room used for the press conferences and every day they bombarded the assembled senior police officers, forensics expert and coroner with their questions safe in the knowledge that they were doing the public a real service. Haukur Hauksson's introduction to life at the top could not have been any more dramatic. The scandal that had cost Ævar his job had become the biggest story the police would in any likelihood ever have to deal with. In sharp contrast to his overworked and stressed-out colleagues Haukur revelled in the demands of the assembled media. He silenced his many critics with ease and made the arduous task of putting the nation's collective minds at rest seem as though it was one he had been waiting his whole life for, which just might have been the case. And when things occasionally became overheated or unnecessarily uncomfortable the newly-appointed Prime Minister Halldór Valdimarsson would appear from out of nowhere at Haukur's side to help out with a few well-chosen words.

'It is almost impossible to see how any police force in the world could have predicted such a hideous sequence of events such as those that have led us to where we are today. Haukur has the Alþingi's full support, on top of which we shall be looking into tightening up the procedures which have allowed such vulnerable young foreign women to enter the country in the first place. We intend to make it as close to impossible as we can to enter Iceland illegally or to stay here beyond the limits of non-EEA holiday visas.'

The women arrested at the champagne club had all been interviewed and identified by now and while a few of them were from countries within the EEA and therefore in the country perfectly legally there were others who had somehow slipped through the net. The net that Halldór had now vowed publicly to close. The timing couldn't have been better for the Prime Minister's right-wing agenda. If he'd attempted the sort of clampdown he had in mind even a few months earlier he would have woken every day to protests in Austurvöllur Square but the way the public were feeling now he could push through his reforms and sell them as being for the protection of illegal aliens and not actually discriminating against them which is how they would have been seen otherwise. If he could make people fear for the safety of these foreigners then he could do almost anything he wanted to keep them out of the country or remove them once they were caught and not be derided publicly for doing so. The reason why he loved these press conferences so much was because he could have sworn that Christmas had come in April for the first time in his life.

CHAPTER FIFTY

Thursday 9th April

Grímur's first month back at work had been much tougher than even he could have imagined. He had half expected to be fired as soon as he walked back through the door but the fact that he'd taken a bullet in the line of duty had made him something of a hero on top of his ever-present role as resident pariah. It seemed that almost dying might just have saved his career. For the time being. When the sensationalism surrounding the shooting had died down attention would inevitably refocus on the mechanics of the night on Öskjuhlíð. More questions would be asked about what he had been doing outside the club asleep in his car and why he'd followed Janko onto the hillside without letting anyone know where he was. His explanation that he was simply keeping an eye on Janko and that he hadn't seen the gun until it had been too late to call for back-up had already been met by several raised eyebrows. And now Halldór Valdimarsson was Prime Minister he felt sure that their little spat on the doorstep of headquarters would come back to haunt him sooner rather than later. The bottom line was that he was not anticipating seeing the year out as a police officer. It wasn't that he didn't want to be a cop any more it just felt as if his time was up. He would accept his fate whatever it may be but he was resigned to losing his job in the next few months. As a result his interest in all things police-related had taken something of a backseat and that hadn't gone unnoticed either. Haukur had called him into his office and asked him what was wrong. Was he unhappy? Did he need more time off? Had he not recovered from the shooting satisfactorily? Haukur had suggested that Grímur take some of the holiday time he was owed and had even offered him the use of his summer house. Grímur had turned the offer down saying that he didn't feel like being on his own in the middle of nowhere at the moment. Haukur had accepted his reasoning but warned him that loneliness could be contagious. It had been meant as a joke but Grímur could see that there was more than a modicum of seriousness behind the comment all the same. The most awkward moment had come when Ævar arrived to collect some of his belongings. Grímur felt guilty for costing the man his job and when he was invited into his old office for one last chat he assumed it would be about the choices he'd made that had led to him getting shot and Ævar losing his job. Much to his surprise Ævar had nothing further to say on the matter. Instead he reached into his desk drawer and pulled a stainless steel hipflask out of it. He placed it on the table between the two of them and waited for the penny to drop. Grímur was puzzled at first and then mortified. He recognised the keepsake but couldn't for the life of him understand how Ævar had come into possession of it. Looks were exchanged across the table as the pair sat in silence. Each of them waiting for the other to say something, not wanting to be the first. Grímur closed his eyes and tried to recall the last time he'd seen the hipflask and slowly it came back to him. The night he'd been trying so hard to forget all about just kept coming back to haunt him. He had been sipping from it in the car just before he fell asleep and had slipped it into his jacket pocket for safekeeping. It must have slipped out when he'd fallen on the ice on Öskjuhlíð. The only way Ævar could have got hold of it was if he had been the one to find it on the icy slope. The implication of exactly what that meant wasn't lost on Grímur. He knew full well that this was the opportunity everyone had been waiting for. Ævar most of all. His boss didn't fool him for a minute with his occasional low-profile shows of support. Ævar finding the hipflask would surely be the last straw. The worst thing was that it was the one Ævar had given him as a Christmas present at some boring work party years ago. Grímur could only imagine what was going through Ævar's mind. Was he waiting for him to make it easy for everybody and resign? He'd been thinking about leaving the police for some time now but he hadn't pictured being forced to fall on his own sword by nothing more than his own stupidity. He reached across the table and took the offending hipflask in his hand. He gave it a little shake. It was still half full. He couldn't look Ævar in the eye. He knew all too well what would be waiting there for him. A cold unfeeling mixture of pity, regret and disappointment. He slid the hipflask into one of his pockets without making eye contact.

'You know if anyone apart from myself had found that there wouldn't be a decision left for you to make,' Ævar said.

Grímur nodded and let out an almost silent sigh.

'I know,' he whispered.

'Grímur, I'm counting on you to do the right thing here. We all are. This has gone on far too long and something should have been done about it a long time ago. Now the perfect opportunity presents itself for us to move on. I know that when you have some free time to go home and think about this you will come to the same conclusion. It's the only way.'

Grímur finally looked up and saw the endgame of his career as a police officer staring back at him the way a disappointed parent looks at a stupid, naughty child.

'Maybe I should take some time off and think things over,' he mumbled.

Ævar smiled and nodded. He finished moving the last of his things into the cardboard box that was sitting on his desk.

'I think that would the best too,' he said. 'You've been through a great deal of late and there's a huge amount of sympathy for you at the moment. That's something you should take full advantage of. This is a chance for you to bow out with your head held high.'

Grímur nodded but he had no idea what he was agreeing with or why.

'Walk away as a hero while you can. You won't get another chance.'

After all their years together this is the way it was going to end. Grímur could feel tears coming to his eyes so he stood and mumbled something about letting them know when he'd made up his mind and walked out of the room. He made a quick stop at his office to pick up a few things and then made straight for the front door. He didn't feel like hanging around one minute longer than he absolutely had to. Outside the air felt cold and hostile. He shoved his hands in his pockets and trudged off towards Hátún feeling as if he'd lost a friend for good.

Rather than sit around the house feeling sorry for himself Grímur took the opportunity to take Bobbi out for a walk. The timing of his early exit from Hverfisgata was perfect for a couple of laps of Klambratún. When they got to the park a familiar face smiled at them from across the grass. Sóllilja was sitting cross-legged and leaning up against a tree. When she saw Bobbi she clapped her hands together and whistled. Bobbi's ears pricked up and he strained against the lead before realising he was going nowhere in a hurry. He looked up at Grímur and whimpered. Grímur knew that technically he had to keep his dog on a leash at all times in the park but he figured that if he'd broken away from him once then it was entirely possible that it could happen again. He took pity on the big brown eyes and let the lead fall slowly from his hand. Bobbi bounded across the grass to get to Sóllilja and dove into her lap bowling the girl over as he did so. She pulled herself to her feet laughing and patting Bobbi until he calmed down. Grímur approached her and apologised for Bobbi's near-lethal levels of enthusiasm.

'He needs to get out of the house more often,' he said. 'Someone might think he's pleased to see you.'

Sóllilja managed to stop laughing just long enough to reply.

'He certainly is,' she said.

'I guess he does need to get out more often,' Grímur chuckled.

Bobbi barked right on cue as if to agree.

'You know, I've been hoping our paths would cross again,' Grímur said.

Sóllilja nodded and looked down at the grass as she continued patting Bobbi.

'I've been wondering why you hadn't come looking for me,' she said.

'I still have dreams about that night and not very pleasant ones either,' Grímur said.

'I can imagine.'

'Can you tell me what you saw, Sóllilja?'

'Okay, but you've got to remember it was very dark and I had a gun pointed at me most of the time. I wasn't even aware there was anyone else there until he started shooting at you.'

Grímur looked around awkwardly as if unsure of where to let his gaze fall.

'I've been wanting to say thank you,' she said. 'I probably wouldn't be alive right now if you hadn't shown up when you did. You're a very brave man.'

'I don't feel like a brave man. I feel like a foolish old man.'

'You did what you thought was right. And you saved my life,' Sóllilja said. 'If you hadn't turned up when you did he was going to kill me and drop me down one of those old manhole covers. I wouldn't be here any more. You would have pulled my body out of one of those old drains. Don't you understand what you did?'

Grímur looked down at the grass and shook his head.

'I still don't understand exactly what happened after I was shot.'

Sóllilja reached into one of her pockets and pulled something out. She handed it to Grímur who took it and stared at it for a while.

'I thought I'd lost this,' he said.

'When Janko let go of me I froze. I was so scared I couldn't even move. Then this other guy shows up out of nowhere and shoots Janko in the back. I didn't need a second invitation to get the hell out of there but when I'd made it a hundred feet or so I realised you were still there and that he might kill you too. Janko deserved it but you didn't. You were just trying to help so I doubled back until I could see what was going on. I didn't know what I was going to do but in the end I didn't have to do anything because he just picked you up and carried you down to Bústaðavegur. He even called one-one-two and told them where you were but he didn't stick around for them to show up. He was straight back up that hill to get Janko and then he disappeared over the other side. That was my cue to split and by the time I got back down the path there was already an ambulance coming up the road to get you. You were pretty lucky. Twice.'

'We were both pretty lucky,' Grímur said.

'I guess we were.'

Grímur looked around the park at the young people and families playing in the chilly spring sunshine. As he got older it seemed to become more difficult for him to tell the difference between right and wrong. He'd always thought that it should be clear cut. As simple to tell apart as black from white. Nothing was ever that simple though. There were moments in his life when he'd done what he thought was the right thing and wound up hating himself for it. Then there were other times when he'd let his emotions get the better of him and ended up doing hopelessly stupid things. And yet he felt that some of those moments were among the few times in his life when he'd actually done something he could be proud of. It was always easier to see things clearly from a distance whether that distance be in space or time. All it took was a few steps back from what was going on around you and everything became simpler than it had been before and easier to understand.

'Are you okay?' Sóllilja asked.

Grímur felt a tear run down his cheek and he realised he had drifted away for a moment. He wiped his hand across his face and tried to smile.

'Yes. I think so.'

Sóllilja nodded but didn't say anything.

'Things have been too dark for me for far too long now,' Grímur said. 'I've become worse than ineffective. I've become useless. I've let everything inside me become corrupted. Not by the things I've done but by the things I haven't done. My life has become a mess. One I no longer know how to clean up.'

There was a moment of silence between the two of them as Grímur stared out into space.

'Do you ever think there's someone whose job it is to look over your shoulder?' he asked.

'You mean like a guardian angel?'

'Yes.'

Sóllilja patted Bobbi's head while she thought about it for a while.

'I think we make our own angels in this life. Our decisions create them and the ones we make through our good decisions look after us and the ones we make through our bad decisions lead us astray,' she said.

'How do you mean?' Grímur asked.

'I mean that when we get out of bed each day we have a string of choices ahead of us. A lot of them will seem so small that we'll think they're insignificant but the thing is that they're all really important.'

Grímur nodded as if he understood.

'Every choice we make either makes us a good angel or a bad one and all those little angels become one big angel sooner or later and whether that angel is a good one or a bad one will decide whether you get to walk away from things like what we've been through and play another day or not. When I realised just how lucky I was to have walked off that hill alive something hit me. All I'd been doing was killing time. That's what my life had become. So I found a shelter and they said that they'd take me in as long as I stayed clean and I've been off smack for sixty-one days now and I'm building that angel every day. And you know something? If I can do it, so can you.'

She reached across and took Grímur's hand in her own.

'So can you. You can still help people and that's a wonderful thing to be able to do.'

Sóllilja got up and said goodbye to Bobbi and walked off. Grímur turned his phone over in his hand thinking back to the night on Öskjuhlíð. The phone somehow seemed to be the key. If he'd managed to keep the damn thing in his hand he would have been able to get some help. On the other hand if he hadn't answered it when Ævar had called he probably wouldn't have been shot. He turned the screen on and checked the battery fully expecting it to be flat but Sóllilja had charged it for him. He checked the notifications on the screen and found a number of missed calls. The vast majority of them were from numbers he knew; Ævar's mobile and the main switchboard at the station along with one from Björn Magnússon the forensics technician he frequently worked with. There was only one number he didn't recognise. It was a mobile number and he stared at it wondering who it might be and what they had been calling about. Since he had no social life to speak of he didn't get many calls that weren't work-related. There was only one thing to do to satisfy his curiosity and that was to call it. It was answered on the third ring by a tired female voice.

'Hello?'

'Hello, I have a missed call from this number and I was wondering if it might have been something important.'

There was silence on the other end of the line.

'Hello?' Grímur said.

'I'm sorry, I don't recognise this number,' the tired voice said.

'It's Grímur Karlsson speaking. Was what it you were calling me about?'

'I… I'm not sure… I don't remember…'

The tired voice sounded edgy and nervous and it seemed to Grímur that she was lying but she had said just enough for him to recognise her voice.

'This is Inga Lind isn't it?'

Once again there was only silence on the other end.

'I'm very sorry about Svandís,' Grímur said.

'Thank you but I really don't remember calling you. Maybe I was upset and just wanted someone to talk to,' Inga Lind said.

'Maybe that's what it was,' Grímur said. 'As it happens there's something I wanted to talk to you about so it's worked out rather well.'

'Something you wanted to talk to me about?' she said sounding a little nervous.

'One of my business cards was found in the apartment of a man called Margeir Hallgrímsson. Do you know anyone by that name?'

'What on earth has this got to do with me?'

'Just answer the question, Inga Lind.'

Inga Lind cleared her throat and took a deep breath.

'I'm sorry. What I meant to say was that I don't know anybody by that name.'

'Okay. It's just that you're the only person I've given one of these cards to lately. I don't use them very much any more but I remember giving one to your parents when you came to see me but it was you who left with it. Now it's been found in the living room of this Margeir fellow and I can't for the life of me figure out how it could have got there.'

'I've no idea who this Margeir guy was,' Inga Lind said.

'Why did you say "was" Inga Lind? Did something happen to Margeir that we should know about?' Grímur asked.

Grímur could hear sobbing on the other end. Very quiet at first and then louder. For about a minute he just let her cry hoping that if he did so he would get the truth out of her.

'I didn't know who else to call,' she sobbed. 'Why didn't you talk to me? I could have really done with your help.'

'I was shot that night, Inga Lind. I dropped my phone and someone else found it. I only got it back today. It was them you spoke to not me.'

'Who the hell was I talking to then?'

'That's not important now. The important thing is I still want to help.'

'Then just tell them you have no idea how the card got there. It wouldn't even be lying.'

'But I'm pretty sure I do know how that card got there. That's the problem, Inga Lind. Somehow Margeir wound up in the Hvítá River and we're pretty sure he had some help getting into it. We didn't find his car out there and now there's a murder investigation underway. If I lie about the card then I'm no better than they are.'

'They? Who are "they" exactly?'

'Those who kill, Inga Lind. The people I'm supposed to help catch.'

'Sometimes people just make mistakes though, don't they?'

'Yes. Sometimes they do.'

'Does that make them bad people?'

'Sometimes it does and sometimes they're no different from you and me.'

'Normal people do bad things too then?'

'Normal people do all sorts of things, Inga Lind.'

Bobbi was sniffing at his feet and seemed anxious to get going. He barked once just to make his point. Grímur reached down and picked his lead up off the ground.

'To be honest I don't know what I could have done to help but I would have tried,' he said.

'I'm sure you would have thought of something. I know you tried to help Svandís but she was beyond help. The only surprise about her death was that it didn't happen five years ago. Sometimes bad things happen and there's nothing anybody can do even if you see them coming and try everything you can think of to stop them. They just happen anyway like they were meant to. That's what Svandís was like. An accident waiting to happen.'

Grímur pulled his wallet out of his pocket and looked at the business card Ævar had handed back to him. He folded it up and dropped it in the nearest rubbish bin.

'You're right. Sometimes there's just nothing you can do to help no matter how hard you try. Take care, Inga Lind. I'm sure everything's going to work out alright for you.'

He ended the call and walked off with Bobbi snapping at his heels thinking that he had walked through the centre of a storm and just about made it to the other side.

THE END

Read the other books in this series…

Printed in Great Britain
by Amazon

10591010R00150